Dolly Crystal, Queen of the Circus

Dolly Crystal, Queen of the Circus

Ida Jack

Library of Congress Number: 2001117808
ISBN: Hardcover 1-4010-2139-5
Softcover 1-4010-2138-7

This is a work of fiction. Names, characters, places and incidents either are the product of the author's imagination or are used fictitiously, and any resemblance to any actual persons, living or dead, events, or locales is entirely coincidental.

This book was printed in the United States of America.

To order additional copies of this book, contact:
Xlibris Corporation
1-888-795-4274
www.Xlibris.com
Orders@Xlibris.com

11320

To my husband, Steve,
for his encouragement and support.

To my daughter and my grandson, Colleen and Cody Mesler,
the two special people in my life who bring me joy and
inspire me the most.

To my parents, Walter and Louise Mertens,
for refreshing me constantly.

I must include my bothers and sister, Walter Jr., Judy, Tommy and
Dennis, because they will be looking for their names on this page.

Last, but not least, I would like to make a special dedication to
my best friend, Dixie Wisson, who helped to keep the spirit of
Dolly alive with me.

CHAPTER 1

The ice-cold beer felt good going down as the old woman licked both corners of her half-toothless mouth. The Miami heat was intense on that August afternoon in 1953 as she sat upon her old apple crate in front of the Lighthouse Grocery Store. Her short thin flaming red hair framed her white powdered face and her tiny winter-blue eyes were almost hidden beneath heavy false eyelashes. Her red lips were drawn on over her pitifully thin ones and she wore her stockings rolled down to her ankles.

She spotted two young barefooted girls crossing Twenty-Seventh Avenue, pulling a rusty wagon. Quickly, the old woman reached under the apple crate for the scruffy old scrapbook and opened it onto her lap. She watched as the two girls headed toward the front door of the store, getting ready to make her move. "Do ya remember me?" she asked as they approached her, "I'm Dolly Crystal, Queen of the Circus." The old woman motioned for the girls to come closer.

"Hi Dolly," said the small thin girl, wearing baggy shorts and a Kool-Aid-stained sleeveless blouse, "Look how many bottles we found yesterday. We're gonna cash them in for candy."

The girls passed her by. The old woman's heart sank for a moment in disappointment, hoping that they would have stopped to listen to her stories before going inside. She took another gulp of beer and laid her hands to rest on top of the old scrapbook on her lap. "Maybe it won't take too long before those girls git back," she uttered beneath her breath as she waited.

The two girls often stopped to listen to her tell about her circus days but Dolly would still ask them if they remembered her, even though she'd seen them the day before. The old woman could remember every detail of her past but she'd forget from day to day what was going on around her. The two young girls didn't mind that Dolly was a little crazy. They liked the old woman and found her to be quite sweet.

The treasured scrapbook that Dolly kept with her as she sat upon her apple crate throne with a bottle of beer clutched in her hand as a scepter was proof that she was indeed the Queen of the Barnum & Bailey Circus.

The long minutes passed before the girls came back outside with bags of candy in their hands. The lonely old woman's disappointment lifted when she heard, "Come on Dixie! Lets' go over an' see Dolly." The taller girl unwrapped a Mary Jane and popped it into her mouth.

Dolly felt a heartwarming satisfaction as she welcomed the girls to be her audience. She slipped her right index finger between the pages ready to begin while the girls positioned themselves against the wall of the stucco building.

"Here's a picture of me when I was twelve years old." Dolly's crooked finger pointed to an old yellowed newspaper clipping of a young girl with long ringlets. "I was born on July eleventh, 1866, right after the war ended, down in St. Augustine, Florida. Daddy got shot by some Yankee who didn't know the war was over before I could even walk an' me an' Mama moved up to South Georgia when I was goin' on eight.

Mama had a lot of men friends who gave her money all the time. I don't remember much about her but she always smelt like whiskey an' never paid much attention to me when I was little. She used to tell me to git away an' leave er alone all the time.

I remember one day when I woke up an' my Mama was gone. She jus' up an' left me there an' never did come back home. At first I cried but later on I did purdy damn good by myself. I was jus' lonely, that's all. After a while I ran outta food an' had to leave but I was very capable of takin' care of myself. I didn't take nothin' with me cause I didn't own nothin'. My Mama took jus' 'bout everythin' outta the house with er when she moved out. She even took all the forks an' blankets, so I jus' left with nothin' but the clothes on my back. I found out later that she ran off with some man out to California. I never heard from er again.

I took care of myself from then on . . . but sometimes I couldn't get enough to eat. People used to give me food but sometimes they'd forgit 'bout me an' I'd have to go in back of people's houses an' find food that they threw away er sometimes I'd sneak tomatoes outta their gardens. I even ate horse feed when I could git it. I tell ya . . . that corn is what kept me alive.

I had no place to live an' used to sleep in the woods cause that winter when I went back to our shack there was people livin' in it. They jus' took over but I never let em see me. I jus' saw their buckboard in front an' peeked in the window. It was a very strange feelin' fer me so I jus' went away an' fergot about it.

When it got freezin' cold I would sneak in barns an' lay down under the hay an' sleep. I remember once I woke up an' there was this big ol' giant scorpion layin' right on my chest. I went to brush em off an' when I slung my arm I felt somethin' else layin' there with me too. I looked over an' there was this giant rattlesnake coiled up right next to my shoulder! The poor critter was jus' tryin' to stay warm too . . . jus' like me. I was afraid to move so I jus' laid there an' finally went to sleep with that daggum thing layin' plum-smack against me. When I woke up that snake was still there but he didn't even try to bite me. I jus' slowly moved away an' got up an' ran like crazy!

A real nice couple found me sleepin' under some leaves when I was ten an' found my Uncle Thomas an' sent me up to Marietta to live with em. My uncle . . . he was a nice man. He had two brothers. One was my daddy . . . his name was Walter an' there was Ernest who I never saw till I was twelve," said Dolly as she tapped her finger on the newspaper clipping. "See? This here's 'bout me an' him." Beneath the photograph it read, "Dolly Wafford, age twelve, stabs man in neck."

The taller girl's eyes widened as she gasped, "Did you kill him?"

"Hell no, I didn't kill em . . . but I wished I did! I hated Uncle Ernest! He would beat the tar outta me with a strap when I didn't do what he told me to . . . an' he beat up poor ol' Uncle

Thomas too, who only had one foot cause he got it chopped off in a fight with some Injun back in 1829."

In the distance a voice of a woman called, "Dixie! Ida! Suuuupper!" The girls looked at each other with both jaws bulging with candy.

"We gotta go," said Dixie as she stood up and quickly grabbed the wagon handle.

"Hey Dolly, I almost forgot. Mama said you could have some mangoes off our tree if you want them cause they're just falling on the ground getting rotten," Ida offered. "Do you like mangoes?"

"Oh yeah. Especially when they're real ripe I do." Dolly smiled, exposing the few brownish-orange teeth that were left in her mouth.

"Then we'll bring you some mangoes when we come back. See ya tomorrow," Ida said as they obediently scurried away.

The sun was beginning to sink down far enough to ease the heat and Dolly's beer was gone. She gazed up at the dark blue sky and watched the cotton-like streaks take on endless formations until they turned pink and orange to signal the end of the day.

Dolly stood up, holding her scrapbook, and walked to the curb to cross Twenty-Seventh Avenue. Joe's Bar was directly in front of her across the street. She licked her dry lips longing for another beer and decided to go inside for one more before walking around to the back of the bar where she rented a small efficiency. She moved slowly, stumbling across the street while cars slowed down and honked their horns at her.

Joe's Bar had four small tables up against the wall and the bar sat six. There were four men sitting at the bar. Dolly made her way to the stool on the far end and shouted, "I'll have me a Schlitz, Joe!"

"Guess we'll be gettin' that hurricane after all," Dolly heard one of the men telling Joe, "They said it took a turn an' now it's headed straight for Miami. I think they said eighty-five mile an hour winds. It's kinda early in the year to be gettin' a hurricane but they say this is a freak one."

Not interested in what they were saying, the old woman turned to the man next to her. "Hey Billy, did I ever tell ya about the time when my arm got chewed up by the lion I tamed?" Billy didn't turn around to face her. He ignored her and continued slurping his beer but Dolly could not stop talking. "Yeah . . . it took two hundred stitches to sew it back up but nosiree, it didn't stop me from goin' back in that cage. Big Jack . . . he was the biggest lion we had too. He was the one who tore up my arm," she rambled on, "Anyways, he never hurt me again cause I never trusted em enough to turn my back on em after that." She paused and brushed the thin red strands from her sweaty neck. "Yesiree, I could do most anythin' back then. I wasn't scared of nothin' an' I was real famous ya know." She held the scrapbook up for him to see the picture. "An' here's me on top of my horse, Star, jus' about to do my death-flip through the ring of fire."

Billy finally turned around on his stool and glanced over at the colorful poster that he'd seen a hundred times before of a beautiful young woman with long flaming red hair standing on the back of a big white horse. It read, "Barnum & Bailey's Greatest Show on Earth proudly presents Dolly Crystal, the Queen of the Circus!"

"Yeah," said Billy, "You were the queen alright. Queen of all the whores," he teased while the men all laughed with their backs turned toward her.

Dolly seemed accustomed to being teased by the men at Joe's Bar but it did bother her. Sometimes they would talk to her and even buy her a drink from time to time but mostly they were cruel and made fun of her. She had no other friends and desperately wanted them to like her so she laughed right along with them. After all, she knew they were probably right.

She gulped down the cold beer to the bottom of the glass then slid down from the stool. "Well, see ya tomorrow night fellas!"

She slowly made her way around to the back of the bar and stepped inside of her tiny rented efficiency. There were newspaper clippings and magazine pages, photographs and old posters plastered over every wall. A red silk scarf with fringes was draped over the one lamp in the room and there was a bed against one wall under the window. An old Victrola sat on the table next to her bed and she owned one record but it was scratched and worn out. She must have listened to it a thousand times but she still loved that song. She turned the crank on the old Victrola and laid her scrapbook on the bed.

"Oh you beautiful doll . . . Ya great big beautiful doll," Dolly sang along with the scratchy voice of Billy Murray as she walked over to the stove and lit a small burner. She reached into the icebox where her dishes were protected from the roaches and pulled out a battered aluminum pot. She opened a can of noodle soup, heated it and poured it into a cup then sat on the edge of the bed. Dolly watched a large roach climbing up the wall over the skirted sink as she drank the soup, not seeming to mind. In fact she even welcomed the sight of another living creature because it made her feel less alone.

After listening to her song several times she turned it off. She recalled hearing something about a hurricane that was moving toward Miami with eighty-five mile an hour winds but couldn't remember hearing when it was supposed to hit. She wasn't too concerned because she'd made it through the big one of 1926 and it was twice as big.

After finishing her soup and rinsing out the cup there was nothing for her to do but gaze at the walls papered in her old memories . . . and remember.

Her thoughts drifted back to the day the nice couple found her. Dolly was ten years old when James and Ruth Gunther spotted her in their back yard sleeping under the leaves. She was curled up in a tiny ball and wearing nothing but a thin dress that was too big for her.

"Shhh! Don't scare er," whispered Ruth, "She might run away."

James knelt down for a closer look and noticed the sour smell of the little girl. Cupped in her right hand was a fistful of the dried corn that he had sprinkled out for the chickens the night before. He gently lifted her tangled red hair away from her face and touched her cheek. "How did ya git here Girl?"

"Git away!" Dolly screeched as she thrashed her arms about.

"We ain't gonna hurt ya, Girl," James said as he pulled away.

Dolly sat up and quickly threw the dried corn kernels into her mouth before they could take them away from her. "Don't worry . . . I'm goin'," she mumbled as she rose to her feet.

"What's yer name, Honey?" Ruth asked, "Where do ya live?"

"My name's Dolly an' I don't live noplace."

Ruth looked at her husband. "My God, James, this child's been abandoned." Her eyes turned back to Dolly. "What's yer last name, Honey? Where's yer mama?"

"Mama went away long time ago an' left me. I'm Dolly . . . Dolly Wafford," she answered, beginning to feel less afraid of them. "Mama's name is Ann but they call her Annie." Just then she leaned forward with her hands over her stomach and squinted her eyes tightly. "I got awful hunger pains."

James bent down and swept her up into his arms. "Let's go get ya somethin' to eat, Dolly."

The Gunthers took her into the house and sat her down at the table. Ruth placed a bowl of hot vegetable soup and fresh bread in front of her.

"This is the first hot food I seen since I don't know when." Dolly reached for the spoon and started scooping it into her mouth as she leaned over the bowl. Within moments the bowl was almost empty. With the bread, she scraped the bowl clean and popped the whole piece into her mouth. She wiped her mouth clean with her arm, storing the food in her cheeks before swallowing and mumbled, "There was . . . there was another nice couple who fed me once," Dolly gulped down some of the storage in her cheeks. "But they wanted to keep me an' I didn't wanna stay."

Ruth passed her another piece of bread. "Why not, Dolly?"

"Cause I wanted to find my uncle an' go live with him . . . so I ran."

"Where does yer uncle live?" asked James.

"I don't know. I wish I did." Dolly's sad blue eyes drooped as she spoke. "I heard he was a good man. Mama didn't like em much but I heard er talkin' 'bout how my daddy was gonna take me up to stay with em fer a while cause mama didn't take good care of me. She was real mad about it but I know my daddy liked my uncle. That's why I do."

When Dolly finished eating all she could hold, the Gunthers took the little girl out to the buckboard and lifted her onto the seat. "We'll find yer uncle, kid. Don't ya go worryin' now, ya hear?" said James.

The old-timer lived alone in a shack about a mile from the Gunthers. Tim Mahoney was a drunk and a gossip and knew everything that ever went on around Valdosta. It wasn't long before James and Ruth were getting some answers.

"Yeah, I met Annie one night at Crockett's Saloon about three years ago. She was drunk an' talkin' about how er husband ran off with er baby. Well, I heard from other folks that er husband was dead an' she still had er kid but she'd leave it alone ever night. She was sayin' that jus' to make herself look good." Tim took a swig of corn liquor and wiped his mouth. "An' I knew she wasn't no good. I could tell cause she was all painted up like a whore an' had all the men in the place hangin' all over er."

Dolly shyed away from the old man and stood behind Ruth's skirt, not liking what he was saying about her mother.

"Do ya know where Annie is now?" asked James.

"Hell. Who knows where she might be by now. She said somethin' about goin' out west to California with some man. That's 'bout all I know."

Ruth said, "Tim . . . think hard. Do ya remember her ever mentionin' er brother-in-law, Thomas Wafford?"

Tim pinched his chin and ran his tongue over his teeth before answering. "Well, I do remember somethin' about some brother of er husband's who lived up in North Georgia . . . 'round Atlanta I think. Marianna er somethin' like that. She told me he was a troublemaker too."

"Could it be Marietta?" Ruth said, "I know there's a Marietta cause I have a second cousin who lives there an' it ain't too far from Atlanta."

"Could be," said Tim, "But like I said, that's jus' about all I know."

Before the day was over they located Dolly's uncle in Marietta and made arrangements to put her on the train early the following morning.

Uncle Thomas was there at the station when Dolly stepped off the train. He was a tall man with long salt and pepper hair, leaning on crutches. "Lordy Girl," he said, "Yer a spittin' image of yer Daddy!" He leaned one crutch against the bench, snatched her up with one arm and swung her up to rest on his hip, almost losing his balance.

Dolly immediately slid back down as he guided her with his arm. "I don't think it's a good idea fer you to be pickin' me up, Uncle Thomas," she said when she noticed that her daddy's brother was missing one foot.

As she stared at the stub where his foot should have been he said, "Oh that ain't nothin' child . . . I lost it in a poker game!" And he made her laugh.

It was a long journey before they reached the small town of Marietta. Uncle Thomas stopped in front of Frank's General Store. "I jus' need to pick up somethin' but it won't take too long," he said.

Dolly browsed around, examining all the merchandise while Uncle Thomas went into the back room with another man. She heard the other man saying, "Here's what I owe ya, Thomas. An' by the way, who's the kid with ya?"

Dolly moved closer to the doorway and listened. She heard Uncle Thomas say, "Oh . . . she's my niece born down in Florida. Poor kid. I jus' found out er Mama deserted er a long time ago an' she ain't got a home so I guess she'll be livin' with me from now on."

"Is that Ernest's kid?"

"Hell no. It's my brother who died's kid. Walter . . . that was his name. He got shot in the back years ago when the girl was jus' a baby. Her name's Dolly an' he used to brag on er all the time. He was crazy 'bout his new daughter but his wife,

Annie, she hated bein' a mother an' she was rotten to the core. He told me she ran 'round on em but I know it's his kid cause she got his eyes."

Dolly stepped away from the doorway then spotted the dried beef strips in a jar on the counter. Her mouth watered but she was too afraid to ask for a piece. She took out a strip and held it to her nostrils, wondering how it would feel to bite into it, when she heard her uncle's footsteps behind her. Quickly, she threw it back into the jar.

"Ya ready to go now, Girl?" He took her by the arm and said, "We still got a purdy good piece to go yet an' I wanna git home before it turns dark." He turned to the man and said, "I'll see ya on Friday, Frank. Oh, an' by the way," he turned and faced Dolly, "This here's Frank Smith. He's one of my poker buddies." The tall man scratched the side of his balding head and nodded.

The two-room shack where Uncle Thomas lived was run down but clean.

"Now you sleep in there," he said as he pointed toward his bedroom. "I'll sleep out here on this cot I made. Now go on an' git some rest." He hugged her close and said, "I'm glad yer here, Dolly."

When she stepped into the tiny room she spotted the white cotton nightgown that Uncle Thomas had placed on her pillow. She undressed and slipped it over her head, smelling the newness of the fabric and realizing that she'd never had anything brand new before. She fell asleep as soon as her head felt the soft pillow beneath it.

Early the next morning Dolly opened her eyes and gazed around the room, lit only by the golden hue of the rising sun. There were clothes strewn across the chair and wobbled in a pile in one corner of the room. A framed picture sat on a primitively built dresser of three men standing together. She stood up and walked over to take a closer look and saw that one of the men was Uncle Thomas. In the picture he was much younger and stood without crutches. Dolly examined the faces of the other two men.

One must have been her father and the other must have been the uncle she'd never seen. She wondered which was which since she'd never seen a picture of her father before.

Dolly slipped out of her new gown and put her dirty thin dress back on. She straightened the blanket on the bed then folded the gown neatly and placed it back onto the pillow. She gathered all the dirty clothes that she could find in the room, planning to wash them all, including the soiled curtains that hung on the tiny window above her bed. She stacked them neatly into a basket then crept out to the front room where her uncle was still sleeping.

Dolly quietly rummaged for a black cast iron skillet and found some salted pork and a basket of eggs on the shelf above the old stove. She peered out through the window and spotted the outhouse. Being careful not to wake her uncle she tiptoed out then back again. She found some coffee and sugar then set to work preparing the food.

The aroma of breakfast began to fill the room and soon reached Uncle Thomas's nostrils. He opened his eyes and sat up blinking. "What's this? Do I smell real food cookin'?"

Dolly knew that she had pleased him. She said with a giggle, "Yep. So git up an' let's eat it."

"Well Girl, it appears to me that you need it more then me," He laughed. "Why look at ya. Yer nothin' more then a bunch a skin an' bones."

He reached for his crutches, pulled himself up and hobbled out the front door to use the outhouse and within a few minutes he was sitting in front of his breakfast at the table.

Dolly had already begun eating. It hadn't dawned on Uncle Thomas that she'd not eaten since he'd met her. He noticed her thin tattered dress and remembered that she had no bag with her when she stepped off the train.

"When was the last time ya ate? Ya look like a damn groun' squirrel with yer cheeks packed with food like that." He wrinkled his nose and puffed his cheeks at her.

Dolly smiled back, exposing the food in her mouth.

"Yer dress ain't gonna fit ya no more after yer through packin' in all that food so I'm gonna take ya into town today fer a new one. How'd ya like that, Dolly?" he said while scraping the last bit of egg onto the fork with his fingers.

She mumbled, "Yep. That'll be good," and continued to stuff the overloaded fork into her mouth repeatedly until her plate was empty.

Dolly was gathering the dirty dishes when Uncle Thomas slipped into the bedroom and came back out with a hairbrush in his hand. "All right Miss Wafford. It's time to get those God awful mats outta yer hair." He motioned for her to sit down and Dolly obediently sat in the chair. As he proceeded to brush he said, "Ya got really purdy red hair, Girl. When was the last time ya brushed out all the tangles?"

"Uh . . . I don't remember, Uncle . . . maybe years . . . I don't know," she laughed.

Uncle Thomas handed her the brush. "I'm gonna go an' hitch up the wagon cause we're goin' shoppin'.

"Uncle, kin I ask ya a question first?"

"What."

"In that picture, which one is my daddy?"

"He's the one wearin' the white shirt. The other one's Ernest."

"Is Ernest dead too?" asked Dolly.

"No, he ain't dead but he might as well be. Me an' yer daddy, we hated em."

"Where does he live, Uncle?"

"Ernest lives right here in Marietta. He moved up here after yer grandmama died lookin' fer a handout but I wouldn't have nothin' to do with em an' we ain't talked in years. Now go wash the grease off yer face. I ain't takin' no dirty kid to town with me." He reached for his crutches then looked at her and smiled.

It was a long six miles to Marietta. The sky was clear blue and the air was crisp. They chattered the whole way.

"Are ya cold?" asked Uncle Thomas.

"Jus' a little bit," Dolly said as she crossed her arms to rub her shoulders.

"Well, put this on," he said, pulling off his coat and handing it to her.

Dolly had never been treated as well by anyone in her life, not even her own mother. "Uncle . . . how come ya took me in to live with ya?"

"Why yer my younger brother's kid ain't ya? An' I'm thankful to have ya here. I figured I wouldn't be so lonely . . . that's all. An' besides . . . ya got the purdiest crystal blue eyes I ever seen." Uncle Thomas paused then said, "Why I had no idea yer Mama left an' you was havin' a hard time. If I knew I'da come lookin' fer ya a long time ago."

His words deeply touched Dolly but she felt too self-conscious to say what was in her heart. Instead, she replied, "This is a mighty long trip fer you to be takin' again jus' to buy me a new dress an' I think it's awful nice of ya, Uncle."

"I'm jus' glad I kin do it fer ya an' besides, I'm gonna like havin' a kid 'round." He put his arm over Dolly's shoulder and said, "Guess it was purdy rough, the way ya been livin' an' all. The Gunthers told me how you was starvin' an' had to sleep out in the woods at night. That musta been terrible fer ya. No kid should ever have to live like that. Yer mama oughta be ashamed. In fact somebody outta beat the tar outta her!"

"But she never hit me er nothin' . . . She jus' didn't pay no attention to me. I learned how to take care of myself real young cause half the time she'd been gone. Sometimes when she was home she'd fix me somethin' to eat but if a man was there she would feed him first an'give me what he didn't eat . . . but sometimes it wasn't enough to fill me up. Mama jus' never had much food in the house cause we was very poor. That's why I had to go out an' find food on my own when Mama wasn't home. Of course I never killed no animals er nothin' but I'd find blackberrys an' lots of good fresh vegetables from people's gardens. I got plenty of food that way an' that's how I learned how to take care of myself. But sometimes people caught me stealin' stuff from their gardens and tell my mama. She'd get real mad at me an' would tie my hands behind my back so I couldn't steal. I'd try to tell er it was jus' cause I was hungry but she still tied me up anyways."

Uncle Thomas felt the fury rise. "It jus' boils my guts thinkin' 'bout how a sweet little thin' like you was treated! If I could find yer mama I'd wring er damn neck! Why I could kill that woman . . . that whore!" He had to gulp down the fury and soften his words when he saw his neice's eyes widen with fear. He tried to comfort her and said, "If yer daddy was alive ya wouldn'ta been treated that way. Why he loved ya more then anythin' in the world. Ya been a very brave little girl, Dolly, to fend fer yerself fer all that time an' turn out as good as ya did. Well, ya don't gotta worry no more 'bout takin care of yerself cause I'm gonna take good care of ya from now on."

As they pulled up to the town square in front of Frank's General Store a fat man with a beard man stepped out from the drug store across the street and came over to them. "Thomas, who's this purdy young thing with ya?" the fat man asked.

"This here's my neice, Ed. Her name's Dolly an' I brung her to buy a new dress. She's gonna be livin' with me from now on." Thomas beamed.

"Mighty nice to meet ya young lady. Yer uncle's been talkin' a lot 'bout ya." His eyes glanced over to the drug store as he spoke. "I own that drug store over there so stop in an' see me sometime. I'll make ya the best strawberry ice cream sundae ya ever tasted."

Uncle Thomas helped Dolly down from the wagon. "See ya Friday, Ed," he said as he led his niece toward the door of the store.

"How ya doin' Frank," said Uncle Thomas as Dolly ran past him, "Do ya think ya might have somethin' real purdy fer my niece to wear to church?"

"Oh Uncle Thomas . . . look at this! Ain't it purdy?" Dolly spotted a pink dress with a matching cape.

Uncle Thomas smiled. "It sure would be fancy to wear to church." He reached for the price tag and sighed. "It costs a lot of money. I don't know if I kin . . . .," He turned to Frank and said, "Ya got somethin' jus' as purdy that don't cost quite . . ." He paused and glanced at Dolly's face, noticing that her smile was beginning to fade. "Hell! Go try it on, Girl," he nodded and said with a smile.

When Dolly came out of the back wearing the dress Uncle Thomas's eyes lit up. "Ya look too damn purdy in that dress to be seen with the likes o' me . . . but I'll buy it fer ya anyways."

Dolly loved Uncle Thomas from the start and there wasn't enough she could do for him. She washed the stack of dirty clothes and took over all the housework from then on. Right away she tackled backbreaking chores, including chopping firewood, without minding at all. She was grateful to him for giving her a home and wanted desperately to please him. She never wanted to go back to the kind of life she'd led ever again.

That Sunday morning Dolly walked out of her room wearing her new pink dress. Her hair was brushed and tied back with a white curtain tie she'd found. "Let me look at ya! Why yer pinker then last night's sunset!" Uncle Thomas sang out cheerfully as Dolly smiled and curtsied. He placed his tattered hat across his chest and bowed. "A queen is what ya look like in that dress. Yesireee' Yer a queen all right! Now let's git goin' so we ain't late fer church."

"Uncle Thomas?" asked Dolly that evening while drying the last few dishes, "Tell me how ya lost yer foot in a poker game."

He laughed. "Now, Miss Dolly, I hope ya know not to believe everythin' an ol' man tells ya." He crossed his knee over the other and put his hand over the end of his footless leg. "What I really meant to say was that when I was down in Florida an' workin' on a fishin' boat down on the St. John's River . . . this alligator . . . musta been some twenty-five feet long, climbed right out of the water an' got up on the deck of the boat. I looked at him an' he looked at me. We both stood there eye to eye fer a long time to see who'd make the first move. Well, that gator decided he would. First he looked at me with those mean eyes then he leaped over an' knocked me down an' snipped off my foot with his powerful jaws jus' like they was scissors!" Uncle Thomas's brows lowered to a serious level. "Blood went spurtin' in all directions an' the pain was like I never felt before." His eyes widened as he raised his brows. "But I was a quick thinker! While the gator was chompin' on my boot tryin' to get to the meat inside I slipped off my other boot an' put a whole box of salt in it. Then I held it back out in front of em with just the tip of my foot in fer the gator to grab. Well, that gator, he loved my foot so much he went back fer seconds. He took my boot in his jaws an' I yanked my foot out jus' in time! Well now, he chomped through that boot an' got a mouthful of salt. Then Lo an' behold! Right there in front of my own eyes that gator dried up an' shriveled down to the size of a chameleon . . . an' I picked em up an' I swallowed em whole!"

Dolly laughed, "Oh Uncle . . . yer such a damn liar."

On Friday evenings Uncle Thomas went into town to play poker with his friends, Frank, Ed and Doc Baker and he also joined in every card game in town that he could find during the week. Most nights he made out well but sometimes it left him deep in debt. Dolly could tell by the look on his face when he came in if he had lost or won. She always waited up for him and made sure he had hot food before going to his clean cot.

When Uncle Thomas had a winning streak he generously bought gifts for Dolly every time they went into town. Dolly soon had nice clothes to wear for the first time in her life. She treasured her new clothes so much that she still wore her old cotton dress to preserve the newness of them for church.

Dolly walked outside in the evenings after supper to visit Thomas's horse out by the barn. She'd always loved horses and dreamed of having one of her own. She loved the smell of the horse and would kiss the soft spot on his nose. She wanted to learn to ride. She wanted to run fast like the wind.

"Maybe Uncle Thomas would let me ride him one day," Dolly thought. She finally conjured up the courage to ask, "Uncle, do ya think maybe ya could let me . . . uh . . . ride yer horse sometime?"

"Of course ya can, Girl. Why, all ya had to do was ask." He held his chin, biting his bottom lip and said, "But ya gotta learn how to first."

He took her out to the barn where the horse was tied and said, "Yer gonna learn how to ride today . . . but ya gotta listen to me an' do what I say."

She patted the horse on his neck and asked, "What do ya call yer horse?"

"I never named him nothin' really. I jus' been callin' him Giddy-up Boy."

"He should have a name. Can't we name em, Uncle?"

"An' what do you suggest."

"Pete . . . Pete, after my brother who died."

"Well then, Pete's what we're gonna call em from now on."

"Kin I ride Pete right now?"

"Ya gotta learn how to put a saddle on first. Here, let me show ya. First ya sling it over his back an' then ya gotta pull these straps tight across his belly."

"This ain't hard. I kin do this," she said as she finished fastening the straps. "There! I did it!"

"Hold on jus' a minute! Yer not done! Pete puffed his belly out so now the straps er too loose. Ya gotta wait fer em to suck it in 'fore ya fasten the straps."

Dolly quickly refastened the straps and said, "Now, Uncle?"

"Yep, now all ya gotta do is jus' hop on his back an' take a hold of the reins."

"I never been on a horse's back before in my life but I jus' know it ain't gonna be hard."

"Yep, there ain't nothin' to it. Jus' give him a little kick on his sides an' he'll go an' when ya wanna stop ya jus' tug back on the reins an' holler whoa! Come on. Jus' hold on to me an' just hop on up."

"I kin do this," Dolly said as she anxiously slid onto Pete's back. She gently pressed her heels into Pete's sides and he began to walk. "Oh this is nothin'!" she said with confidence. "Git goin' Pete!" She slapped her legs against his sides until he took of running.

"Wait jus' a minute!" Thomas yelled but it was too late. Dolly was gone. "Hell! That girl thinks she kin do anythin' she wants."

"Whoooa Pete!" She stopped in the woods and slid down to the ground as if she'd done it a hundred times before. Dolly looked up at the horse and stroked his soft nose, saying, "Yer really a fine horse, Pete. We're gonna be good together, ain't we?"

By the end of the summer Uncle Thomas had qualified her as an expert rider. She hurdled over creeks and ran the horse hard until she could make Pete do anything she wanted him to do.

"Ya really got a knack with horses, Dolly," Uncle Thomas said, "Why yer jus' as good as anybody. In fact yer better then most . . . but I watched ya take off this mornin' an' you was runnin' that horse too fast. I jus' want ya to be careful an' not break yer neck. So jus' don't go ridin' too fast ya hear?"

"Oh, Uncle," said Dolly, "I ain't gonna git hurt. Why I feel like Pete's part of my own body."

Months swiftly rolled into winter. Dolly happily cleaned and baked, mended and chopped firewood while her uncle went to his card games. She made bright new curtains and scrubbed the dirty stone floor until it gleamed. The dismal two-room shack soon took on the warmth of a real home.

Every morning before doing her chores, Dolly's first thoughts were about Pete. She could hardly wait to get dressed and out to the barn to saddle up.

Riding soon became second nature to Dolly and she needed more of a challenge. It wasn't long before she was riding bareback, holding onto Pete's mane instead of using the reins.

CHAPTER 2

Old Dolly felt tired. She slipped off her shoes and settled back in the bed then reached over and turned off the scarf-covered lamp. The flashing neon sign from the side of Joe's Bar lit her room with rhythmatic spurts of blue light. As she stared at the hypnotic blue reflections in her dresser mirror she vividly relived the haunting nightmare in every detail.

The Friday night before Dolly's twelfth birthday Uncle Thomas had won enough money playing poker to buy her a horse at the auction. The next day Dolly fell in love with a sixteen-hand high Tennessee walker named Pronto and Thomas's bid of eleven dollars did it.

Dolly mounted Pronto the minute Uncle Thomas handed the money to the auctioneer.

"Ya gonna ride em right now? Without reins?" asked Uncle Thomas.

"Yep. It ain't no problem. I kin do it."

"Ya sure he ain't too big fer ya, Dolly?" Uncle Thomas looked over at her as she rode along side of him. "How's his gait feel to ya?"

"Oh, he couldn't be no better. I love Pronto so much. Why he feels like part of me . . . jus' like Pete does."

They rode into town side by side. She rode with her head high, hoping that everyone in town would notice that she was riding her own horse.

"Let's look at some saddles," Uncle Thomas said as they approached Frank's General Store.

"Oh don't bother gettin' me a saddle . . . er nothin' fer that matter. I like to ride jus' like this . . . with nothin' but my hands an' legs."

"Well then, let me buy ya some ice cream." He grinned as he passed her a piece of thin rope from his saddlebag.

"Ya know, Uncle Thomas?" Dolly said as they were tying the horses to the hitching post in front of Ed's Drug Store. "Today I'm twelve years old an' I jus' can't believe I been stayin' with ya fer this long. I never been happier in all my life an' now I even got my own horse. Nobody was ever good to me like you been. I jus' want ya to know how grateful I am to ya."

He reached up for his crutches and said, "Aw . . . ya don't have to say nothin' . . . I know."

Inside the drugstore Dolly took a seat on a stool at the counter.

"This summer's hotter then it usually is," Ed said to Uncle Thomas as he passed the strawberry ice cream sundae over to Dolly.

"Reckon so," said Uncle Thomas, reaching into his pocket and placing a nickel on the counter. "But it's gonna rain soon . . . I kin feel it in my knees. That'll cool us down a bit."

"Oh Yeah. I almost forgot to tell ya. Ya know my sister up in Tennessee who married that rich fella who owns the glass factory?" Ed said, as he slid the nickel into is cash register and passed back a penny.

"Yeah, I know. What about er?"

"Well anyways, her boy, Matt, went an' dove off a high waterfall an' almost broke his daggum neck. I think he only broke his arm er somethin' but he was sure lucky. I'll tell ya, sometimes I don't think that boy's gotta penny's worth of brains in that fool head of his," Ed said as he shook his head, "Well, he almost drowned too. But good thin' he was with this other boy. I think his name was Josh . . . no. What was his name now? Oh yeah . . . Jacob. Yeah . . . Jacob . . . that was his name. Well anyways, Jacob, he jumped in an' saved my nephew from drownin'." Ed shook his head again and said, "Sometimes I think he shoulda jus' let em drown cause my sister, all she does is complain about how rotten he is anyways."

Uncle Thomas really wasn't interested in what Ed was saying but Dolly absorbed every word.

"Oh Yeah? Hey Ed, we gotta git goin'. See ya Friday," Uncle Thomas said as he nudged Dolly to leave.

As they were riding away Uncle Thomas said, "Ed talks too

much. If ya let em git goin' he never stops. He'll stretch the truth an' gossip like an ol' woman."

That following Friday afternoon Uncle Thomas invited Dolly to come with him into Marietta for the poker game. "Ya ain't invited to play, ya hear? Jus' watch. But I think yer gonna enjoy what ya see cause yer gonna be seein' yer uncle pullin' in all the chips!"

Dolly was excited about going. "Oh, I'll stay outta yer way, Uncle. I'll jus' bring ya good luck . . . that's all."

The supper dishes were washed and put away when Dolly realized that she was still wearing her old dress. "Give me some time to git dressed, Uncle. I forgot how late is was."

"Oh ya kin go jus' like ya are. It's too damn hot to wear anythin' good. Oh! I almost forgot! I wanna give ya somethin' 'fore we go." Uncle Thomas stepped into the bedroom to retrieve his surprise then came back out and handed her a small black beaded purse. "Now open it up."

Dolly pulled it open and took out a tiny box of lip rouge. She looked up him and said, "Do ya think I'm old enough to wear this stuff? I mean . . . I really love it an' the purse is real purdy . . . but am I really old enough fer this?"

"Yep," Uncle Thomas said as he grabbed his battered felt hat.

"Kin I ride Pronto to town?"

"Nope. I got Pete hitched to the wagon ready to go so let's get outta here before it get's too late an' they start without me."

Dolly quickly ran to put the purse back in the bedroom then hurried out the door to the wagon.

The smoldering sun was beating down hard as they began their journey toward town. Dolly's thin dress was soaked with sweat. "It sure is hot, ain't it Uncle?"

"Yep, it's hotter then hell out here."

"Ya reckon it'll cool down later?"

"Yep. Always does."

"Hey, Uncle. Thank ya fer the nice gifts. I should'na said what I did."

"Well Girl, ya jus' growin' up an' I figured ya might like somethin' grown-up-like. That beaded purse really caught my eye an' I figured you kin use it when ya git all dressed up. I jus' threw in the lip rouge, thinkin' it would make ya feel more grown-up. Besides . . . ya kin jus' practice with it if ya want."

With only two more miles left to go on the rocky red clay road, the sun's intense rays were beginning to soften. They were passing a wide grassy field when all of a sudden a black bear cub ran out in front of the wagon. Uncle Thomas pulled hard on the reins but couldn't stop the wheels from crushing it's little neck.

"Oh, Uncle Thomas! A baby bear! The poor thin'! Do ya think we killed em?"

They climbed down to examine the cub. Thomas used his crutch to poke at the small black mound of fur under the wagon but it did not budge. "Oh, he's deader then a doornail alright!"

As he used his crutch again to push the dead cub away from the path of the back wheel they heard a loud human-like groan. Dolly and her uncle turned around and there stood a four hundred pound black beast ready to tear them apart.

"Oh shit!" howled Uncle Thomas, "It's the mama bear!" He poked at her with his crutch while Dolly scrambled to get back up to the wagon seat.

"Uncle Thomas! Be careful! She's mad!" Dolly took the reins in her hands and watched the angry mother lash out at Uncle Thomas with her mighty claw.

"Run Dolly! Git . . . .," His voice trailed off into silence as he fell to the ground.

Dolly's heart was pumping so hard she could hardly breathe. The horse reared up but didn't move from his spot. She sat frozen, not believing what she was watching. Sprawled across the rocky road face down, Uncle Thomas was motionless. Unable to move, Dolly watched as the giant black female backed away from him. From not more than six feet away, she stared down until the bear's eyes met hers. Not knowing what to do and feeling fear beginning to mix with anger, she glared back into the eyes of the huge bear and began to scream, "Get outta here bear! Git! Shoo! Git outta here ya damn bitch bear!" The bear took off running back into the field.

Dolly jumped down and knelt by her uncle's side, crying, "Oh Uncle Thomas, please don't die! Oh please don't leave me!"

She managed to roll him over onto his back. His shirt was drenched with the warm red liquid as she tore it open to look at his wounds. She felt her stomach juices rising and turning to vomit when she saw the four long, deep gashes oozing blood. Then she shuddered with relief to see his chest rise and fall to the rhythm of life.

She was unable to lift her uncle onto the wagon and wept out of frustration as she tried. An idea suddenly struck her. She managed to pull the heavy canvas tarp from the back and spread it out onto the ground next to her uncle. She tied two corners of the canvas with a rope and tied the rope to the back of the wagon. She kept saying over and over to herself, "This is the best I kin do . . . the best I kin do," as she rolled Uncle Thomas's limp body onto the canvas. Dolly was afraid he was dying so she hurried back up to the seat and took the reins. "Easy now boy . . . come on, Pete . . . Let's git!"

As the wagon started to move so did the canvas holding Uncle Thomas. Dolly walked the horse slowly trying to avoid stones in the road but when she looked back she could see his head bouncing back and forth with every step the horse took. She ached inside for him with every rock and bump that tossed his body around on the canvas but it was the best she could do.

She pulled her uncle slowly on the canvas for two and a half hours before she finally reached the town square. By then the sun was pink and she was relieved that she had made it before dark.

People came running out when they saw the little girl dragging the canvas with a man on it. Two men picked Uncle Thomas up and rushed him into Ed's drug store where Doc Baker had a clinic upstairs.

Doc Baker said, "Dolly, your uncle's torn up pretty bad and he's lost a lot of blood. I'm gonna have to keep him here for a while. You might outta stay with your uncle's brother. He's in town. I'll send somebody to fetch him for ya."

Dolly cried as they carried Thomas up the stairs. She overheard Ed saying, "Well Thomas, don't reckon we're playin' poker tonight, huh?

Dolly waited on the stool downstairs in the drug store. She had never laid eyes on Uncle Ernest before, except in the photograph on her dresser. She'd heard from Uncle Thomas that he was a bad man. He lived about five miles south of the town square but Uncle Thomas hadn't spoken to him in over twenty years. They hated each other.

Minutes later a man approached her. "Are you Dolly Wafford?"

"Yes," she answered politely.

"Well, they got me to come git ya an' take ya home with me." Ernest, a lot younger than Uncle Thomas, had a long beard and wore a beat up dusty black hat. He moved closer and put his fingers under her chin and grinned, displaying his yellowed decaying teeth. He spit a wad of brown slimy chewing tobacco on the floor and, slurring his words, he said, "So yer Walter's kid huh?" He pulled out a dirty bandana and wiped his sweaty neck then took a big gulp from his flask. "So I guess yer goin' home with me now." He reached for Dolly's hand but she pulled it away, not wanting to touch him. He smelled of whiskey and filth and looked evil to her.

Ernest led her to his buckboard and she reluctantly climbed up onto the seat. She turned to her uncle and asked, "Do ya mind if maybe I kin jus' stay here in town an' wait till Uncle Thomas gits better? Then ya won't have to take me with ya. I kin take care of myself . . . really. I did it before fer a long time an' I was jus' fine."

"Shut yer mouth girl!" he snapped as he shook the reins hard to make the horses move.

Dolly was afraid to say another word.

When the sun was completely gone Ernest stopped just long enough to light a lantern while the thought of another bear nearby crossed Dolly's mind and made her shudder. Without a word he shook the reins and continued on the long five-mile journey to his shanty.

When Ernest opened his front door the stench was overpowering. There was only one room and in the corner was a bucket filled with human waste. The dirty glass windows were tightly closed and the odor was making her feel sick to her stomach.

Her uncle motioned for her to lie down on the one bed in the room. A large rat scurried across her foot while Ernest was lighting the lantern. She screamed and startled him into dropping the lantern on his foot.

"Damn it girl! It's only a rat!" He picked up the lantern and said, "Ya almost made me burn the damn place down! Now git on that bed!"

Dolly plopped down onto the edge of the filthy bed and watched her uncle as he went over to open the window.

"Damn! It's hot as hell in here!" He unbuttoned his shirt and took it off then sat down onto the one chair in the room to remove his boots. "I need a Goddamn drink," he said as he reached for one of the bottles on the table. He took a few generous gulps and said, "Ah . . . that's better." He raised his brows and held the bottle out to offer Dolly a drink.

"No thank you."

"Well ain't ya gonna undress?" he asked as he stood up to take off his britches. He pulled off all his clothes until he was completely naked. He deliberately stood in front of her, making her squirm with embarrassment.

The sight of her naked uncle frightened her and she couldn't answer him. She took off her boots then hesitatingly reclined back onto the dirty rumpled bed.

"Okay Girl . . . now roll over," he said as he climbed into the small bed with her.

Dolly inched her way so far over that she was in the crack between the bed and the wall.

Within minutes she could hear the sounds of his sputtering snore. She stared up at the ceiling, afraid to look down at his naked body that was fully exposed in the moonlight. She was afraid to move and afraid to close her eyes but soon fatigue and sleepiness overruled her will to stay awake.

When Dolly awoke the next morning he was gone. "Thank God," she muttered to herself and slipped out the door to urinate onto the ground by the side of the shanty.

She was hungry. She went back inside to look for food and found a sack on the table with a half of a loaf of hard bread and two eggs. She hurriedly lit a small fire in the fireplace and heated the black skillet. She found only one plate and one fork but they were dirty. She scraped them off then cracked the two eggs into the hot skillet. The scent of rotten eggs filled her nostrils but they looked so good to her that she scrambled them anyway and slid them onto the dirty plate. She broke the hard bread before quickly swallowing the rancid eggs. She gulped down a cup of water then ate the bread fast to kill the taste in her mouth.

Dolly heard Ernest step through the door in back of her and turned around. The sight of him disgusted her. She knew now why Uncle Thomas wouldn't have anything to do with him."

"Girl, I want ya to take off that dress so as I kin look at ya," He said as he began unbuttoning his shirt.

"No! I ain't gonna undress in front of the likes of you!"

Ernest shoved her onto the bed and pounced on top of her. "Yer gonna lay still an' like it, Girl," he said as he held her down.

"Git off of me ya nasty bastard!"

Ernest held her down with his right arm while he fumbled for the slit in the crotch of her bloomers. "Jus' shut up! Ain't nobody kin hear ya anyways!" he said as he pressed hard with his right arm against her small sensitive breasts.

Pain mixed with rage shot through her as she screamed, "What are ya doin!" I'll tell Uncle Thomas! Git offa me, ya ba . . ."

Suddenly her words stopped as Ernest reached up with his left hand and punched her on the side of the head. He hit her so hard that blood started to trickle out of her ear. Dolly became limp as he unbuttoned his pants and forcefully guided his erection into her tiny opening. She finally lost consciousness to escape the pain while he finished relieving himself inside her.

When Dolly regained her senses she could not move. There was blood between her thighs, on the pillow and all over the bed. Her small developing breasts were tender and still throbbing from the pressure of his weight.

"That'll teach ya not to argue back with me, Girl," Ernest

said as he stood up to pull up his pants. "Ya jus' stay put . . . ya hear?" he said while slipping back into his soiled shirt and grabbing his dusty black hat. "I'm ridin' into town fer some food. Ya try to leave from here an' I'll track ya down an' skin yer ass like a jackrabbit," he said as he pulled the door closed behind him.

Once she heard the sound of hoofs growing faint in the distance Dolly wailed out loud to relieve her anger. "Oh Dear God!" she sobbed, "Why did ya let em do that to me? Why!" She slid down from the bed onto the floor, feeling the burning pain like she had been turned inside out over a blazing fire. She struggled to get to her feet and ran straight for the door. She tried to push it open but it was locked from the other side. Her heart began to pound as her eyes darted from one window to the other, remembering his last threatening words, "I'll skin yer ass like a jackrabbit!"

Dolly knew that if she ran he'd find her and kill her. She was too terrified to move and collapsed helplessly back onto the rumpled blood stained bed. She drew her arms and legs in and tucked her head down into a fetal position then cried loud and hard until her head was throbbing.

Just before sundown the door opened and Ernest staggered in. Dolly could feel her muscles stiffen, locking her into an even tighter fetal position.

"I thought ya might be gettin' hungry by now, Girl. I got some dried beef an' some beans an' coffee an' plenty more stuff to eat." He almost had a gentle tone in his voice but Dolly did not respond. Ernest gazed lustfully at her small body curled into a rigid ball and positioned against the wall, licking his slobbery lips and saying, "I never knew I had such a sweet young niece before. Has yer Uncle Thomas tried ya out yet?"

Dolly uncoiled her body in rage and stood up. "Ya better shut yer filthy mouth, ya damn son-of-a-bitch!" she screamed. "I'm gittin' outta here before ya . . .,"

Suddenly she felt the sting of the back of his hand as he struck her across the face, throwing her onto the floor.

"That'll teach ya to mouth off like that again," he said as he rolled her over with his foot.

Ernest continued raping Dolly that night. She tried to fight him but he brutally beat her until she had cuts and welts all over her body. Everytime she screamed from the pain he would strike her again. She finally gave up and became limp. From that time on she would not put up a struggle.

He used the little girl's body several times a day, often whipping her with a strap that added to his pleasure. Numbed by the excruciating pain, Dolly became like a rag doll, not moving from the bed and staring at the ceiling, hating his sweaty naked body and his horrible mean face. Hating the stench of his slimy mouth. Hating him more each day.

Her uncle offered bits of food but Dolly refused to eat. Her stomach ached from the emptiness but could not stand the thought of putting food into her mouth that came from his hand.

On the sixth night, after the routine rape, Dolly realized that she was going to die unless she could find a way to escape. She decided to make an attempt that night. Once he was asleep she would run. She was scared of him but the thought of being caught was even more frightening. She prayed she could find the courage to do it.

Afraid to move for hours, she finally decided that it was time. She listened for the steady rhythm of his breathing that produced his snoring and grunts then slowly pulled herself away from his hairy naked body and tiptoed toward the door. Dolly's legs were weak beneath her and her hands trembled as she quietly reached for her thin cotton dress on the floor. She made her way to the door handle and very slowly pulled up the latch. The door made a loud squeak and she froze for a moment. She looked back, waiting for him to wake up but his uninterrupted snoring continued. She managed to get the heavy wooden door opened just wide enough to slip out. She could hear him beginning to stir and darted out as fast as she could, leaving the door open behind her.

She ran into the woods without looking back and continued to run until her breath was almost gone. She had to stop to rest then realized that she had no idea where she was. The moon was almost gone and it was pitch black amongst the tall pines. She slipped into her dress then dropped to the pine needle covered ground. Resting just long enough to catch her breath, she had to keep moving for fear he would be chasing her soon. Her bare feet were filled with blackberry thorns but she did not want to stop long enough to pull them out. She would find her way back to town and tell Uncle Thomas what Ernest had done to her. She thought for a moment. She felt so dirty and ashamed. Maybe she shouldn't tell anyone.

Dolly was tired and hungry. Her insides ached where Ernest had violated her with his large penis. She felt like vomiting and fell down to her knees. Her stomach was so empty that she threw up nothing but bitter green bile. Sudden fear that he might be near prompted her to jump back to her feet to continue moving. There was no way she could see in the darkness so she had to move slowly through woods, groping through the blackness and stumbling over fallen branches. Finally she dropped to the ground and wept.

Dolly sprang to her feet the moment she saw the first hint of morning light. She made her way through a clump of blackberry bushes that snagged her skin, leaving bloody trails on her face, arms and legs. She wandered through the thick pines for the rest of the day, collecting more painful cuts and thorns with her bare feet.

Just before dark she spotted what appeared to be a road and ran toward it. It was the road that led into Marietta. She was careful to stay off to the side in the woods so she wouldn't be seen by Ernest and followed it into town.

She made her way toward the storefront, dragging her feet until she reached the door. It was locked. She pounded on the door screaming, "Please let me in! Help me! Somebody help me!" Then she collapsed onto the wooden walkway, weakened by hunger and exhaustion.

The door opened and there stood Doc Baker. He had heard her from upstairs in his clinic where Uncle Thomas was.

Ed came running over. "I thought I heard a kid screamin'. He looked down and cried, "Oh my Lord it's Dolly!"

Doc Baker snatched up her small limp body, noticing that she was as light as a feather, covered in dried blood and reeked of Ernest's sweat and dried semen. He knew immediately what had happened to her. Ed followed as Doc Baker carried her up the stairs to the clinic.

"It was Ernest. He's been usin' this girl. But don't say anything to Thomas cause he's not ready for this just yet," whispered Doc Baker. He laid her down on the bed next to Uncle Thomas's and used ammonia to try to bring her out of her daze. He listened to her heart but there was nothing he could do but clean her up and dress her wounds.

Dolly slowly opened her eyes and began to cry, "Please help me, Doc . . . I hurt so bad I . . . .", She suddenly silenced her crying when she saw Uncle Thomas in the bed next to her. "He's gonna be alright, ain't he Doc?" she said as she tried to choke back her sobs.

Uncle Thomas heard his niece and opened his eyes to look at her. In a weak strained voice he said, "Lordy girl! What happened to ya?" He struggled to sit up and reach for Dolly but he couldn't move. His pale face began to twist with anxious curiosity. "Did Ernest hurt ya? Tell me! What did he do to ya!"

"No . . . No, Uncle," still trying to choke back the tears, "I . . . . I got lost in the woods an' I fell down . . . an' . . . got all cut up . . . that's all," she lied with a half smile.

Thomas stretched his trembling arms out to her and said, "Come on over here, girl . . . next to yer Uncle Thomas."

She managed to climb over to him and fell into the comfort of his arms. He held her close, stroking her long hair back away from her dirty tear-stained face and whispered, "Shhh . . . Shhh, now, now, Dolly, yer safe now . . . . Shhh . . . Shhh."

CHAPTER 3

Old Dolly opened her eyes and welcomed the morning light to come in and flood out her dream. Her old bones creaked as she sat up. Carefully sliding her feet to the floor, she slipped into her worn out shoes and made her way to the tiny bathroom.

While the old woman was sitting on the toilet she reached over to the sink for her hairbrush and started brushing her thin red hair. She couldn't see very well but she could feel the strands falling onto her bare thighs. She picked the hair out of the brush and flushed it down the toilet.

She slowly shuffled over to her dressing table where she applied thick white powder over yesterdays' makeup. Dolly spent time painting her lips and smearing red rouge in a circular motion on each cheek until they looked like candy apples then she re-glued her false eyelashes and added more black mascara to what was there. Gazing at the reflection of her painted face, but not seeing the smudges and crooked lines, Dolly imagined that she was just as beautiful as she always was. She rolled her stockings neatly down to her ankles and stood up to smooth her wrinkled dress then picked up her scrapbook and out the door she went.

Within minutes she was fetching a cold beer from the icebox at the Lighthouse Grocery Store.

"How are things Dolly?" Mike Stern said from behind the counter. It was unusual for him to say much to Dolly because he never cared for her but he was in an especailly good mood that day. "Have you heard anything from your son lately?"

"Nope. Not a word . . . an' I reckon I don't expect to neither." Dolly replied as she counted the pennies in the palm of her hand. "I need a pack of Old Golds too, Mike."

"Dolly, don't you ever eat?"

"When I git hungry I do," she said as she slapped the coins down on the counter, "Be back in a while, Mike."

With her scrapbook clutched in her arms she went back out to her apple crate throne where she waited for anyone to stop and listen to her stories. But people only stared as they went by.

A small child came up to her and pointed his finger, saying, "Mommy! Look at the funny lady!"

The mother yanked the boy by the hand and with an embarrassing smile she said, "Joey! That's not polite!"

Dolly did look funny with her flaming red hair and painted face with a cigarette dangling from her lips. "Well, that's alright. I guess he jus' don't know who I am," grinned the old woman.

Once the mother and child were out of sight she opened her scrapbook to the newspaper article about stabbing her uncle and her thoughts drifted back to that day.

Dolly and Uncle Thomas had been home two days when she remembered the black beaded purse and lip rouge that she had put away. She needed an escape from the horrible memories of Ernest. Maybe if she kept busy it would help. She went into the bedroom and snatched them from the drawer. She grabbed the small mirror that hung on the wall then sat on the bed and gazed at her reflection. Her bottom lids were lined with red and there were dark circles beneath them. Tears swelled as she said to herself, "Dolly Wafford, yer gonna be real purdy in a minute." She dipped her pinky finger into the lip rouge then ran it over her thin lips over and over again until they were bright red. "There!" she said as she smacked her lips. But she still felt ugly and even more ashamed than ever. She tossed her purse and lip rouge back into the drawer and ran out to visit Pronto.

"Poor ol' fella." She kissed his nose. "I'm so sorry we left ya fer so long. I'm glad yer doin' fine." Pronto nudged her cheek as if he understood every word. She mounted his back and walked him over to the creek where he could cool his feet and drink the refreshing cold water. "We ain't doin' no hard ridin' today. I jus' want ya to git strong again."

Before going back to the house Dolly gave him a pat on the neck and whispered, "I promise I'll never leave ya ever again, Boy."

"Poor Pronto. He's so skinny, Uncle," said Dolly as she stepped through the door.

"Now don't ya go worryin' so much. He didn't die from starvation, an besides, we'll fatten em up again."

"But that was a long time to go without eatin'. Do ya reckon he'll be alright?"

"Yeah, he'll be jus' fine." Uncle Thomas looked up from the kitchen chair. "Hey, what's that red stuff on yer lips? Ya look like a damn clown."

"It's what ya bought fer me. Don't ya like it?"

"Oh yeah." Uncle Thomas tilted his head to examine her face. "Maybe not so much next time an' only put it on when yer home. I don't want folks thinkin' yer older then ya are."

Ignoring his disapproving remarks, Dolly learned over to hug her uncle's neck. "It's so good to be home, ain't it Uncle?"

"I need to run over to see Ed over at his place fer a little while," Uncle Thomas said as he reached for his crutches. "There's somethin' he wants to tell me."

"What's he wanna tell ya, Uncle?" she asked nervously, twisting her fingers together behind her back.

"Hell, Girl. If I knew I wouldn't be goin' over there to find out now would I."

Feeling guilty, she kept busy with house chores while Uncle Thomas was gone. "What if Ed says somethin' 'bout what happened? What would I say? I'm gonna look like a liar," she mumbled as she swept the orange sand out the front door. "It's already embarrassin' enough jus' with Ed an' Doc Baker knowin'. He's gonna be disgusted with me an' hate me." She tried to stay calm. "Maybe they won't say nothin' 'bout me. Maybe it's jus' some stupid thing he wants to tell em like maybe he owes Uncle money an' don't have it." She wiped her sweaty palms on her skirt after leaning the broom against the wall in the corner then began wiping the lip rouge from her lips.

"I'll kill that damn stinkin' bastard!" Uncle Thomas screamed as he stormed in slamming the door behind him. "Dolly! Why in the hell didn't ya tell me!" he yelled as he stumbled toward the gun rack. "Ya jus' wait here, Girl." He snatched out his shotgun and forgetting his crutches, he charged out through the door, hobbling on his stubbed leg and so overwhelmed with anger that he felt no pain. He climbed onto the wagon and took off in a burst of red dust.

Dolly, afraid for her uncle, ran for the long-bladed knife and tucked it into her boot then dashed out the door. She made a promise to herself that she would get to Ernest before Uncle Thomas did. She jumped onto her horse and shouted, "Git goin'! Git, Pronto! Git!"

She ran the horse hard through the woods to pass her uncle's wagon on the road. She held tight to Pronto's mane as she they hurdled over fallen trees and crossed the wide creek until she knew that she was far ahead of Uncle Thomas. She crossed over onto the clay road, through town, and straight to Ernest's shanty.

"Thank God!" she breathlessly panted. "Thank ya Lord fer getting' me here before Uncle Thomas did."

Quickly and fearlessly, Dolly jumped down from her horse and darted toward the door that she had once escaped through. She barged in and caught the ugly sight of Uncle Ernest lying on the bed in a drunken stupor with his britches off.

"Hey Girl, so ya come back fer more?" he said with a thick-tongued speech.

Oh, how Dolly detested him. She blurted out, "Ya bastard! Ya ain't gonna hurt me no more an' ya ain't gonna lay a hand on Uncle Thomas . . . cause I'll kill ya first!"

To Dolly's surprise the drunken man swiftly leaped off the bed and grabbed her by the arm, throwing her onto the floor.

"Do ya want this?" He said nastily as he held her down and slid his hand down to his hairy crotch.

The young girl was pinned down and helpless against Ernest's powerful arms. She thought about the knife in her boot but couldn't get to it. As he tore off her bloomers and violently tried to push himself inside of her she screamed, "Dear God! Help me! Please don't do this to me again!" She desperately squirmed and twisted her body, slinging her legs from side to side, trying to prevent him from entering.

"Hold still ya little bitch!" he yelled as his face grew redder.

The door flew open and there stood Uncle Thomas with his shotgun aimed at his brother's head. "Git offa that girl, ya fuckin' bastard!" Uncle Thomas limped closer to his brother and held the shotgun to his face.

Ernest, still on top of Dolly, reached up and slapped the gun back, making it go off. The whiskey bottles on the table shattered from the force. Ernest jumped up and Thomas stumbled and fell. Ernest pounced on top of him and began smashing his head against the stone floor.

In shock, Dolly watched as Uncle Thomas's body became limp. The blood began to drain out onto the floor around his head. Ernest stood up and looked down at his brother's lifeless body.

She quickly reached for her knife and from behind, lunged forward and jabbed the back of his leg, causing him to stagger then fall to the floor. She yanked out the knife and rolled on top of him, stabbing the side of his neck. "I'm gonna kill ya!" she screeched in a violent storm of rage. Blood spurted into her eyes as she pulled the knife back again ready to stab his chest.

"Please! Please don't do it! Please Dolly . . . Don't!" he begged.

She let out a scream as she plunged the long blade into his shoulder then yanked it out again.

While holding his neck with one hand, Ernest's other hand quickly moved down to his shoulder. He moaned, "Don't kill me! Aghhh . . ."

Without mercy Dolly continued her attack. She looked down at his penis to see that it was still slightly erect and with one heavy whack of the huge sharp blade it was split down the middle. He grabbed his crotch and red ooze spurted between his fingers. His eyes rolled back before they closed.

Dolly stood up, "Die . . . . ya worthless hunk o' dog shit!" Trembling, she threw the knife down and looked down at her Uncle Thomas. His head was lying in a muddy red pool. "Uncle Thomas!" she screamed. She knelt down and picked his head up to rest on her lap. "Please don't be dead. Uncle, kin ya hear me?"

Thomas slowly opened his eyes and gazed up at her. "Are ya all right girl?" he asked in a weak voice as his eyes moved toward his brother lying on the floor. "Is he dead?"

Dolly looked over at Ernest's motionless body and answered, "Yeah, he's dead."

Dolly helped the old man to stand on his one foot then finally made it out to the wagon. He held the back of his head trying to stop the blood but it kept trickling through his fingers until his shirt was saturated.

"I feel kinda dizzy-like," he said.

"Try an' see if ya kin git yer foot up here. Jus' hold on to me." Dolly had found the strength to help him up onto the wagon. She tore off a piece of the bottom of her dress and handed it to Uncle Thomas to hold against his head before she took the reins.

As Pete began to pull the wagon, pronto followed. Dolly glanced back at the shanty one last time. Flashbacks from the horrible nightmare made her shudder. "It's all over now," she sighed.

When they reached home Dolly helped her uncle off with his clothes, cleaned off the blood and examined his head. She saw several deep cuts and used a clean piece of linen to bandage his head. He still felt dizzy so she helped him into the bed. "He'd be better by tomorrow," she thought to herself. "I jus' know he will."

Within minutes Thomas drifted off to sleep. Dolly looked down at her blood soaked dress then ran outside toward the creek. She stripped off all of her clothes and shoes then tossed them into the rushing water. As she stood shaking, she watched them float away downstream leaving a red trail behind them. She stepped into the cold water and began rubbing her skin with sand and pebbles, trying to rid her body of all traces of Uncle Ernest. She repeatedly scrubbed the same areas of her body over and over again. After ten minutes of scrubbing she stepped onto the bank, shivering but still feeling dirty.

When she came back into the house Uncle Thomas was still asleep. She checked to make sure he was breathing by watching his chest rise and fall. Dolly took a deep breath and sighed, "He seems to be peaceful now. "Oh thank You, Lord."

Her heart was still pounding as she slipped into her nightgown then knelt by her bed to pray, "Dear God . . . please forgive me fer what I jus' did. Please let Uncle Thomas be all right . . ." She paused when she heard voices coming from outside.

She went back into where her uncle was sleeping. The door flung open and there stood three men. One of them was the Sheriff.

"Ya better come into town with us Dolly," he said.

CHAPTER 4

The old woman closed the scrapbook and gazed out at the palmettos on the vacant lot across the street where the kids were out playing. Dolly felt so alone and yearned for them to come over to visit with her again. She thought about how she loved children because they were so full of innocent wonder then she suddenly was overwhelmed with shame. She remembered her own baby . . . the son she could never love.

The awning that shaded her apple crate wasn't much help. The sweltering August sun heated the air like an oven, causing the rouge on her cheeks to slide down with the sweat, leaving streaks behind as the flies swarmed around Dolly's face and legs. She was so uncomfortable but had nowhere to go. Her small efficiency was hotter than outside. Dolly's only relief was to step inside the Lighthouse Grocery Store and stand under the ceiling fan.

"It sure don't look like no storm's comin' this way to me. It's mighty hot out there an' the sun is jus' as bright as ever," Dolly said to Mike as she reached into the icebox. "This cold air sure feels refreshin'. If I wasn't so dern fat I'd climb right in!" she laughed.

"Well, you better close it up cause you're letting out all the cold air." He scrunched his face, showing no sign of a sense of humor as he counted the pennies on the counter.

After cooling off inside she stepped back out to her apple crate and spotted the two young girls tiptoeing across the hot pavement on Twenty-Seventh Avenue in their bare feet. They broke out into a run, pulling the wagon fast behind them. Dolly sat up straight and mopped her sweaty face and neck with her dirty handkerchief.

"Maybe they'll stop to listen again today," she muttered to herself. She took a swig of the ice-cold beer and gently wiped her mouth, being careful not to spoil her painted-on lips.

The girls finally made it to the relieving shade of the building. Dolly's eyes lit up as she began, "Do ya remember me?"

Ida darted past Dolly, without answering and ran into the store but Dixie dropped the wagon handle and had to sit down to rub her stinging feet. "Boy, that tar's steaming hot!" she squealed. She glanced up and noticed the disappointed look in Dolly's eyes and felt sorry for her and said, "We'll be back in a minute, Dolly." She jumped up and ran into the store after Ida, pulling the wagon behind her.

The old woman waited impatiently for them to come back out. She reached down for the scrapbook and held it anxiously on her lap.

Within minutes they came out of the grocery store and walked over to her. "Hi Dolly. Will you tell us another story?" The blond girl bit into a Three Musketeer bar and plopped down onto the concrete next to Dixie.

"Oh Ida! We forgot Dolly's mangoes!" Dixie remembered as she turned to look up at Dolly's face. "I'm sorry, Dolly. We had em all in a bag but Ida forgot to put em in the wagon."

"It's alright. Ya kin bring em next time." The old woman was delighted as she opened her scrapbook again. She moved her wrinkled hand over the page until her index finger rested on a photograph of the same pretty girl with ringlets standing next to an old man with crutches. "This is me an' my Uncle Thomas when we was at church. See? He ain't got a foot on one leg. This was taken jus' before I joined the circus. Oh . . . an' that's Ella standin' in the back by the wagon. That Ella, she was somethin' else too. She was real good to me an' really did love my uncle."

Ida noticed that Dolly's long red fingernails had dirt under them and her white powdered nose was covered with blackheads. She silently wondered, as she twirled a strand of her long strawberry blond hair around her finger, if the old woman ever bathed. Ida was one of four kids but her mother would not let any one of them go to bed without a bath first.

As Dolly went on with her stories, Ida's mind wandered. She was curious about how Dolly lived. She tried to picture the inside of her home as she stared at Joe's Bar across the street. Her mother told her that Dolly lived all alone and had nobody. Ida couldn't imagine not having a family.

Dixie sat there soaking in every word that Dolly was saying. She was a year younger than Ida but much smaller with dark brown stringy hair and big black-brown eyes. She was one of seven kids but one of her older sisters, Barbara, had died the year before from lockjaw. She'd cut her foot on a coral rock that was in the yard and the doctor didn't think to give her a tetanus shot. Ida remembered the funeral. That was the first time she'd seen anyone dead. She remembered Dixie's mother's red eyes and how sad it was because Barbara was only nine years old.

Ida's stray thoughts vanished when she heard Dolly talking about Uncle Ernest again. She leaned in closer to listen and got a whiff of Dolly's odor of heavy sweet perfume mixed with sweat and alcohol.

Dolly flipped the page and said, "Uncle Thomas used to tell me about how mean Ernest was when they was kids. He said Ernest was jus' born mean. If fact in a way, he even killed his own mother." She moved her crooked finger to the top of the page and said, "This here's Uncle Thomas. See? An' this here's my daddy who I never saw . . . an' this one is Ernest . . . the one I stabbed."

"Dolly, did you ever get put in jail for stabbing your uncle?" Dixie asked.

"Hell No!" she said, thrusting her fist forward in a punching motion. "Everybody in town was on my side. They said he deserved it. Yessireeee . . . Bob! I got em good an' I got away with it too! I wished I did kill him though. He was in bad shape but he was strong as an ox an' determined to live. Why, he managed to git hisself to his buckboard an' git to town fer help." Dolly's tiny blue eyes sparkled as she went on with her story.

"Me an' Uncle Thomas had to git outta that town so we packed up all we had an' hitched up Pete an' Pronto . . . They was our horses. We hitched em to the wagon and took off up to where Ed's sister lived . . . to a small town called Ridgetop . . . jus' north of Nashville to start all over. Let's see . . . that musta been aroun' 1879 cause I was almost thirteen. Well anyways, we jus' had to get outta

Marietta cause there was too many people there who knew what happened an' they'd all talk about us.

We got a letter from Ed jus' after we moved an' he told us about uncle Ernest. It turned out that Uncle Ernest ended up in a wheelchair cause of the nerve damage in his neck an' they had to remove his private parts cause they got infected. We even got word later that he tried to kill hisself once by tyin' a rope around the top banister at the home he had to stay at an' then tied the other end around his neck. He tried to push hisself down the stairs in that wheelchair but it got stuck an' he only fell down to the third step. He didn't even get hurt an' somebody found em. I remember it did my heart good to know he at least tried to kill hisself!

Ridgetop was a good town to start over in. We didn't know a soul there an', except fer Ed's sister of course, an' Uncle Thomas got a job at Kilgore Glass Company. Ed's brother-in-law owned it so he helped git em the job there. My uncle was a real good speller an' he was in charge of writin' down all the orders an' everythin'.

Ed promised me an' Uncle Thomas he wouldn't tell his sister cause my uncle worked fer her husband. He promised he wouldn't tell nobody about what happened in Marietta with Uncle Ernest an' all.

Uncle Thomas got me in school an' we lived in town at the boardin' house till he saved up a little money an' got a loan to buy a house. It was a purdy nice place too. Of course it was old an' run down but it was real roomy. It had a small parlor but the livin' room was real big an' we had our bedrooms upstairs. It had a big front porch an' a back porch too. Me an' Uncle Thomas fixed it up an' was real proud of it."

"There was this boy named Jacob Turner . . ." Old Dolly had to pause for a few moments after saying his name and looked up at the hazy summer sky. The two young girls sat patiently waiting to hear more as they opened more candy and shoved it into their overfilled mouths. The old woman silently reflected back to the day she first met Jacob . . . remembering every detail like it was yesterday.

Everyone had gathered on the lawn in front of the church after the service ended.

"Hello Thomas," said Mr. Turner standing next to his wife and a young boy, just about the same age as Dolly. "I hear you have your niece staying with you."

"Oh, that's Dolly. She's with those girls jumpin' rope right over there. The one in the pink." He cupped his mouth with his hands and called, "Dolly! Come on over here. Somebody wants to meet ya!"

Dolly dropped the jump rope and ran toward him. "Oh Uncle, I jus' met a new friend an' her name is Abby an' she's real nice too."

"That's nice, Dolly," said Uncle Thomas, "Now I want ya to meet these good folks."

Dolly stood in front of Mr. and Mrs. Turner and struck a pose as if she were on stage, with her head tilted and hands clasped over her chest, waiting to be introduced.

"This is her," said Uncle Thomas, "Dolly's my brother's girl but he's dead now so she lives with me." He turned to Dolly. "Say hello to Mr. an' Mrs. Turner an' this here's their son, Jacob."

"It's a pleasure to meet ya." Dolly held her skirt up in the front, exposing her worn out boots, and curtsied.

"Why she's just beautiful and so well-mannered, Thomas," smiled Mrs. Turner, "And look at those eyes. Their just as blue as the sky."

Dolly stared at the skinny boy with the big ears and smiled but Jacob would not look at her. He stepped behind his father where she couldn't see his face.

Mr. Turner was a quiet handsome lawyer with dark wavy hair. He had an office in Ridgetop and one in Nashville.

"Yer boy's shy, ain't he," Dolly said in a loud precocious voice.

"Come on around here and say hello to Dolly, Jacob," his father ordered as he pushed the boy forward.

Jacob stepped over to Dolly with his hands behind his back and looking down. "Nice to meet you too," then quickly stepped back away from her again.

"Give Jacob a little time to warm up to you, Dolly. He really is a very sweet boy. Maybe you two can become friends," said Mrs. Turner, "Why don't you come visit us sometime? I see you met Abby. She comes to our house often. You could come with her if you like."

"That'd be nice," said Uncle Thomas, "But we gotta git goin' now."

Uncle Thomas took Dolly by the arm and led her to the wagon. "Looks like yer gonna have some friends here. It'll be good fer ya. Now let's git home so we kin git all that dirt off yer new dress."

She thought about the new friends she had just met and knew she was going to be happy in Ridgetop.

The old circus queen returned to the present, noticing that the young girls were staring blankly at her, and said, "Oh yeah . . . this boy, his name was Jacob Turner, who I'll tell ya more about later, used to come over after school an' help me with my school work. He was real smart in school but I was real behind cause I never went before. He lived over on the nice side of town in a big house, real close to his friend, Matt Kilgore, whose father owned the glass factory where Uncle Thomas worked. He would tell me Matt was an only child an' real spoilt. He didn't like to play with em much an' thought he was a brat. He used to call him "Matt the Brat." Jacob was my age but a lot shorter then me an' had real big ears. Anyways . . . he was really nice to me.

I reckon I was a real tomboy back then. I wore ridin' britches an' was always getting' dirty. I loved ridin' my horse, Pronto. It seemed like that horse understood every word of the English language. He always did jus' what I told him an' it was like he always wanted to please me. I taught myself how to ride while standin' on his back. Why, I could do anythin' with that horse includin' jumpin' an' doin' triple somersaults in mid air while I was ridin' em. I called that my death-flip. Why I did thin's nobody else could ever dream of doin'!"

I loved wild critters too. I used to go out in the woods an' sit fer hours jus' watchin' fer deer an' squirrels to come up. They wasn't even scared of me er nothin'. I'd take corn out there with me an' sit it on the groun' an' they'd jus' look at me like I was one of them an' jus' eat. They had no fear at all an' would come within jus' a few feet from me. In fact once I was out in the woods sittin' under a tree an' I looked up an' there was a huge black bear right over my head! At first it scared me but then I jus' remembered that he was jus' another wild creature too. I knew he didn't want to do me no harm so I jus' slowly got up an' walked about ten feet away from the tree an' stood there watchin' em. An' sure enough that bear jus' moseyed on down that tree, looked right at me an' walked away real slow like he wasn't scared of me. Yesssiree! I had a way with animals that nobody else ever did!

Times was real good at last. Me an' Uncle Thomas was livin' good fer the first time ever. He even quit gamblin' an' we started goin' to church regular again. That's where he met Ella Ryan. He got married to Ella not too long after he met er. He'd tell me it was love at first sight. She was only twenty-nine an' he was almost sixty but they was very happy. We all lived together in that nice house . . . not too far outta town.

I kin remember the first time I ever went to see the circus when it came to Nashville. Why I never seen anythin' more beautiful in all my days. There was clowns an' people swingin' high on the trapeze an' a man who could walk a tightrope without usin' a net . . . but he did finally fall, I heard later, an' died.

I loved the circus. They had this giant elephant named Jumbo but he wasn't near as big as they showed em in the pictures. Everbody was dressed in sparkles an' colors. Oh, it was all so magical to me. I always loved the lion tamer the best . . . an' of course, the bareback rider. That's when I decided I wanted to be in the circus . . . an' I knew I would one day.

That first few years life only seemed to git better an' better. Abby Mitchell an' Jacob Turner was my best friends. They was real smart at school but I had to quit school cause I was so far behind all the other kids cause I missed too much. It was humiliatin' to me. Couldn't even read. Jacob an' Abby liked me a lot anyways an' always was nice to me. I reckon I was kinda like the leader.

Once we found this big ol' rattlesnake by the back door an' it was all curled up an' shakin' it's tail. I was never scared of snakes but they got all excited an' killed it with Uncle Thomas's hatchet. I got real mad cause I didn't like to see any critter git killed but her an' him wanted to cut it open jus' to see what was inside of it. I kinda thought it was gruesome but they was always curious about what the insides of livin' creatures looked like. If we even ran across a dead possum on the road they'd squat down an' examine it up close fer a long time. Abby an' Jacob always talked about bein' doctors one day.

Matt Kilgore never hardly associated hisself with us though. He was a year older an' was never nice to us . . . but I remember he was real cute. I always had a crush on Matt Kilgore . . . even if he was a snob.

Uncle Thomas would say to me, "Girl, ya gotta learn to read. It's important cause ya can't get along in life if ya don't know how." He started teachin' me hisself. Every night he'd sit with me till I learned. In fact he was better then the teacher they had at the school. An' he was so proud that I was a fast learner. I practiced every day an' I read all I could get my hands on till I had it licked.

I got a job at Gracie's Café when I got bigger an' used to give my money to Uncle Thomas to help out. We always had plenty of money too. Yep, those times was really good fer us. I started carin' what I looked like an' wore dresses more then my britches. Uncle Thomas made sure I had lots of purdy clothes to wear an' I blossomed into a real purdy young woman by the time I was sixteen. That's when I started wearin' lip rouge on a regular basis . . . jus' after I turned sixteen.

Yessireeee Bob! Life was sure good . . . that is . . . till I fell in love . . . er at least I thought I was in love. Matt Kilgore grew into a tall an' handsome boy with blond hair an' straight teeth. He never paid much attention to me til I turned sixteen. He was a good catch fer any girl cause he would inherit his father's glass factory one day an' he lived in the biggest house in town. It was twenty-three rooms. He was sure perfect an' all the girls swooned over em . . . includin' me. I even got Abby to get me the picture of his graduation class from out of the newspaper an' used to look at it all the time.

Matt was goin' away to college after that summer an' I was afraid I'd never see em again but one day he came to Gracie's Café' where I worked.

When I saw em walk through that door I ran to the back to look at myself in the mirror to make sure I looked good fer him. I fluffed my long curly red hair an' smoothed down my apron. I was quite a purdy thing too. My eyes was big an' my mouth was small. My bosoms never got too big an' my waist was so tiny that ya could put yer hands 'round it.

I went back over to the counter where he sat an' said, "Hello Matt . . . what kin I git ya." I was shy back then an' could feel sweat under my arms when he spoke to me.

"I'll have just a sugar cookie and coffee," he said.

I reached in the cookie jar an' got out the biggest sugar cookie in there an' poured his coffee. I could feel my knees knockin' together under my long skirt an' my heart was flutterin' an' skippin' . . . but he never knew it.

Then he said to me, "Uh . . . can I ask you about something, Dolly?"

Then I said to him, "Why certainly, Matt." I was anticipatin' somethin' really big then. I cocked my head to the side an' fluttered my long eyelashes at em.

"Dolly, will you go with me on the Heavenly Hayride the church is having tomorrow evening?" He spoke real proper English.

I looked up like I had to think about it fer a minute an' finally answered em. "Why that sounds like fun, Matt. Uh . . . yeah, I'll go with ya."

He got up without even takin' a bite of his cookie. On his way to the door he turned an' said, "I'll meet you at your house at seven." He seemed so calm about it while I was all in a whirl an' then he left.

All the rest of that day I floated 'round on a cloud, not thinkin' 'bout anythin' but what I was gonna wear that next evenin'. I poured coffee on customers an' dropped plates of food. It's a wonder Gracie didn't fire me!

At closin' time I couldn't wait to run home an' tell Uncle Thomas an' Ella. I ran through the front door a hollerin', "Uncle Thomas! Ella! Where are ya!" I ran upstairs an' banged on their bedroom door. An' it seemed they spent most of their time in the bedroom. Well anyways, Ella opened the door an' said, "What in the world are ya hollerin' about, Dolly?"

"Yer never gonna guess who I'm goin' to the hayride tomorrow night with, Ella!" I sang out all excited-like.

"I reckon it's Matt Kilgore," she said in a matter-of-fact manner . . . cause she knew I was crazy about em.

"Yep. He asked me early today . . . an' Ella I'm quiverin' all over. Will you help me pick out somethin' real purdy to wear? I wanna look my best. No . . . I want to be the purdiest girl on the ride!" I rambled on like a cacklin' hen.

Ella just smiled an' said, "Go to bed an' git yer beauty sleep. We'll make sure yer the purdiest thin' he ever laid eyes on. Now git!" She was jus' grinnin' from ear to ear.

I undressed an' opened the window to let in the cool night air an' went to bed but I couldn't sleep. I finally got back up an' played with my hair an' decided to wear my purple dress. After an hour er two I went back to bed but I remember I never did git to sleep that night.

Next evenin' when I got home I dashed upstairs cause I only had two hours to git dressed. I decided to take a bath so I'd be real fresh an' smell good fer Matt. I snuck into Ella's bath stuff she kept in the kitchen an' poured some of her perfumed oil into the tub that was in a small room off the kitchen. I had to heat the water on the wood stove to git that small tub filled up. I musta sat in that water fer a whole hour makin' sure I cleaned every inch of my body.

Then I heard Ella callin' me an' I yelled, "I'm in here Ella! I was just about to git outta the tub." Ella came on in an' saw me naked . . . an' I felt funny cause I never let nobody ever see me naked. I pulled the towel aroun' me an' Ella helped by emptyin' the tub fer me.

"I hope ya don't mind if I used some of yer perfume oil," I told her before I ran up the stairs. I slipped into my undergarments, which back then was bloomers, camisoles and corsets . . . . very flatterin' but they was also very hot an' uncomfortable too.

Ella came up to help me tie my corset as tight as we could git it. "My, girl, ya got the tiniest waist I ever seen on anybody. What I'd give to have a waist that small." Ella went on, "This purple dress will be jus' perfect."

Ella looked older then twenty-nine. She was kinda plump an' had thin brown hair an' bulgin' bug eyes. She was envious of my looks but still acted like she loved me. She was more like a sister to me then a step-aunt.

We got me squeezed into that purple dress an' Ella buttoned up the back fer me an' said, "Let's do somethin' with that hair." She pinned it on top of my head an' used a rat-tail to pull down the tendrils in front of my ears. My hair was naturally curly an' easy to work the ringlets in. When I looked at myself in front of er full-length mirror I thought I was beautiful . . . an' I was!

I couldn't help but to think about Sarah Martin. She always liked Matt too. In fact she even went out once with him. I wondered what Sarah musta done to lose his interest so quickly. Sarah was purdy too but her daddy had a lot of money cause he owned the biggest department store in Nashville so of course she dressed real nice. The girls at school . . . they didn't care much fer Sarah. She wasn't very friendly to me neither. In fact she ignored me most of the time. Oh, I was so pleased to think that Sarah might be jealous of me when she saw me with Matt Kilgore.

It was after seven an'Matt was late. I was all ready an' sittin' up in my room when Uncle Thomas knocked on my door an' yelled, "Hey Girl . . . kin I come in?" An' then he jus' pushed it open.

"Look at ya!" he said. "Why yer the most beautiful thin' I ever laid my eyes on! That Matt sure is a lucky fella."

Jus' then we heard Ella's voice a callin', "Dolly! Yer beau's here!" I wished she hadn'tna called em my beau. It was embarrassin' to me.

Uncle Thomas gave me a tight hug an' I had to take a long breath before I could go down those stairs.

When I finally went down, Matt was standin' there at the bottom an' lookin' up at me. He was so handsome standin' there in his black coat with his hat in his hands an' his blond hair all plastered down. He was holdin' somethin' else too. A small package. I smiled at him, wantin' to get a compliment 'bout how I looked but he didn't say a damn thin'! Then Matt held out the small package an' said, "This is for you, Dolly."

I tore it open an' there was this red silk scarf with fringes 'round the edges. It didn't go with my purple dress but I smiled at em an' told em, "Oh Matt, this is the purdiest thing ever! I love it!" An' then I draped it over my shoulders."

Dolly took another slug of beer and paused. Not wanting to tell the details of her story because it was not suited for innocent young ears, she abruptly changed the subject and said, "Well, love ain't all it's cracked up to be anyways. I never married em or nothin'. Of course one day he finally did see me in all my glory when I was queen of the circus. No man could resist me back then . . . . not even Matt Kilgore."

Just then they all heard the sound of a woman's voice calling, "Dixie! Ida! Come hoooome! Suuupper!"

"We gotta go home now, Dolly," said Ida, but will you finish telling us about how your Uncle Ernest sort of killed his own mother and what happened with Matt when we see you again?"

"Yeah. An' will you tell us about how you joined the circus an' all about when you were the queen?" asked Dixie as she slowly rose to her feet, pulling the seat of her baggy shorts out of the crack in her fanny.

"We'll bring those mangoes next time,"said Ida.

"Yep . . . that'll be good," replied the old woman.

"Okay, then we'll bring you some real ripe ones," the girl

smiled. "Oh yeah, did you hear about the hurricane that's supposed to hit us?"

"Yep. But it don't worry me none." Dolly said as she closed her scrapbook.

The two girls walked back across Twenty-Seventh Avenue toward home, deserting her once again. Dolly staggered back inside for another beer.

CHAPTER 5

When Dolly came back out to her throne she opened her scrapbook to the picture of Matt's high school graduation. There was Matt Kilgore. Last row, third from the end. Seeing his face took her back to the night of the Heavenly Hayride.

By the time she and Matt arrived at the church everyone was there. Dolly spotted Sarah Martin glaring at her. It was a good feeling knowing that Sarah Martin was actually jealous. Dolly turned her nose up while holding Matt's arm as they passed her. Matt ignored Sarah as if he'd never seen her before. Dolly wondered why. Sarah was with a man Dolly had never seen before and wondered who he was.

"Hey Dolly! Hello Matt!" Abby said as she walked up from behind them. "Did you see Sarah with that older man? I wonder who he is."

Dolly noticed that Jacob Turner was standing in back of Abby.

Matt turned to Abby and said, "She didn't have a date, since she thought she was coming with me, so her brother fixed her up with his piano teacher."

"I didn't realize she was that desperate. The man's ugly as sin!" contributed Jacob, making them laugh.

Everyone liked Jacob. He was still slightly small for his age and his big ears stuck out but even though he was shy he possessed a great deal of charm and wit. Dolly had often caught Jacob staring at her and enjoyed watching him blush when she'd stare back. But this evening was different. Dolly could only see Matt.

The night was lit by a full moon and the stars seemed to be only inches out of reach. About twenty young chattering people piled into the hay-filled wagon hitched to six horses.

A young man began playing the harmonica as the wagon started down the bumpy road. Abby and Jacob sat up front with the harmonica player where everyone, including Sarah and the piano teacher, was singing while Dolly and Matt sat in the back corner of the wagon where they would be unnoticed. Dolly giggled as she and Matt buried their legs into the deep bed of hay. They could hear Abby's off-key singing voice stand out from the others during a chorus of "Oh My Darlin'." Dolly and Matt inched as far as they could get to the back corner of the wagon. Dolly glanced over at a young couple embraced in each other's arms then her eyes darted back to Matt . . . waiting for him to make his first move.

She pulled the red silk scarf up over her hair and said, "There's a wind kickin' up. Don't reckon there's a storm comin' do ya?"

"Don't think so. But I know there's a storm kicking up inside of me right now," said Matt, as he slid his arm around her shoulder.

She longed for Matt to kiss her but instead he slid his hand down to her thigh that was partially hidden beneath the hay as they continued down the rocky clay road. She felt uncomfortable but said nothing.

"Dolly, you look beautiful tonight," said Matt, finally giving her the compliment that she had been looking for earlier.

She gazed straight ahead, imagining every feature of his handsome face without looking at it. Dolly silently thanked God for that moment. "Thank ya Matt. So do you," she giggled.

Still running his fingers lightly up and down her thigh, he leaned over and whispered into her ear, "You do things to me, Dolly. I'm so glad you came with me tonight." He gently bit her earlobe then slid his tongue into her ear, making her shiver. He blew his hot breath lightly then moved slowly, with his lips, to the back of her neck.

"Why don't he kiss me?" she thought, then decided to lift her face and offer her lips to him.

"Oh, Dolly." Matt leaned forward to kiss her. His parted lips were only an inch away from hers when he paused and turned his head.

"It's startin' to rain!" someone shouted from the front.

Dolly felt a few drops hit her face but she did not move her inviting lips away from his, still waiting for her kiss.

Matt became distracted and turned his face upward toward the sky. "Why I didn't even notice that the moon went away. Did you? It was so clear when we left. Oh well, we'll probably head back soon." Matt squeezed her shoulder and whispered, "It'll still be early. Do you want to go someplace else, Dolly?"

Dolly couldn't think of the right words to say and didn't answer him. She was still interested in that kiss. She'd never been kissed on the mouth before except by her Uncle Ernest. Her thoughts drifted back to the time when her wicked uncle held her captive. His mouth was stinking and slimy. She hated him . . . still. She wondered what it would be like to kiss someone she loved. She began to shiver and moved closer to Matt, trying to erase the thoughts of her evil uncle but Ernest's horrible image kept creeping back into her mind. She wondered if he was still alive. She wanted to forget but it was impossible to keep him out of her thoughts.

The heavy rain began to pour down and all the girls squealed, including Sarah Martin. Dolly didn't mind if she got wet. She felt the urge to kiss Matt, no matter what, and leaned in with her eyes closed and her lips closely available. The night was now black and she could barely see around her. It was like she and Matt were alone at last. His face was wet with rain as he pressed his full lips against hers. She kissed him back hard and wrapped both arms around him. His lips slowly moved down the side of her neck, making her tingle with excitement. Dolly all at once felt his hand on her breast.

"Let's go someplace where nobody will see us, Dolly. I want you to be alone with me tonight . . . and I know you want to . . ."

Surprised and confused, she tried to figure him out. She wanted romance and tenderness, not for Matt to be so forceful and aggressive. He was moving too fast. But then again, she didn't want to lose him.

As the wagon finally pulled up in front of the church she felt his two fingers brush across her nipple, signaling a strange twinge of arousal, that she'd never felt before, spread throughout her entire body. "This ain't proper, I know," she thought, as she tried to hide her shameful thoughts from Matt, "But I jus' can't help it. I don't want em to stop."

The wagon was emptied of all its' passengers in a matter of seconds. Matt and Dolly were the last ones to get off.

"Dolly, come with me . . . now," Matt begged. His hot breath penetrated her ear. At this point she had no choice.

They climbed into his carriage and rode away in the direction toward Franklin. Matt hardly said a word to her until they were about a mile out of town. He stopped the carriage and turned to her. "Well, here we are Dolly . . . and we're all alone out here."

He helped her down onto the muddy roadside. The sky was beginning to clear enough to see the moon and the rain had stopped but they were both drenched to the skin. He reached into the carriage, pulled out a blanket and a candle then led her into the edge of the woods. Dolly couldn't help but wonder why he was so conveniently prepared by carrying a blanket and candle with him but she pushed it out of her mind. She felt her heart pounding so hard that she was afraid he'd hear it. They found a spot where the pine needles were thick beneath their feet.

"This is perfect," he said as he spread the blanket down then stuck the candle into the muddy ground and lit it.

Dolly didn't know how to react to all that was happening. She knew that she wasn't supposed to be out in the woods at night with a young man. It was improper. But then again, it was too late.

She stood face to face with Matt in the soft candlelight that was magically glowing from the ground, feeling sensations she'd never felt before. She took a step forward into his outstretched arms and pressed her body hard against his, feeling with her abdomen the hardness in his britches. His hands slid down her back as they kissed, sending chills up the backs of her legs. She wrapped her arms up around his neck as the red silk scarf tumbled to the wet ground.

Dolly's heart beat faster with his every movement and every touch. He kissed her mouth hard then slid his lips to her neck as he started to unbutton the back of her dress. Soon her dress was open enough to pull it down and expose her small firm breasts. He slid off his coat, unbuttoned his britches and pulled her down onto the blanket. He lifted her dress to her waist and slid off her bloomers then guided himself in. He gyrated rhythmically until he stiffened and moaned. Without shame, Dolly openly shuddered and moaned until she felt Matt's body go limp.

"I never had that feelin' before in my life, Matt. It felt all warm an' tingly like I can't describe."

"Dolly . . . Dolly . . . Beautiful Dolly," he whispered as he rolled off to her side, "I've never known a girl like you. You are so unbelievable."

"Am I?" she said as she as she took his hand.

Matt let go of her hand then stood up to button his britches. "I better take you back before your uncle comes out looking for you."

It was over too fast for Dolly. She wanted more but Matt seemed to be in a hurry to leave. He put his coat back on and handed her the muddy red scarf that had fallen to the ground.

Dolly slipped into her bloomers and fastened her dress. "I never dreamed we'd do what we did. I never knew it would feel so good an' it don't even feel embarrassin' to me. Have ya ever done this with a girl before, Matt?"

"No, you're my first, Dolly," he answered as he helped her back onto his carriage.

"Yeah . . . Yer my first too." Dolly thought of Ernest for a moment. The guilt made her quickly push the thought away. Her pale eyes glistened as she watched Matt climb up beside her. She held his arm, savoring the afterglow and said, "Ya know, Matt? I never did think I'd ever do that before I was married but I ain't sorry."

The puddles on the road caught the shimmering light from the moon as they traveled down the dark road and the musty fragrance of the wet earth filled the air as she lightly stroked the back of Matt's blond hair back into place.

Matt did not say much during the ride back while Dolly

chattered the whole way. "I sure hope my uncle ain't too upset. I know he'll be worryin' 'bout me. I sure did enjoy this evenin', Matt. Did you? That moon came out big an' bright didn't it? An' I can't believe how wet we got. My shoes are soaked to my toes! When do ya think I'll see ya again? I hope ya don't think bad of me now. Are ya goin' to church on Sunday, Matt?"

When they reached Dolly's house they kissed. "Good night Dolly," said Matt as he stepped down off the carriage. He reached up and put his hands around her tiny waist to help her down. "I want to see you again."

"Yeah, I wanna see you again too," she said as he lifted her down to the ground. "It was a wonderful evenin', Matt." She batted her lashes at him, hoping that she still looked beautiful to him, even though she was wet and her lip rouge was gone.

"I'll see you tomorrow at church, Dolly. Goodnight."

She stood watching her darling Matt's carriage sink away into the darkness of night before running into the house.

Uncle Thomas was standing in the parlor waiting for her, just as she knew he would be. "Do ya know how late it is?" he scolded.

"Oh, me an' Matt took a ride after the hayride got rained out." She paused and glanced down at her muddy clothes. With her head down she looked up with her eyes and gave him a shy smile. "Uncle Thomas . . . I love him . . . I do!"

Uncle Thomas sensed what she'd done but Dolly curiously showed no shame. "Well Little Miss Wafford . . . ya better be careful . . . ya hear?" he said sternly. "Now get yer little ass up to bed!"

"Goodnight Uncle." she sang out as she happily skipped up the stairs.

Uncle Thomas worried, knowing how naïve and gullible she was, and didn't want anything to happen to her. He wasn't surprised with her attitude. He'd never taught Dolly about the shame that a girl was supposed to feel with a boy because she never really had a chance to keep her innocence.

The next morning Dolly couldn't concentrate on anything but Matt Kilgore. She sang while she dressed for church, knowing that she'd see him again that morning. She carefully pulled her long tresses back into a thick braid and tied it with a pink ribbon to match her pink bustled skirt. Her shoes were still wet but they felt good on her feet . . . taking her back again to the night before.

Matt wasn't in the pews. "He's jus' late . . . that's all," she told herself as she sat anxiously watching for him to walk through the church door.

Twenty minutes into the church service Dolly's disappointment was so obvious, with her fidgeting and restless squirming, that Uncle Thomas scolded her with a look of disapproval. "Yer in God's house now, girl. So show some respect an' stop thinkin' 'bout that boy an' think 'bout where ya are. Ya should be prayin' fer forgiveness right now."

CHAPTER 6

Once they were back home Dolly decided to take Pronto out for a run. She hadn't had much time to ride since she'd gotten that job working for Gracie. She threw on her riding pants and ran back out to the barn. "Well there ya are boy. I missed ya! Do ya wanna git some exercise? Then come on, let's go Pronto." She pulled off her boots and tied them to the horse's mane then straddled his bare back and tore off like the wind down the clay road.

"Alright now Pronto. Slow down a bit cause now I'm gonna stand up." She pulled herself to her feet on the horses back and spread her arms out to the side. "Jus' a little bit faster now." As Pronto sped up Dolly's incredible balance was as poised as a graceful ballerina's. "Now slower . . . slower." She bent her legs to a half-squatting position then sprang into the air and spun into a summersault. "I'm flyin'!" she yelled then landed in a handstand on Pronto's back. "Keep goin' Boy! Faster now . . . don't slow down yet." She slid upright from a handstand and landed gently on his back. "You did perfect, Pronto! Now let's ride!"

She ran her horse hard for several miles before she stopped by a small stream so he could drink. Dolly jumped down to the wet grass and put her boots back on. She led Pronto over to the water and noticed a beaver sitting on the bank chewing on a twig.

"Why hello little fella. Whatcha makin' there?" Showing no intimidation, the fat little beaver looked up at Dolly and continued chewing. She watched him as he chewed then carried his finished carving to add it to the pile of twigs in the stream.

While Pronto was drinking she walked over to a tall oak tree, sat down and leaned against the trunk and looked up at the sky. Her thoughts drifted back to Matt. "Why hadn't he come to church?" She wondered where he was. She longed to see him again and remembering his words, "I want to see you again," sent shivers running up and down the backs of her legs again.

A squirrel scampered across the ground in front of her. Dolly sat, not moving and watched it as it paused for a moment to look back at her. Just then another squirrel ran down the tree next to where she was sitting. It cautiously peered up at her then began scraping the earth's surface, looking for acorns, without minding that Dolly was there. She was no threat to the wild creatures and they somehow sensed it.

She respectfully waited for the small animals to finish gathering their harvest before she began to pull her boots off again. She tied them together and slung them over Pronto's neck, tying them to his mane, before mounting him. "I'm ready, Boy . . . let's ride!"

"Run fast like the wind, Pronto!" she ordered him. "Go Pronto! Faster . . . faster!" Pronto loved to run and Dolly loved the feel of the wind blowing back her long thick ringlets as they picked up speed.

She slowed his pace and said, "Alright, Boy, I'm gonna stand up now so go slow . . . slower." She drew up her legs and pulled them up under her until she secured a squatting position then slowly stood on the horse's back, holding both arms over her head. "I wish Matt could see this," she said. "Now git ready, Pronto." Dolly moved her arms down to her sides then to the back as she bent her knees into a half squat. She leaped into the air and did a somersault but Pronto was moving too fast. She landed too far on his rear side, startling him, and he stumbled and fell to the ground, taking Dolly with him.

Pronto rolled over on top of her with the full weight of his body to get back to his feet. She lay there unable to move as the numbing pain shot through the lower half of her body. She tried to scream but her mouth was packed with red clay and only a muffled sound came out. She sputtered and spit until she could get out the sound, "Go home, Pronto! Go git Uncle Thomas! Git!" And he took off toward the house.

Dolly tried to move but the paralyzing pain kept her pinned to the ground. She prayed, "Dear Lord, please help me. I'm scared." She closed her eyes and waited. She knew Pronto would go straight to Uncle Thomas.

Ella was out hanging the wash when she spotted the horse running toward the barn without Dolly. She gasped as she dropped her bag of clothespins then ran toward the house screaming, "Thomas! Thomas! Come quick! Somethin's happened to Dolly!"

Thomas came hobbling out in his one socked foot. "What is it Ella? Where is she?" A strong jolt of adrenaline shot through his body when he saw the horse standing there without Dolly. He quickly jumped onto Pronto's back and rode out to find her.

"Dolly! Dolly! Where are ya? Answer me! Dolly!" He called over and over again. "Come on Pronto! Take me to her, Boy!"

Finally, he spotted her lying on the side of the road. He knew right away that she had broken her leg by the way it was bent in back of her. He knelt down by her and cried, "Dolly. Talk to me!"

Her eyes were closed and there was no movement. He held his breath when he noticed her mouth was opened and filled with wet clay. She didn't seem to be breathing. "Dear God! Don't let her be dead!" He laid his head on her chest and wailed, "Please, Dolly . . . Jus' talk to me!"

Dolly's chest moved and she began to cough. "Uncle . . ." she moaned in a slurred weak voice as her pale eyes began to open. "Uncle? Where's Pronto?"

"Praise God! Ooohh thank You, God!" he bellowed as he raised his face to the sky. "Yer alright, Dolly. Yer gonna be jus' fine . . . Yer gonna be jus' fine." He quickly wiped both eyes with one hand before looking back down at her and saying, "Kin ya tell me what happened out here, Girl?"

"Pronto fell on top of my leg. It won't move an' it hurts real bad," groaned Dolly, as mud mixed with the tears on her face.

Thomas pulled her up, not thinking about where his sudden strength came from. Dolly blacked out from the pain. He lifted her onto the horse and rode slowly back home.

When they reached the house he tried to lift her down from Pronto's back but could not find the strength that he had before.

Without using his crutches for balance, he stumbled and almost dropped her.

Ella came running out. "Thomas! Ya can't carry er! Now, let me do it!" She snatched Dolly's full weight away from him like she was a doll and carried her into the house. She laid her gently onto the settee' in the parlor and said, "I'm leavin' now."

Ella quickly hitched the wagon to Pete and was ready to go. "Take good care of er till I git back with Doc Wilson!" she yelled.

Ella ran Thomas's horse hard all the way into town. "Doc! Ya gotta come right away! Dolly's hurt! I think she busted er leg!"

Doc grabbed his bag and followed Ella down the stairs and out the door.

"I'm purdy sure it's broke." Ella went on, "Thomas found er on the ground where she fell off er horse. She's all bloody too."

When they arrived back at the house Dolly was still lying on the settee'. Her face was distorted in agony and her leg was bent out in an abnormal direction.

The doctor cut away her blood soaked riding pants and examined her leg. Her right thighbone was protruding through the skin. "It's definitely broken," he said. "Ella, hand me some warm blankets. Dolly, you lay back now. You're gonna be just fine."

Doc Wilson set her leg while Thomas and Ella waited in the kitchen. As they listened to the screams, Thomas's eyes filled with stinging tears while Ella draped her arms around him in a comforting squeeze.

Soon the screaming stopped. Doc Wilson opened the door and announced, "You can come in now."

Dolly was as white as a sheet but her eyes were opened. "How's Pronto? Is he alright, Uncle?" Dolly's leg was in bandages and her eyes still wet with muddy tears.

"Pronto's jus' fine. Now don't ya worry. We want fer ya to relax an' settle down now. Yer gonna be fine . . ." He turned to Doc Wilson and said, "Won't she, Doc?"

"Well, I think so. We just gotta look out for the concussion but I think she'll recover fine. Now let's get her up to bed."

Ella and Doc gently lifted Dolly and carried her up the flight of stairs to her room while Thomas went for a clean rag to wipe her face.

"It still hurts bad, Doc." Dolly cried.

"Jus lay yer head back an' rest now," said Doc. "It'll hurt for a day or two but it won't be forever. I'll be back to see ya tomorrow."

The minute Doc Wilson left the room Uncle Thomas knelt down beside Dolly and buried his face in the bed next to her. Dolly placed her hand on his head while Ella held her hand on his shoulder. He picked his head up then began wiping the mud off her face.

"Now open yer mouth an' let's get all the dirt off yer tongue." He finished cleaning her mouth and neck then dropped the dirty rag to the floor. "When I first saw ya layin' there like ya was dead it scared me . . ." He sniffed back then blew his nose hard into his handkerchief.

"Oh Uncle, I'm so sorry I fell." She wiped his eyes with the sheet. "I saw the pure terror in yer face an' I know I scared ya."

"I jus' don't know what I'd do if somethin' was to happen to ya, Dolly. I love ya so much." He buried his face in his hands and wept.

That was the first time Dolly had ever seen her uncle cry.

Again, there was no sign of Matt at church the following Sunday. Dolly's wheelchair sat in the isle near the back. Feeling very confused and depressed as the minister preached, she did not hear a word. She didn't know how she'd make it through another day when all her thoughts were of nothing but Matt Kilgore. Surely he must have heard about her accident. The pain shot through her body every time she tried to move but the pain of not seeing Matt was more unbearable.

After the church service ended, Thomas wheeled Dolly to the front yard of the church where they all congregated in the late morning sunlight.

"Dolly!" Abby Mitchell came running over waving a newspaper in the air. "I got ya what you asked for."

Dolly knew what it was. She'd asked Abby to get it for her months before. "I knew ya'd bring it!" Dolly squealed as she reached up and snatched the paper from Abby's hand.

"Open it up and look at it. There's Matt in the last row . . . the tallest boy at graduation." Abby pressed her finger to Matt's face on the front page.

Dolly closed the paper then folded it and tucked it down by her side in the wheelchair. "I'm so grateful to ya fer gettin' it fer me, Abby. Oh, an' how come ya ain't been comin' to church lately?"

"I had to go to Washington with my folks right after the hayride. Just got home yesterday." Abby put her hand on Dolly's shoulder, "I'm real sorry to hear about your accident. I would have written to you but we kept so busy sightseeing and all. Forgive me Dolly?"

It was good to see her old friend again. Abby was a short girl with a large nose and plain brown straight hair, but to Dolly she was beautiful in her own way. "I forgive ya." Dolly looked down at the paper and said, "Ya didn't miss too much aroun' here an' I didn't have no news to write to ya anyways. Oh, by the way, ya seen Jacob lately?"

"As a matter of fact he stopped by yesterday." She leaned over and whispered, "I think he likes you, Dolly."

"I thought he was yer beau."

"Heavens no! We're only just friends . . . I thought you knew that," laughed Abby, "It's just that we both plan to study medicine that's all. In fact, all we ever talk is the anatomy of the body and how to fix a chicken's broken wing."

"Well, you was with him at the hayride an' yer always together. I thought the two of ya liked each other."

"He is sort of sweet but no. I never thought of him in that way."

"Well then, what makes ya think he likes me?" Dolly was curious to know what he'd said about her.

Abby bit her bottom lip and her eyes darted back and forth before saying in a low voice, "Now Dolly, don't go telling him that I told you because he'll get mad and never forgive me." She leaned down to Dolly's ear and whispered, "He told me that he thinks you're the most beautiful girl he's ever seen and that he only wished he had the courage to tell you. He said he thinks about you a lot. He didn't come out and say he liked you but it was the same thing. You know Jacob . . . he's so shy."

Dolly's face flushed. "Oh hell! That don't mean nothin'. Jus' cause a boy thinks a girl's purdy don't mean he's in love with 'er. An' besides, he knows how I feel 'bout Matt."

"By the way, have you seen Matt since the hayride?"

Dolly lowered her eyes. "Nope."

"How come?"

"I really don't wanna talk 'bout it, Abby."

Uncle Thomas appeared from nowhere. "Are ya ready to go now Girl?"

"Yeah, I guess," she answered, even though she wasn't really ready to leave. She and Abby had so much to talk about. "Will ya come see me soon Abby? I get so bored an' besides, I missed ya."

Abby placed her hand on Dolly's shoulder. "You know I will, Dolly."

As the wagon pulled up in front of the house Dolly spotted her horse lying on his side in the sun. "Pronto looks like he's gettin' lazy don't he? Jus' wait till my leg heals an' I'll git em up off his ass!"

Thomas and Ella laughed. They enjoyed seeing Dolly in good spirits.

"How ya feelin', Honey?" Ella said as she carried a tray into Dolly that evening. "I want ya to eat all yer supper now. I made everythin' ya like. I even fried up some okra that ya love so much . . . . an' some stewed tomatoes too."

"I'm grateful to ya, Ella, but I ain't very hungry." Dolly was sitting up with the newspaper in her lap.

Ella placed the tray at the foot of the bed. "What's that yer readin'?"

"Oh, it's jus' that newspaper Abby got me," Dolly said as she folded it and laid it on the table next to the bed.

"Well, ain't that the one with Matt Kilgore's graduation class in it?" Ella picked it up and examined the front page. "Yeah . . . there he is . . . the tallest boy there in the back row. An' look. There's Mr. Fox. He was my teacher too." Ella paused and looked up. "I remember back when my mama got real sick an' I had to stay home an' take care of er. I had two little brothers who I had to take care of too. Mr. Fox told me not to quit school . . . an' I really didn't want to . . . but I had to."

"What was wrong with yer mama, Ella? What ever happened to er?" Dolly asked curiously, realizing that she knew nothing about Ella's past.

"The doctor never did find out exactly what it was but Mama, she jus' kept getting' more tired an' er hands would shake all the time. She got so weak she couldn't git up nomore. An' my two baby brothers was a handful too. They was twins." Ella moved the tray of food up onto Dolly's lap as she spoke and signaled with her finger for Dolly to eat.

"Well, where's yer family now?" Dolly picked up her fork and stabbed at a fried okra.

"Oh . . . all except fer my older sister, they ain't livin' no more."

"Well . . . what happened to em?"

"Ya see, my Daddy, he got killed by lightnin' on his way home from the mine where he worked jus' 'bout the time Mama started to git sick. The twins . . . they was only two years old. Well . . . anyways . . . after I had to quit school when I was thirteen an' Mama was real bad off, I was too busy washin' clothes an' cleanin' an' cookin' to keep a good eye on em. It was hard to take care of Mama cause she couldn't get outta bed no more. I had to do everythin' fer her. I was washin' up my Mama an' left the boys in the kitchen by theirselves. Only fer a short time too. Well I heard a scream an' dropped the wash pan an' ran. Billy was on the floor an' there was blood all around his little head. It was Davie who was doin' all the screamin'. Billy fell down off the kitchen table tryin' to git to the cookies, cause the table was on it's side an' there was cookies all over the floor an' he had one in each hand. He landed on his head . . . . right on the stone floor."

Ella had to stop for a moment to take a deep breath. Her eyes became glassy as she sniffed back tears to the back of her throat. "Billy's eyes was all white, like they jus' rolled to the back of his head an' his tongue was hangin' out real far. Well, I was so scared I couldn't even help em. Why, I couldn't even look at em so I snatched up Davie an' ran over to fetch the Doc. When we got back he said that Billy was already dead. I ran to my Mama and she was layin' there with her eyes wide open . . . an' not breathin'. They both died at the same time. The doctor said her heart gave out. I guess she was scared too but she couldn't git up off the bed to see what happened to er babies an' er heart jus' couldn't take it." Ella's eyes closed as she folded her hands under her chin.

Dolly put her fork down onto the tray as her jaw fell. "Oh how awful, Ella. Where was yer sister an' whatever happened to Davie?"

After a moment of silence, Ella took another deep breath and wiped her eyes before she could continue. "Well . . . Margaret . . . she was a lot older then me . . . well . . . she got pregnant an' ran off to Knoxville with George Whitmore an' married him way before all this happened. An' . . . as fer Little Davie . . . I took good care of em. I was always scared he'd git hurt an' I never took my eyes off em even fer a minute. It was about six months after Mama an' Billy died that Davie got sick too. He got the fever an' one mornin' when I woke up he wasn't breathin' an' was pale an' gray as a ghost. I picked em up and shook em, trying to shake the life back into em again . . . . but it didn't work. He was gone too."

"Poor Ella. Ya musta felt real bad. Yer whole family . . . gone in such a short time an' all. Did ya ever see yer sister again?" Dolly asked, wanting to put her arms around her.

"I ain't seen Margaret since she went away an' got married. She sends me letters sometimes an' sometimes she sends me her dresses that she don't want. Anyways, she lost her baby before it was born. An' yeah . . . I suppose I did feel bad . . . I felt like it was all my fault. If I never left the twins by theirselves . . . well, anyways it's all in the past now an' the good Lord forgave me fer it." She forced a gentle smile and said, "Now Dolly . . . don't ya go feelin' sorry fer me cause I'm happy now. Yer Uncle Thomas an' you er my family now."

Just then Uncle Thomas called from downstairs, "Dolly! Ya have a visitor!"

"It's Matt! Hand me that brush over there! Oh Ella, how do I look? Do I look awful?"

"You could never look awful."

Dolly's heart sank when she heard a girl's voice from downstairs. "Who do ya think it is, Ella?"

Ella left the room to find out.

A few moments later Abby appeared in the doorway. "I brought you some fresh warm blueberry muffins. Are you feeling any better Dolly?" Abby said as she handed her the box.

"Oh Abby, I love these kind!" Dolly giggled as she tore open the box. "Now I'll get fat as a pig!" She tried to be cheerful so that Abby wouldn't suspect her disappointment that her visitor wasn't Matt.

Abby sat down in the wicker rocking chair next to the bed. She wore a tailored dress with her long straight hair pinned in a bun and wore glasses. Dolly always thought she should have done more with her looks. Maybe wear brighter colors. She always looked so plain.

"Your Uncle says you've been depressed, Dolly. Is there anything you want to talk about?" said Abby.

Dolly's smile vanished. "Not really. I . . . I don't wanna talk about it right now."

"It's that Matt Kilgore, isn't it."

Dolly picked up a cold piece of okra and plopped it into her mouth. "Umm . . . Ella made my favorite. Want some?" She chewed then spit the okra into her hand and started to cry, "Oh Abby . . . Yeah, it's Matt Kilgore . . . . it hurts too bad to even think about em."

Abby reached over and took Dolly's hand. Patting it gently, she said, "Well, I think it's time that you do talk about it. It'll do you good."

"Uh . . .", Dolly began, "Remember when he took me to the

Heavenly Hayride the church had? I ain't seen em since. Now I can't think of nothin' else but him."

"And you have no idea why?" asked Abby.

"Oh I don't know. All I know is he acted like he loved me one minute an' the next thin' he's gone outta my life. Maybe it's cause I can't walk. Maybe he jus'don't wanna see me this way." She didn't dare tell Abby what had really happened that night. She knew that Abby wouldn't have said a word to anyone but Dolly was afraid that she would think less of her if she knew what she and Matt had done. Uncle Thomas was the only person in the world she could trust with her secret. She took a blueberry muffin from the box and took a small bite. "Maybe he jus' don't wanna see me no more er maybe he loves me an' . . . Oh I don't know!" She started to cry.

Abby wrapped her arms around Dolly and tried to encourage her to pour her heart out to her but Dolly would not say more.

CHAPTER 7

The weeks that followed were long. Ella ran up and down the stairs all day long bringing Dolly her meals and visiting with her between loads of wash. She and Uncle Thomas carried her down to the parlor every evening to be with them.

Thomas tried to make her smile by saying, "Hey Dolly, did I ever tell ya how I got my foot chopped off by an Injun?"

"No Uncle, ya never told me 'bout that. I suspect yer lyin' again cause . . . well, in fact I don't think ya kin ever tell the truth."

"Damn, Girl! Yer eyes twinkle like blue ice crystals when ya git mad," he teased.

Dolly couldn't stop the smile from creeping onto her face. Uncle Thomas always knew how to make her feel better. He was the nicest man she'd ever known. Her thoughts wandered back to Uncle Ernest and wondered how they could have possibly been brothers.

"Well . . . Did I ever tell ya 'bout the time me an' yer Daddy used to pick on poor little Ernest back before he got mean?" He knew that Dolly despised him and thought she would enjoy hearing the story.

It seemed strange to Dolly that Uncle Thomas brought his name up just when she was thinking about him. "Ya never told me that story before, Uncle. What did you an' my daddy do to em?" She anxiously squirmed as her eyes grew wide.

Thomas pulled up a straight-back chair and sat down next to her. "Well, we was a lot bigger then Ernest an' we used to take em with us when we went fishin' down at the Saint John's River. Mama always thought we was lookin' out fer our little brother but when we got em to the river we'd tease em just to watch em cry. He musta been only six er seven at that time an' me an' Walter . . . we musta been in our teens. Anyways, we hated crybabies an' he was a real sissy. We never let him touch the fishin' pole an' we'd tell em it was cause he was too little an' might git stuck with the hook. We'd tell em to jus' sit there an' watch us fish. He always got his way at the house cause he was the baby an' he was awfully spoilt. I never liked em . . . even back then. Well . . . he would always yell an' scream when we told em that. Fer some reason . . . I don't know why . . . but he was unlikable . . . even when he was jus' a baby. Walter an' me wanted em to cry. We'd tell em there was monsters in the river that ate little kids an' he believed us. He'd sit way far away from the water . . . scared to death. Sometimes we'd tell em there was dead people walkin' 'round in the woods so he didn't feel safe anywhere he sat. We never hit him er nothin' but sometimes yer Daddy would, accidently-on-purpose, bump em with his hip an' knock em over on the rocks. He cried 'bout everythin' an' had tantrums but we didn't care. In fact we sorta liked the sound. Once me an' yer Daddy accidently-on-prupose shoved Ernest in the river. We knew he couldn't swim an' we only wanted to scare em but he went under right away. It scared us cause we didn't see em come back up an' I jumped in an' couldn't find em. Then yer Daddy jumped in an' got em out. He was chokin' real bad. He took one leg an' I took the other one an' we turned em upside down an' shook the water out of em. Jus' think . . . we coulda killed em!"

Uncle Thomas laughed with a devilish look on his face and Dolly had to laugh out loud.

He took a deep breath and went on. "Well . . . when me an' Walter got older an' moved away he got really mean. We'd come home to visit Mama an' she'd tell us that Ernest was hard to handle an' he'd punch her in the stomach er cuss at 'er. Once he kicked er in the stomach an' blood came a pourin' out of er mouth. Not much later then that she got real sick an' almost died. After that she was never the same. Our Mama was in pain all the time an' used to spit up blood but Ernest kept on a punchin' 'er in the stomach. One time I threatened to beat the tar out of em if he did it again but it only made em mad that I said it an' he beat the hell outta me. Mama finally jus' up an' died one day but we knew why. An' Ernest got away with it too! He beat anybody up that disagreed with em, especially me an' Walter. But once me an' Walter got him down an' we'd take turns punchin' the shit out of em! Then we had to run like hell to git outta there fast. Ernest was the only person I ever knew who got pleasure outta hurtin' folks. Anyways, it makes me wonder if maybe me an' yer daddy was the ones who made em turn out mean."

"Huh! Sounds like he was born mean." smirked Dolly. "I wish ya coulda drowned em that day." She curled her lips and giggled, "I jus' wish I coulda been there to git some punches in with Daddy an' you. I kin jus' imagine how much fun it was!" Then with an evil squint, she punched her right fist into her left palm.

All at once the thought struck them both funny. They looked at each other and began to laugh so hard Dolly had tears in her eyes. Ella walked into the room and said, "You two at it again? What's so funny?"

Still laughing uncontrollably at their sadistic sense of humor, they could not find the breath to answer her.

Dolly awoke before the sun rose without feeling the usual pain. Matt crept into her mind again. She theorized that he would love her again if she could walk. She decided to try to walk across the room. "I kin walk . . . I know I can," she whispered to herself as she slowly moved to the edge of the bed. "I jus' know I can, I jus' know I can," she repeated to herself as she took two painless steps before collapsing to the floor with a loud thud.

"Help me!" she cried. "Oh Lord it hurts! Please make it stop hurtin' dear Lord!" The pain was worse than ever.

Ella heard the cry and scrambled out of bed toward Dolly's room across the hallway and slung the door open. Dolly was sprawled across the floor in the moonlight.

"What in the world are ya doin' on the floor Dolly? What happen to ya?"

Uncle Thomas appeared at the doorway behind Ella. "What's goin' on? Are ya alright Dolly?"

Dolly couldn't answer. The crushing pain had silenced her into unconsciousness.

"We gotta git her back on the bed Ella. Help me."

Together they carefully lifted Dolly's light limp body back onto the bed.

"Ya better go fetch Doc again," Ella's voice quivered as she pulled the covers over Dolly's shoulders.

Thomas lit the oil lamp by Dolly's bedside. "My God! She's bleedin' again!" Then he limped over to the doorway. "I'll go fetch Doc now!"

Without putting clothes over his nightshirt, Thomas hobbled out to the barn, mounted Pete and tore away in a burst of orange dust.

"Doc! Get up! Dolly needs ya!" Thomas was hammering on the door. "Hurry up Doc! She's bleedin' real bad!"

Within seconds there stood Doc Wilson up at the front door in his long johns.

"Jus' let me grab my bag. I'll ride with you." Doc threw on his britches and boots then retrieved his medical bag from upstairs before climbing up onto the horse with Uncle Thomas.

When they arrived Ella was sitting by Dolly's bedside wringing her hands. Dolly's eyes were open and there was blood on the blanket that covered her legs.

After examining Dolly, Doc Wilson said, "It popped out again . . . I'll have to reset it. Ella, go fetch some water and some clean rags."

Doc placed a rag over the young girls nose and mouth. Her eyes rolled back and she was unconscious again.

When Dolly woke up she felt as if a thousand knives were stabbing her thigh all at once. "I'm sorry Doc. I jus' thought I could walk . . . that's all. Oh! It hurts so bad!"

"If you'll stay off that dadburn leg, Dolly, you'll heal a lot faster!" Doc Wilson scolded. "I'll tell you when you can try to walk again. Ya got a bad infection an' I want you to take this medicine two times a day." He held up a bottle and placed it on her night table. "Now stay in that bed till I tell you to get up!"

Thomas looked at Doc Wilson and said, "That girl thinks she kin do anythin'. She's so determined but I'll do my best to try to keep er down. Come on, I'll take ya back." He turned to Dolly, "An' girl ya better listen this time. Ya set yerself back again . . . now stay offa that leg!"

That month passed even more slowly for Dolly. She could do nothing but wait. There was no word from Matt, making each day harder to face. Abby came to see her on Sundays and Doc stopped in to check on her from time to time but she had no other visitors.

One morning Uncle Thomas came into her room and found her in front of the window with her head down. When she turned her face up he saw that she had been crying again. His heart ached for her.

"Dolly . . . ya gotta stop actin' this way," he said with his hands behind his back, "The doc said yer gonna be walkin' an' ridin' Pronto in another few weeks so stop yer frettin' over that boy an' start thinkin' 'bout other thin's!" He moved his arm from behind his back and held out a small blue box.

"What's this, Uncle?"

"Well open it up an' see!" he said playfully as he placed his hand on his hip trying to sway it but instead stumbled.

Dolly held the box to her ear and shook it. "I wonder what it could be?"

"Well ya ain't gonna know till ya open it . . . so go on an' open it an' look!" Uncle Thomas laughed, feeling just as excited as Dolly.

She carefully opened the small box and pulled out a heart-shaped locket on a gold chain. "Oh Uncle Thomas! It's jus' so beautiful!" she exclaimed as she held it up. She smiled as she examined the outside of the locket first then slowly opened it. Inside, there was a photograph of Uncle Thomas and Dolly on one side and a picture of a small baby that Dolly had never seen before on the other. Her mouth fell open and a curious frown appeared. "Who's baby is this?"

"That baby is you, Dolly. Yer Daddy sent it to me right before he got killed. I kept it all this time hopin' I'd get to see ya one day. Yer the only kid in the family an' I always wanted a kid." A teardrop glistened in the corners of each eye, "Dolly, it's like ya was mine all the time."

She held it up for her uncle to put it on her. "I'll wear it forever, Uncle. Oh, I love ya so much. Thank you." She reached up and hugged him around the neck, almost pulling him over. She lowered her brow as her bottom lip protruded into a cute pout. "An' I promise . . . I promise I'll act better from now on."

Summer ended. Dolly missed her job at the café' and felt useless and bored. Matt never showed up at church and Dolly could not stop thinking about the night of the Heavenly Hayride. "Oh, why did I let this happen," she thought, "Maybe if I hadn'tna gone to the woods with em that night thin's would be different." The more she thought about him the more the anger set in. "I'm gonna forgit all about Matt Kilgore," she promised herself. "From now on I ain't gonna cry an' I ain't gonna mope no more. He kin jus's go to hell fer all I care."

CHAPTER 8

September leaves soon were covering the ground. Dolly felt stronger and began to stand on both legs without pain. She was healing fast, just like Doc said she would. She was anxious to ride again and wondered how much longer it would be before the doc would let her walk.

"Someone's at the door, Thomas," Ella called from the kitchen.

"I'll answer it!" he yelled.

Dolly heard Doc Wilson's voice downstairs and waited impatiently for him to come up.

After examining Dolly, Doc Wilson looked at her and said with a wide smile, "Well Dolly, you seem to be as good as new. The infection's gone an' the bone has mended nicely so I reckon it's time for you to start riding again. You can give it a try in a day or two."

"Do ya really mean it, Doc?"

"Yep. I really mean it." He smoothed his beard and said with a grin, "But no falling off this time."

Dolly could not walk fast enough to reach to the barn. "Alright Pronto, are ya ready? Did ya miss me boy?" she kissed his soft nose then grabbed his mane and jumped onto his back.

Uncle Thomas and Ella watched her as she flew off down the trail. "Be careful Girl!" they both yelled then smiled at each other because they knew that she'd be all right.

Dolly rode Pronto hard for a while then stopped. The wind was cool and the red leaves from the dogwood trees covered the ground. She took a deep breath and couldn't get enough of the chilled clean air. A charge of adrenalin gave her a shiver as she gazed up at the blue sky realizing that there was so much beauty all around her and she was a part of it. She was ready for anything.

Dolly decided to do something new and different while riding on Ponto's back. She wanted to try a double somersault this time but at a faster pace. She imagined herself flying through the air.

"Pronto, that's what I wanna do . . . I wanna fly! Git Pronto! Fly like the wind boy!" she yelled. "Easy now . . .," she finally got Pronto running fast but on an even pace. "Now Pronto . . . . I'm gonna jump up so don't ya slow down, Boy, ya hear?" She pulled herself up to a standing position on the horses back, keeping her balance with graceful ease, and raised her arms. With her legs bent she slowly brought her arms down and then back. "One . . . two . . . three . . . up!" she counted and sprang high into a double somersault and landed back onto her feet again. In amazement she said, "My God Pronto! We did it! First try an' we did it perfect!"

Dolly could hardly wait for the mornings so she could run off into the woods to practice her jumps and somersaults again. Within two weeks she had her double somersault flawlessly mastered and began working on a triple. She couldn't seem to get it just right at first. She was a little clumsy with her landing. She knew she'd have to work on it until she was able to do a triple gracefully and with as much ease.

Not a soul, including Uncle Thomas, knew about Dolly's incredible talent. She wanted to keep it a secret until she was ready to reveal it to the world and she knew that she was almost there.

After an early practice one morning, Dolly said to Pronto, "I think I'll call this my death-flip when we git in the circus one day . . . an' I think I'll call myself Dolly Crystal cause Uncle Thomas says my eyes look like ice blue crystals . . . an' besides . . . it's purdier then Wafford." She jumped down and patted Pronto on the nose and said, "I'm gonna go git dressed now so we kin get to town."

Dolly rode into town to buy a dress for the party that Uncle Thomas was planning for Ella's thirtieth birthday. It would be quite an affair. He had invited every person they knew, including the Kilgores. He did not want them to come but had to invite them because he worked for them. Dolly doubted that Matt would come but just in case, she wanted to look her best.

She bounced into Betty's Dress Shop, just down the street from the boarding house where they'd once lived and began snatching up dresses to try on. The first one she put on was the one she wanted. It was white with lace sleeves trimmed with rows of tiny pink rose buds. She picked out some white satin ribbon for her hair and threw it onto the counter along with the dress.

"Jus' charge it to my uncle, Betty," she said as her eyes wondered out to the street through the display window.

While Betty was wrapping the dress Dolly caught a glimpse of Matt Kilgore walking past the shop. Excitement filled her heart with sudden pain. At first she had to remind herself to ignore him but the pain in her heart told her to run and catch him. She snatched up the bundle and panted, "Thank ya Betty . . . I'll see ya later."

She swiftly headed for the front door, not even thinking about what she would say to him. When she reached the walkway Matt was twenty feet in front of her. She sped up her pace to try to catch up with him. "He looks older . . . an' taller," she gulped and paused before running up to him. She watched him as he stopped in front of the bakery and peered inside.

Dolly was just about to move toward him when she spotted Sarah Martin coming out of the door of the bakery. Dolly heard herself gasp as Sarah went up to Matt and took him by the arm. Dolly stood dead in her tracks as rage and jealousy sent hot stinging tears streaming down her face. She wanted to hide. She dropped her package where she stood then turned around and began to run. She reached for Pronto's mane and jumped on. "Git! Git goin' . . . Let's git the hell outta here!" She tore off as fast as possible before Matt and Sarah could see her.

Dolly didn't know where to go. She just had to run as far away as she could to hide but her own shame would follow her no matter where she went. She passed her house and continued down the road. She eventually found herself miles from home and had no idea where she was but didn't really care. She just wanted to die. She stopped by the edge of the woods, slid off and fell to the ground sobbing.

After a long hard cry she sat for a long time trying to piece things together. She finally decided that her pride was worth more than anything. "I'm a fighter. I ain't gonna let Matt Kilgore ruin my life. I'll jus' pretend I never even knew em . . . that's all," she told herself, "I'll jus' go on home now. It's jus' the best I kin do fer now."

The next day Dolly went back into town to find the package that she had dropped. She went into Betty's Dress Shop and sure enough, the package was there, waiting for her.

"Dolly, what in the world were ya doin'?" Betty asked. "Why did ya drop yer new dress an' run like that? Yer lucky cause Carl brought it in here when he saw ya drop it."

Dolly felt embarrassed and couldn't think of what to say to Betty. "I . . . I appreciate it . . . well . . . I gotta go," she stammered. "The party's tonight . . . . an' there's a lot to do. Goodbye Betty." She took the package and left in a hurry.

Uncle Thomas and Dolly had decorated the house with flowers and bows for the party. Everyone started coming over just before dark. Her uncle had asked Hank and Joe Williams if they would come play some music and sing. Hank played the banjo and Joe played the fiddle. There were only the two of them but they made a lot of music together.

Dolly was breathtaking in her new white gown and when she walked into the room every head turned. Dolly felt confident and it showed. Her eyes combed the room but she did not see Matt.

It seemed like just about everybody in Ridgetop showed up. There must have been at least sixty people, shoulder to shoulder, throughout the main floor. The living room, which was the largest room in the house, had plenty of room for dancing. The chairs were lined against the walls and chairs were set in the kitchen and on the porches.

The Williams boys started playing their music, triggering everyone to start moving to the middle of the floor to dance.

After Jacob Turner finished a dance with Abby he stepped up to Dolly. "May I have this dance?" he asked shyly.

Dolly held her arms out and they began to glide across the floor to a waltz. Her red curly hair hung down to her waist and swung out as he turned her around and around in the middle of the floor. Jacob was a good dancer and Dolly followed his lead with ease.

"He's not very handsome," Dolly thought, "But he was so polite and always was the smartest boy in school." Dolly liked him but her thoughts drifted back to Matt.

Another young man cut in and soon Dolly was dancing with every boy there. They all seemed to want Dolly's attention and she loved it.

As she was twirling with the music her eyes caught a glimpse of Matt's father and mother dancing together across the room from her. Her heart stopped beating for an instant, thinking that maybe Matt was there too.

Dolly and Jacob danced their way across to where Matt's parents were dancing. "Hello Mr. an' Mrs. Kilgore," she smiled. She looked at Mrs. Kilgore and asked, "Have ya heard from yer brother, Ed, lately?"

"Yes, Dear, we write on a regular basis," answered Matt's mother in a not-so-warm-tone as she turned her nose up.

Dolly found her eyes searching the room until she spotted Matt standing against the wall across the room staring at her. "Oh my God! He's here!" she whispered breathlessly into Jacob's ear.

Jacob turned his head to look at Matt and smiled. "Yes, and it looks like he's watching us."

"Don't look at em, Jacob!" Dolly snapped.

"I suppose you'll need to go talk to him huh Dolly?" Jacob loosened his hold on Dolly's hand.

"Hell no. He kin go someplace an' die fer all I care!"

Before the waltz ended another young man cut in. "Jacob, may I have this dance with Dolly?"

Jacob looked down and backed away from Dolly without a word.

She began whirling around the floor with Ned Allen and before the dance was over Benjamin Ritts cut in. Dolly kept glancing over to make sure that Matt was still there. He was so handsome in his black suit and his blond hair was even blonder than she'd remembered. When Matt's eyes almost caught hers she blushed and pretended not to notice him. She boldly teased and flirted with every boy she danced with, in hopes that Matt was still watching her every move. She continually glanced over to confirm that he was indeed watching her.

Uncle Thomas got up and hobbled to the middle of the room. "I have an announcement to make! Everybody! Hush up now!"

The music stopped and everyone turned to see what Thomas was about to say. "My Ella is thirty years old tonight. An' she's catchin' up with me cause I'm gettin' younger jus by bein' married to er. Well, anyways . . . I jus want everybody in this here room to know that I love my wife!"

He looked at Ella as everyone laughed and applauded. They all joined in with a clapping rhythm and chanted, "Speech! Ella, speech!"

Ella's face lit up as she turned to Thomas and said, in a sturdy, loud voice, "I can't think of nothin' to say except turnin' thirty don't make me feel so old when I'm married to this ol' coot! Well. I want all y'all to know that I love this ol' coot too! Even if he is fallin'-down drunk!"

Uncle Thomas limped across the floor to Ella to deliver a long hard kiss while everyone whistled and cheered. He dropped one crutch and held on to Ella's shoulder as they began to stagger around to a gentle waltz.

Dolly loved seeing them both so happy but her mind was on Matt. Ned Allen grabbed her hand and began twirling her around. She noticed that Jacob was standing against the opposite wall watching her too. She smiled at him but he did not smile back. Moments later he was dancing with Abby again.

"I gotta catch my breath a minute!" Dolly pleaded to Ned. "Will ya walk me over to my chair?" she panted.

Moments after Dolly was seated, Abby came over and sat in the chair next to her.

"Are ya havin' a nice time, Abby?"

"Oh it's a wonderful party. Did you notice who's here?"

"Yeah, I know he's here. I jus' don't wanna talk to em." Dolly leaned closer and said, "He keeps lookin' at me an' I wish he'd leave."

Just then Jacob approached them. "Abby, would you care to dance with me again?"

"My goodness, Jacob, I'm still out of wind but I'm willing if you are," Abby laughed as she stood up and took Jacob's hand.

As Dolly watched them waltz away together, she felt alone and vulnerable. She self-consciously smoothed her skirt over her knees while her eyes darted across the room to check on Matt. She saw no sign of him and assumed that he had deserted the party. Her heart began to sink as her eyes wandered to the floor in front of her.

"Well it suits me jus' fine," she mumbled to herself. Without glancing up, she spotted a pair of legs in men's trousers, standing directly in front of her.

"Hello Dolly. How have you been?" Matt's voice struck her poor heart like a torch but that same fire ignited the angry fuse that made her nostrils flare. As soon as she looked up and saw his handsome face, her anger turned to a desperate yearning to fall into his arms but she also desperately needed to scream. Her palms became moist and her heart pounded as she forced a pretentious smile.

"You are the most enchanting creature in this room Miss Dolly Wafford. Would you care to dance?" Matt said as he extended his hand.

Dolly stood on the fine line between love and hate and didn't exactly know how she should react but she immediately extended her hand to him. The hunger that had been stored up inside for so long made it difficult to hide her excitement when she felt his touch but she fought hard to remain as aloof as possible.

"I reckon so," she answered as she stood to her feet.

Matt took her by the waist and swung her around the floor to a square dance. Each time they passed each other in a doe-see-doe he smiled at her but she would not smile back.

When the music stopped Matt walked her over to the chairs that were lined against the wall and motioned for her to sit down next to him.

"Dolly . . . I know you must hate me for not coming over to see you after our night together but don't think . . . don't think I haven't thought about you." His nervousness showed.

"Well what in hell makes ya think I even care," She answered in a quivering voice as the butterflies in her stomach violently fluttered.

"Because I know you, Dolly." He took a deep breath and said, "I need to tell you what happened but you must promise not to say a word to anyone."

Dolly sat quietly listening to every word and trying hard to maintain her frail composure.

Matt leaned down and whispered, "Dolly, what I'm about to say may make you upset but I have to say it. Sarah . . . Sarah Martin got pregnant . . . by . . . by me . . . I had to take her down to Franklin for . . . you know . . . to get rid of it."

The crushing words sounded like blasts from a cannon, as they struck hard against her chest. She wasn't sure if it was because she despised him for humiliating her, because she still loved him . . . or both.

"It was the only thing to do, Dolly." His eyes dropped to examine the toe of his shoe. "So many times I wanted to see you but I just couldn't." He lifted his eyes and said, "Sarah was going to tell my father and he would have made me marry her. How could I marry her when all I can think about is you."

As he wrung his hands together Dolly noticed the small beads of sweat on his upper lip.

"Well, Sarah lost the baby . . . and now . . . now it's all over . . . Oh Dolly, will you please forgive me?" He reached for Dolly's hand but she pulled it away.

"Why didn't you jus' tell me, Matt!" Dolly snapped as she glared back with her crystal eyes in a half squint. "Why did ya jus' leave me hangin' in mid air like that? Ya told me I was yer first!" Ya lied an' jus' used me . . . that's all!"

"Oh Dolly. I just didn't know what to say to you. I didn't want you to know about Sarah and me. I really am sorry I hurt you." He sat up straight and nervously smoothed his hair back. "I found out that she was pregnant the day after I saw you and I had to leave town right away."

"So where ya been all this time?"

"I wanted to see you but I was afraid."

Dolly could feel her throat tighten as she tried to hold her feelings inside. She managed to maintain a stone-like expression on her face and said, "So ya used Sarah too . . . . jus' like me . . . . an' that means she was pregnant all the while you was makin' love to me. I thought ya loved me . . . Oh Matt . . . what a fool ya musta thought I was!" She could no longer fight back the tears that rose from her lower lids. They rolled down her cheeks and she caught one with the tip of her tongue as she positioned her hands on the chair in an attempt to stand up.

Matt reached for her arm, "Dolly, don't. Please listen to me. I'm leaving tomorrow morning to go to college up in New York."

She shook her arm loose and folded it into the other arm in front of her. "So? Why should I care? I thought yer suppose to start in September jus' like everybody else."

"I couldn't . . . because of Sarah."

They sat silently for a moment. Gently, he placed two fingers under her chin and guided her face toward his. "I want you back again, Dolly, I . . . I'm in love with you."

Dolly's head began to swim and she began to feel weak. She had been longing to hear those words from him for a long time . . . but the painful thought of him getting Sarah pregnant was unbearable. She opened her lips to speak but instead choked on the words that she really wanted to say from her heart and pushed his hand away from her face. "Oh Matt . . . I don't know how to believe ya. I want to be with ya . . . yeah . . . but how do I know ya really mean it?"

Matt stood up. "I don't know how to make you believe me. All I know is that I think about you all the time . . . and about that night. I'll be gone for quite a while and I couldn't stand it if you were with someone else." He paused and took her hand, "Will you wait for me?"

In the midst of her confusion she'd almost forgotten the promise she'd made to herself. She would have to be strong. She was a fighter and she would not allow him to hurt her again. "I don't think ya know what love is Matt Kilgore!" she snapped hatefully as she yanked her hand away. "Ya think I'll jus' wait aroun' again like a damn wallflower? Jus' forgit me Matt. Jus' go off to New York to that fancy college an' forgit all 'bout me. I don't care if I never see ya again!"

"If that's the way you want it." He leaned down and whispered by her ear, "I'll miss you, Dolly Wafford."

She sat with her arms folded while her bottom lip formed a stubborn pout. She made no effort to move from her chair as she painfully watched him turn and walk toward the door. Dolly had to fight back the sudden urge to run after him then she had to remind herself again to be strong. She would not be made a fool of again. Without looking back he opened the door and disappeared. Dolly's shoulders fell to a slump as she sniffed back the few unnoticed tears before she rose from the chair.

With a pasted half-smile she walked over to her uncle and said, "Matt left. Did ya see em?"

"Yep, but I was hopin' he wouldn't show up. But he's gone now, huh?"

"Well it don't matter none."

"Oh I kin see straight through yer lyin' blue eyes, Dolly. Ya gotta git over Matt Kilgore cause he ain't good fer ya. He ain't worth it an' besides he jus' thinks he kin do anythin' an' git away with it. Well, he ain't gonna git away with hurtin' my girl now is he?" Uncle Thomas smiled and took her by the arm. "Come on . . . let's go dance."

Early the next morning Dolly slowly opened her eyes and suddenly remembered that Matt was leaving. "New York was so far away," she thought. Her body stiffened as the fear set in that she might never see him again. The desperate urge to see Matt overruled the self-promise she'd made to forget him. She quickly jumped out of bed and ran over to open her wardrobe. She slipped into her yellow wool dress then hurried to apply the red lip paint. She tucked her long locks under a yellow ruffled bonnet and headed down the stairs and to the front door.

"I'll be home soon!" shouted Dolly as she ran out the front door, not knowing if Uncle Thomas or Ella even heard her. She mounted Pronto and headed into town, riding slowly so she would not lose her bonnet.

The train wasn't due to leave until daylight and the sun was only just beginning to show signs of rising. As she reached Broad Street where she would wait for Matt she knew she had plenty of time. She slid down from her horse and tied him to the hitching post in front of Carl's Feed Store, just across the road from the train depot. Dolly had regreted wearing her yellow dress because she could not sit down on the walkway without getting it dirty. It was cold and the stars were still hanging thick in the dark blue sky. Her underarms begin to perspire as she thought about what she would say to Matt as she stood waiting.

A rat darted across the clay road as she watched for Matt in the distant morning light. Soon there were the sounds of horses' feet and she could smell coffee from the sandwich shop down the walkway.

Carl stepped out of the front door with a broom in his hand. "Good mornin' Dolly! What are you doin' here so early?"

"Oh, I jus' came into town to do some shoppin' fer Ella," she lied as she spotted Matt's carriage down the street. "I'll see ya later, Carl."

She began her stroll toward the train depot carefully moving at a casual pace when she heard, "Dolly! Wait up!" She turned her head and saw Jacob coming up from behind.

"Good morning!" Jacob shouted as he ran to catch up with her.

She felt her face turn hot. She didn't feel like talking to Carl . . . or Jacob. She wondered where Matt was as her eyes bounced from Jacob back to the depot. "It's nice to see ya Jacob," Dolly said without looking at him.

"You come to see Matt off? Me too. He told me he was leaving for New York City today and I guess he'll be gone for quite some time." Jacob pointed, "I think I see him right over there with his folks."

A carriage pulled up beside the stage and a young woman with long blond curls stepped down.

"Why it's Sarah Martin!" Dolly heard her own voice screech. "What in the world is she doin' here?"

"Oh . . . Sarah's seeing Matt off too. They've been seeing each other. You didn't know that?" he answered as he started to walk faster toward the depot.

"Yeah, I found out about it. Why didn't ya mention it to me last night?"

Jacob didn't answer.

Sarah's eyes met Dolly's for an instant and Dolly felt her face turn red with shame for being there. She wanted to run away but instead she stood there for a moment and thought, "Why should I feel shame? He loves me . . . not her!" Jealously she glared back at Sarah, who was dressed in dark pink velvet with a bonnet more beautiful than hers. She watched Sarah as she raised her head high and gracefully glided toward Matt to take his arm.

"Are you coming Dolly?" Jacob yelled back as he moved toward Matt and Sarah.

"Why was she with Matt again?" Dolly thought. She stood motionless for a moment, not sure of what she should do next, then courageously started to approach them both. Consciously using her casual stroll, she made it over to where they were standing and smiled.

Mr. Kilgore glanced at Dolly then back to Matt and said, "You say goodbye to your friends, Son. Your mother and I will meet you inside."

Mrs. Kilgore smiled at Sarah but did not look at Dolly.

"Matt, I jus' wanted to say goodbye to ya." Then, being careful not to appear jealous, she turned to Sarah and said, "Oh, Sarah, Hello."

Ignoring Dolly's greeting, Sarah let go of Matt's arm and turned toward Jacob. "Jacob, how are you? Oh, I heard you went to that dreadful party last night on the other side of town. Matt said it was just awful. What did you think of it?"

Jacob could only blush.

"Enough Sarah! Don't start trouble!" Matt yelled.

Stunned by the way Matt had snapped at her, Sarah stepped back and glared hatefully at the back of Matt's head as he turned to face Dolly.

Matt cleared his voice and said in a high pitch, "Of course I never said that to Sarah, Dolly. It was a lovely party and I had a wonderful time." His voice then softened. "I knew you'd come this morning."

"Matt," Jacob interrupted then cleared his throat, "I suppose we won't be seeing you for a while, huh.

"Guess not, Friend." Matt extended his hand, "I won't be home for the holidays but I'm coming back in the spring. We'll see each other then."

"Yeah . . . see you then." Jacob nodded and shook his hand. His eyes darted back and forth from Matt back to Dolly then turned to Sarah and said, "Come on Sarah . . . I'll walk you to your carriage."

"Goodbye Matt, I'll see you when you come home in the spring." Sarah's mouth curled into a false pout as she stepped up to give him a light hug before walking away with Jacob.

Matt barely made an effort to hug her back.

Once Jacob and Sarah were out of ear range, Dolly said, "Whatever happened to that piano teacher Sarah was with?" She raised her brows high. "Is she still seein' em?"

Matt toyed nervously with the school ring that he wore on his right finger. "Sarah told me that he wanted to marry her . . . but she told him she couldn't because she was still in love with me . . . . but I don't love her!"

"Oh, I didn't mean to pry." Dolly played with the heart shaped locket that she wore, feeling embarrassed for asking.

Matt took Dolly's hand, raised it to his lips and kissed it

gently. "I meant what I said last night about wanting to be with you Dolly . . . I do love you. Maybe you don't believe me now but when I come back I'll prove it to you. And you know there's nothing left between Sarah and me anymore, don't you Dolly? You're the one I want."

Dolly felt all the warmth of his love in the kiss on her hand. "I . . . I guess I love you too, Matt. I didn't really mean what I said last night about . . . about not wantin' to ever see ya again. But sometimes ya make it so hard fer a girl to try to figure ya out." She smiled, "Yeah Matt . . . I'll be here in the spring when ya git back. How are ya goin' to prove ya love me?"

"You'll just have to wait and see." Matt squeezed her hand and said, "This is goodbye until spring. I'll write to you. Wait for me."

She wanted to kiss his soft lips more than anything but couldn't. Not in full view of everyone in town, especially not his parents. It wouldn't have been proper. Instead, she squeezed his hand back then let go. "Now don't go missin' yer train . . . Git goin'."

Matt went inside.

"All aboard!" the conductor shouted.

Dolly ran over to the tracks on the other side of the boarding station to wave goodbye. As the wheels began to turn she spotted Matt through the window looking back at her. She waved until the train was out of sight, feeling the warm stream of tears wetting her cheeks.

She wiped her eyes and glanced up to see Jacob standing next to her. "I thought ya left, Jacob."

"Not yet. I just walked Sarah to her carriage but I wanted to come back to make sure you were going to be all right."

"Why wouldn't I be? I got better things to think about other then Matt Kilgore."

"I just know how you feel about him," Dolly. "That's all. If you ever need a friend to talk to, I'm here." Jacob reached over with his pinky finger and brushed a tear from under her eye.

"Thank you but I'm jus' fine . . . really," she sniffed.

"Come on. You can tie Pronto to my buggy and I'll ride you back to Ridgetop."

CHAPTER 9

The days that followed were empty for Dolly. She waited for a letter but no letter came. She had no interest in anything except riding Pronto and thinking about seeing Matt again in the spring. She decided to write the first letter. Her hands trembled as she wrote.

> "My Darling Matt,
>
> I do hope you like college in New York and suppose you are staying very busy with your studies. Maybe that's why you have not found the time to write to me yet.
>
> I think about you every minute, even while I sleep. I believe you now, Matt. I believe you really do love me. I've loved you since I first laid eyes on you when we were kids. Did you know that I loved you all along? I'll wait for you and promise to save myself for you. I can't hardly wait to see you in the spring. I can't hardly wait to see how you are going to prove you love me.
>
> I hope Sarah doesn't bother you anymore. I know you love me and not her.
>
> Do you remember the night of the Heavenly Hayride? I cherish the memory of that night but I want more memories to cherish like that one. I want to be with you forever. Let me hear from you soon.
>
> Love Always,
>
> Dolly"

The letter was too brief but she didn't know what else to write. She sealed it and placed it into her top dresser drawer.

Dolly held the letter for days before she had the courage to mail it. As she slipped it to the Post Master she wished that she had worded it differently. She knew her grammar wasn't perfect like his was but once it was mailed there was no changing it.

Autumn was always Dolly's favorite time of year. She loved the smell of firewood in the air and the leaves that crunched beneath her feet as she walked. But that fall the air was too cold and the crunching of the leaves as she walked made her melancholy.

Every morning she went to the post office to see if a letter arrived. Nights became sleepless for her. It had been over two weeks since she'd mailed her letter to Matt and still there was no word from him.

Ella said, "We're invited to Knoxville fer my brother-in-law's younger brother's weddin'! Margaret said we could stay with her an' George. I ain't seen my sister fer so long. It's gonna be a big celebration an' should be fun . . . will ya come with us Dolly?"

Dolly knew she couldn't leave home. She was waiting for a very important letter. "Thank ya anyways, Ella, but I think I'll jus' stay around here. I gotta lotta practicin' on Pronto to do . . . . an' besides I wanna git some things done aroun' the barn. You an' Uncle Thomas go an' have a good time. By the way . . . when er ya leavin'?"

"In two weeks . . . an' we'll be gone about ten days." Ella, suddenly sounding less excited said, "I wish ya could change yer mind an' come with us."

"Oh . . . I jus' can't, Ella. I'm sorry."

The next two weeks seemed to drag by before the morning finally came. Uncle Thomas and Ella were leaving for their trip and Dolly was looking forward to time alone.

As soon as they hugged each other goodbye and shut the door Dolly all at once felt the freedom of the empty house and slowly walked through every room crying out loud, "Oh Matt!

How could ya make me wait so long to hear from ya? Dear God . . . Please make em love me. Please don't let em hurt me again!"

She kept busy. She cleaned the house until it sparkled, organized the barn, baked and mended all the torn clothes that she could find. She checked for a letter at the post office daily and was beginning to give up hope of ever getting a letter from Matt.

"All right Pronto!" Dolly grabbed his mane. "Git ready fer the ride of yer life! I wanna fly faster then a tornado today!" She sprang up onto his back and headed straight for the woods.

Within minutes she was standing on the horses' back with both arms held high yelling, "Like the wind, Pronto! We're jus' like the wind!" She jumped high into the air and spun around landing on his backside on one foot. "Slow down boy! Easy now! Git ready fer my death-flip!" She bent slightly forward and leaped up doing a triple somersault in mid-air. "That was perfect!" she squealed.

Pronto slowed to a walk then stopped and Dolly slid down to the ground and sat on the leaves to look out over the hills in the distance. There was a waterfall that she'd never seen before. She took a deep breath and was overwhelmed by the serene beauty that surrounded her.

"Dolly! Dolly Wafford, is that you?" a voice called.

She looked up at the top of the ridge and spotted Jacob Turner then yelled back, "Yeah, it's me!"

Jacob rode down from the ridge to where she was sitting. "I never saw anyone ride like that before!"

"What in the hell are you out here fer?" she snapped, resentmenting him for invading her privacy.

"I'm sorry, Dolly. I didn't know you owned this place," he said arrogantly as he slid down from his horse. "I just never saw anybody ever do what you just did. I was watching you way back there and I followed you." Then his face beamed. "You surprise me Dolly."

"Well, I jus' keep it private, that's all. I'm gonna be in the circus one day an' I gotta practice till I git perfect." Dolly lost her anger and said, "An' I feel like I'm gettin' purdy close."

"You look pretty perfect to me already," Jacob said as his face turned pink. He sat on the ground next to her and gazed out over the valley at the waterfall. "Matt and I used to go swimming over there by the falls when we were younger," he said, "It's really beautiful down there. Wanna go see?"

"Yeah . . . I never even knew it was there before today. It looks mighty big. Let's go."

They could hear the rushing water before they reached the falls. "It's cold here," said Dolly as she slid off of Pronto's back. She looked up to see the mighty waterfall gracefully pouring down the side of the mountain. "It is beautiful here, Jacob."

"Here, put this over your shoulders," Jacob offered as he slid his arms out of his coat.

They sat down on a boulder overlooking the waterfall where endless tons of white water tumbled down over the rocks.

"Matt-the-brat and I used to come here a lot when we were kids. There's some good deep water down there," said Jacob.

"Why did ya call em the brat?"

"Matt was a brat back then. He was a showoff and thought he knew everything. He used to jump off that big rock over there into the rough water where the deep hole is. He really wasn't that much of a swimmer and we all thought he was crazy. I never had a desire to jump off that high rock myself. I guess either I was coward or I was just too smart. Anyway, Matt broke his arm doing it once. He was sucked under so I had to jump in and pull the stupid fool out before he drowned."

Dolly vaguely remembered hearing about that incident but had to think hard about where she'd heard it. Then suddenly it hit her that it was when Ed told Uncle Thomas about it in the drugstore back in Marietta. "My gosh, Jacob! That was you they was talkin' 'bout!"

"What do you mean?"

"I heard Ed tellin' Uncle Thomas a long time ago about you an' Matt an' how ya jumped in an' saved his life."

"Yeah, and just to think," Jacob complained. "Matt used to try to drown me all the time." He looked at Dolly and added, "I guess you're still smitten with him aren't you."

"Yeah, I reckon I am. But I sure can't figure em out. It's like he's two different people. One minute he says he loves me an' the next minute he acts like I ain't even alive."

"Well, I think you're too good for him."

"Maybe I am, Jacob. I guess ya heard 'bout Sarah Martin an' him, huh?"

"What about them."

"Well . . . that he got er pregnant."

"I didn't know that you knew about that."

"Yep . . . he told me all about it." She gazed up at the falls and said, "Where do ya think all that water comes from?"

"Out of the rocks I guess. They say there's a big spring up on top of that mountain."

"Yeah, but how does the water get in the rocks when they're up so high?"

"Hell . . . I don't know Dolly. I've got something more important to tell you." Jacob stood up and let out a long breath. "I'll be going off to college next fall. I've been accepted at Harvard. I plan to study medicine and become a surgeon."

"That's real nice, Jacob. I hope ya do real well. I know yer gonna make an excellent doctor some day."

"What are you're plans, Dolly?"

"Oh, I plan to join the circus one day . . . and I will . . . . jus' as soon as I git good enough."

"Dolly . . . I told you . . . you're good enough right now. I watched you. I could hardly believe my eyes. How come you never let anybody know that you could ride like that?"

Dolly rose to her feet. "I don't know . . . Maybe it's cause I want to know I'm the best before they see me." She cocked her head and asked, "Do ya really think I'm good, Jacob?"

He stood up and pulled the coat snugly around Dolly's neck and looked into her eyes. "I think you're more than good, Dolly. I think you're the best right now. I've never admired anyone more."

Remembering what Abby had told her, Dolly teased him by tilting her face up toward his and saying, "Jacob . . . do ya think I'm beautiful?" She knew she was beautiful but she wanted to hear it and even though her heart belonged to Matt she still adored the attention she got from Jacob.

"Of . . . Of course I do. Why you're the most beautiful girl I've ever known . . . and the prettiest blue in all the world is painted in your eyes." Jacob's face turned pink again, realizing that he may have sounded a bit corny.

Dolly was pleased with what she heard. "Do ya really think so?" She moved closer with her mouth only inches from his. She wondered how it would feel to kiss his rigid, thin lips, and caught the scent of his sweet breath. It smelled like cucumbers . . . only sweet like sugar. She loved the way he smelled and saw that Jacob was not at all as homely as she used to think he was.

He slowly moved his arms around her tiny waist and closed his eyes. He parted his lips and tilted his head, anticipating that long awaited kiss that he'd been dreaming of.

Dolly quickly turned her face and his lips tenderly met her cheek. "I think we better go now, Jacob."

Jacob dropped his arms to his sides and his face flushed. "Can I come see you sometime, Dolly?" he asked. "Since Matt's not here . . . as a friend of course!" He looked down and blushed again.

"Why that would be real nice, Jacob," she replied girlishly as she moved toward Pronto and tossed his coat back to him.

"I'll come over to see you soon then."

"Well, I gotta run over to the post office now, Jacob." Dolly mounted her horse. "I'll see ya later!" she called back as she rode away.

Jacob knew why she was going to the post office. He stood by the boulder and sadly watched her ride away until she was out of sight. Without looking back, Dolly knew that his eyes were on her.

When she ran into the post office she found the letter from Matt that she'd been waiting so long for had finally arrived. She anxiously wanted to tear it open right then and there but decided to take it home to read it so she could savor every word. She hurried back to the house, holding the letter in her fist as she rode hard.

Out of breath when she reached the front door, she tore it open and ran toward her room. Her knees began to buckle beneath her as she read.

> "Dear Dolly,
>
> It took me a long time to work up the courage to write this letter to you.
>
> My parents came to visit me recently and we talked quite a bit about you and me. I've done some thinking since they left and I don't know how to put this into nicer words. I don't want to hurt you anymore, Dolly, but I have my future to think about. My mother told me that she found out from my Uncle Ed, in Atlanta, that your uncle raped you. I'm sorry, but I must admit that I knew about this long before the night of the hayride.
>
> I don't think it would work out for us. Dolly, I had no intention of marrying you but I was and maybe still am, in love with you. Still, I have no choice. My family says it would not be a good idea for us to see each other again. Since everyone in Ridgetop knows that you are not a virgin it would affect my family's reputation. My father told me I would not inherit his business if I continued seeing you. Please forgive me.
>
> Matt"

Dolly tore the letter into tiny pieces and bursted into tears then fell across her bed. While clutching the bits of paper in her fist the fury rose as she remembered Ed's promise not to tell her secret. He had betrayed her too.

After a long cry she went over to her desk to write him one last time. She dipped the quill into the inkwell and began to write.

> "Dear Matt,
>
> If you loved me you would not care about what your family says. Why didn't you tell me you knew? I could have explained it all to you. What happened to me was not my fault and besides I was only twelve years old. Think about what you are doing to us. You should listen to your own heart, not the heart of others. Maybe I'll see you in the spring if you decide to change your mind. I know that I'll never . . . ."

Dolly could not finish the letter. She threw herself onto the bed and cried herself to sleep.

"Dolly! Dolly! We're Hoooome!" Uncle Thomas's cheerful voice filled the room, startling her from a deep sleep. "Dolly!" he repeated. "We're home! Give me a hug, Girl!" He sat on the edge of her bed and squeezed her tight. Dolly started to cry as she nuzzled her face in his chest "Well I know those tears ain't fer me cause I know ya didn't miss me that bad. What's the matter?" asked Uncle Thomas as he patted her back gently. "Ya look like ya need to empty yer heart out on me before it explodes."

"Yeah, Uncle . . . I do. I got a letter from Matt an' he don't wanna see me no more cause I ain't good enough fer his damn family. Yer friend, Ed, blabbed about Uncle Ernest to em all! He broke his promise to ya! He ain't our friend no more!" She wiped her eyes with her two index fingers then calmly said, "Now I'll be jus' fine. Don't worry about me no more Uncle."

"Well . . . to hell with that damn snot-nosed snob! I jus' don't think he's good enough fer you . . . . er our family! An' to hell with Ed too!"

Dolly forced a smile. "Now ya jus' go back outta here an' let me freshen up a bit. I'll be down in jus' a few minutes."

Uncle Thomas gave her one more squeeze then left the room.

Dolly remembered the letter that she had started to write to Matt before she fell asleep and picked it up to read it. It angered her to think that she could write such a pathetic letter. It made her sound desperate and weak. She tore it into as many pieces that she could and stuffed it into another piece of paper, wobbled it and threw it into the wastebasket.

CHAPTER 10

It became easier for Dolly that winter. Christmas was almost there and she kept busy by helping Ella with the holiday baking and decorating. They adorned the house with festive holly branches, pinecones and red ribbons. Everyone was floating around humming Christmas carols, including Dolly. There was so much to keep her occupied that soon she was having days when did not think of Matt Kilgore at all.

Dolly continued riding every day, concentrating on her death-flip but always attempting new tricks. She finally mastered jumping from one side to the other, touching her foot to the ground while Pronto was in a full run. She knew that she was almost ready for the circus.

Every day that she went into the woods to practice she would routinely stop to visit with her beloved wild critters. Where she sat upon the ground, the deer curiously came out of their hiding to examine her while the birds fearlessly lighted upon her shoulders. Squirrels would come down from their nests high in the trees and chatter to her. Dolly knew that they were all telling her goodbye for the winter. She knew the relationship she possessed with the wild animals was something no other person in the world could possibly have.

"What er you two bakin' up fer me thet smells so good?" said Uncle Thomas as he swung the kitchen door open.

"Sugar cookies an' we got some pecan bread bakin' but ya can't eat any of it till we git done." Ella swatted the dishrag at him. "Now git outta this kitchen an' leave me an' Dolly be!"

Uncle Thomas reached over and snatched up a cookie then

quickly popped it into his mouth. "Ya can't do this to a man! My stomach's in agony . . . jus' screamin' fer these sugar cookies," he grinned with a mouthful then reached for another.

"Uncle!" yelled Dolly, "Yer gonna ruin everthin'! We wanna decorate em before ya eat em! Now go on!" she screeched as she smacked his hand with the spoon.

He pulled up a chair and sat down. "I promise I won't steal nothin' else if ya let me sit here an' watch," he begged. "Maybe even I kin help ya."

Dolly licked the spoon. "Should we let em, Ella?"

With her tightly clamped lips, Ella passed the icing to Uncle Thomas and said, "Ya gotta do it right . . . an no stealin'."

He picked up the first cookie and began slathering icing over it but as soon as the girls' heads were turned he tossed it into his mouth. After decorating and sneaking his fill of them he announced, "I done enough. I'm goin' back outside to finish choppin' down that tree." He grabbed one more cookie and stuffed it into his mouth. "This is women's work . . . call me when yer done."

It wasn't long before they were all sitting at the table with a hot pot of coffee and a plate of cookies and warm pecan bread in front of them. Uncle Thomas ate until his stomach was bulging. "I gotta go sit an' rest. I think I got a belly ache," he moaned.

They followed him out to the parlor to sit down down. Ella sat on the setee' next to him then reached over and patted his stomach saying, "Ya ain't gonna have no room fer supper now so I don't imagine I'll waste my energy cookin' it cause me an' Dolly still got a lotta bakin' to finish 'fore Christmas."

Dolly went to the window and looked out over the white ground. "It looks mighty cold out there today."

Uncle Thomas burped before answering, "Why-Lord-no! I was so hot out there choppin' that tree that I had to take my shirt off!"

"A damn liar is what you are!" Dolly giggled.

"Then why do ya even bother askin' me anythin'?"

"Cause maybe I figure ya know but ya jus' ain't tellin'!" Then a solomn expression crossed her face. "Hey Uncle, how come ya never say much'about my brother, Pete, who died?"

"Why I was wonderin' when ya would ever ask about em," he replied.

"That's cause I knew it was somethin' ya never wanted to talk 'bout. I been wonderin' 'bout Pete fer a long time now." She walked over and sat in the chair across from him.

"Let's see now . . . Yer brother, he was born two years 'fore you was," he began. "I told ya yer mother was a selfish woman. Annie drank all the time an' was mean to yer daddy. An' poor little Pete . . . he was jus' a little baby an' she'd go off an' leave em alone a lot. Yer daddy, he did most of the work. He'd stay home with that baby while she went out an' sometimes didn't git home till it was way past dark. He never knew where she went but he did know that she was cheatin' on em. He really loved that woman too. One day he left er there with Pete an' he wasn't but maybe two years old. When he got home he found er in the bed with some Yankee soldier an' Pete was on the floor cryin'. He picked em up with one arm an' pulled out his gun an' aimed it at the Yankee's head while he was still on the bed with yer mama. She yelled at yer daddy to put down the gun but he pulled the trigger. He told me there was blood everywhere . . . even splashed on yer brother's face. Yer mama helped em to drag the body outside an' bury it in the woods. She promised she'd never do it again an' he believed er. It wasn't too long after that that yer mama got real sick. It turned out that the Yankee had some kinda sickness that spread to her. She got better an' then little ol' Pete got it. He got a real bad fever an' I guess it musta affected his brain cause after it went away he never was the same after that. He would drool an' his little eyes was crossed an' he'd cry all the time. An' as I remember he was a real purdy little baby too. He had those crystal blue eyes like you an' yer daddy. I moved up to Marietta about then an' never saw Walter er Pete again. Yer daddy wrote me later that little Pete died one night in his sleep. He told me that yer mama never even cried cause she seemed glad he was gone."

Dolly gasped, "Well, does that mean she was pregnant with me durin' that time?"

"Yep. That's why yer daddy didn't run er off. He wanted to make sure you was gonna be alright."

Dolly looked down for a moment, preparing herself for the answer to a question that she'd harbored for so long. "Uncle? Was . . . was I his?"

"Oh yeah! No doubt he was yer daddy cause he wondered too till he saw ya. Then he knew right away you was his. That was when he sent me that picture of ya."

"So I look like my daddy?"

"Yep. Jus' like em . . . eyes an' red hair an' all."

Dolly took a deep sigh of relief. "Ya know, I always knew she was a bad woman. I don't ever remember er ever huggin' me er nothin'." She looked at her uncle and took a deep breath then let it out again. "How come my daddy got killed?"

"Well, yer mama, she was out late again when you was a tiny baby. Yer daddy put ya in a blanket an' took ya with em to go find er. She was in a saloon with some other Yankee getting' drunk. Of course I wasn't there but I heard that Walter got real mad an' pulled his gun on em an' yer mama begged em not to shoot but he jus' told er to go outside an' wait fer em. He kept you in his other arm cause she was too drunk to hold ya. He jus' glared at the soldier an' told him to stay away from his wife. When he turned to walk outside he shot yer daddy right in the back."

"Ya mean he was holdin' me when he died?" asked Dolly.

"Yep . . . he was." Uncle Thomas's lips began to quiver as he wiped both eyes "He was only jus' tryin' to keep his family together. He shoulda shot first."

"I'm sorry I asked ya, Uncle. I didn't mean to make ya sad." She stepped over and hugged him.

Two days before Christmas Jacob Turner came to call. Dolly opened the door and greeted him with delight. He looked good to her as he stood on the front porch wearing a heavy black riding coat opened in the front with a thick red pullover sweater beneath it. His nose was red from the cold and his dark green eyes sparkled in the afternoon sunlight. Dolly realized then how much she had missed him.

"Dolly?" he said. "Perhaps you would like to go to the church play with me this evening?"

"Why I'd love to, Jacob. I'd invite ya in but I'm real busy helping Ella with the holiday bakin' right now," she lied, knowing she'd need some time for herself to get ready so that she'd look her best. "But I'll see ya when ya come back fer me this evenin'."

"Alright Dolly. I'll look forward to seeing you at six o'clock," he chirped cheerfully as he turned to leave.

"Ella!" Dolly called out as she ran toward the kitchen. "Do ya mind if I don't help ya right now? I gotta lot to do to look good fer tonight. Jacob asked me to go to the play with em at the church. Do ya mind?"

Ella turned around with flour all over the front of her apron, holding a rolling pin in one hand and smiled. "Honey, I'm so happy yer finally goin' out with Jacob. He seems like like such a nice young fella."

Dolly ran upstairs to get ready for the evening. She couldn't understand why she was so excited about going out with Jacob. After all she'd known him for so long. He was even a pest at times but now she felt some kind of odd attraction. She decided that is was only her curiosity . . . nothing else.

Before she was finished dressing she heard Uncle Thomas's voice shrill from downstairs, "Dolly! Jacob's here fer ya!"

She wasn't going to rush and wanted to look just right for Jacob. She took a moment to gaze into the mirror and study her reflection. She was wearing the yellow wool that she had on the last time she saw Matt. It looked good on her and she was pleased with the way she looked. She stepped into Ella and Uncle Thomas's room and splashed some of Ella's cologne behind her neck before beginning her nonchalant descent down the stairs.

When she spotted Jacob at the foot of the stairs looking up at her she felt an unusual twinge of excitement but couldn't figure out why. "It's only Jacob," she thought as she stepped over she took his arm. "Let's go, Jacob." She'd noticed that he'd gotten taller. "Goodnight Uncle an' Ella!"

The church was lighted by a thousand red candles and there were rows of red carnations and greenery on each side of the room. A red velvet curtain hung from the ceiling, covering the altar that was used for a stage.

As Jacob led Dolly to her seat he turned to her and said, "Sarah Martin is in the Christmas play . . . and guess what part she's playing." With a wicked grin, he paused as Dolly tilted her head to listen. Then he whispered, "The Virgin Mary."

Dolly had to giggle out loud as they sat down, "Oh my God, Jacob, I jus' gotta see this."

When the lights dimmed and the curtain rose there stood Sarah Martin on the stage holding a doll in her arms. Dolly smirked, "Jus' look at er up there actin' all holier then thou."

"I know . . . Hey look, she's holding that doll upside down." He tried to muffle his laugh by cupping his hand over his mouth.

Dolly glanced up and caught Jacob's profile. "Jacob was a true gentleman," she thought, "He's got what any girl would want but he ain't at all like Matt. Jacob ain't as handsome as Matt. Damn!" Dolly thought to herself. "Why can't I git em outta my head!" Every time she thought about Matt she felt the rage and then the hurt. She didn't like it that she was comparing Jacob to Matt. She examined Jacob's face again as he watched the play, not noticing that her eyes were on him. She saw that his ears weren't as big as they used to be. She never realized before what a nice straight nose and strong chin he had. In fact, he was extremely handsome. He was one of three boys but two of his brothers died before she and Uncle Thomas moved to Ridgetop. Jacob's family was very wealthy but Mr. and Mrs. Turner were very nice people. Jacob was unspoiled and a much better person than Matt. He was sweet and sensitive. She wondered, "Why couldn't I fall in love with him instead."

When the play was over, before standing up, Jacob turned to her and asked, "Well, Dolly? What did you think of the play?"

"Oh . . . I loved it! But Sarah was the best one up there . . . don't ya think?"

"Oh yes," Jacob rolled his eyes up and made a face, "So sweet she was . . . and so stupid she was. Holding baby Jesus upside down like that. It was so embarrassing it made me sick to my stomach. He leaned over Dolly's lap, "Oh, I think I'm getting sicker . . . oh wait . . . I think I'm about ready to puke right now."

"Don't ya dare, Jacob Turner!"

"Then let's get out of here before I do puke!"

Jacob made Dolly laugh just like Uncle Thomas always did. She took his arm as he led her to the front door of the church.

They stepped outside and saw that it had begun to snow. The ground was almost covered with sugar-like flakes that sparkled in the light from the doorway.

"Oh, ain't it beautiful, Jacob?" Dolly said, inhaling the cold air deeply through her nose.

Jacob looked at her and said, "Yes, it is. But I know something more beautiful."

Dolly loved the way he threw those read-between-the-lines compliments to her.

"It's going to be a cold ride home so get ready to freeze your behind off, Dolly," Jacob teased as he helped her onto his buggy before climbing up beside her.

Dolly moved over close to him, "I don't care if my fanny does does freeze off . . . I love the snow. An' I really enjoyed the play, even with Sarah in it. It was really nice, don't ya think? Hey Jacob! Look! It's startin' to stick to the trees!" She stretched her arm out pointing her finger.

Jacob reached over and grabbed her outstretched arm with his hand and slid it down until it was holding hers. "Your hands are like ice!" He brought her hand up to his mouth and blew warm air into it as Dolly snuggled closer to stay warm.

When they reached Dolly's house she expected him to try to kiss her again, but instead, he immediately jumped off and walked around to her side. He reached up and took her by the waist to help her onto the ground. To Dolly's surprise, he caught the backs of her legs and swept her into his arms.

Dolly brought her arms up around his neck and giggled, "What er ya doin'?"

"I'm going to carry you over the snow," he said gallantly.

Dolly waited for him to try to kiss her, but still he made no attempt. She turned her face up to his and said, "You wanna kiss me . . . don't ya, Jacob."

"Nope," he said as he carried her across the front yard. His sweet breath was warm against her cold cheeks, as he playfully teased, "Not tonight." He reached the front porch and dropped her to her feet. "I'll see you in a few days . . . Merry Christmas, Dolly," he nodded.

Dolly stood there, stunned by what he had just said, and could do nothing but smile back. Slightly puzzled, she hesitated before replying, "Merry Christmas to you too, Jacob." Then quickly kissed him on the cheek then ran into the house.

On Christmas Eve Dolly put on her new red dress and came downstairs to join Uncle Thomas and Ella in the parlor. They poured wine and sang Christmas carols before passing out the presents.

"Ella, you open yer's first," Dolly said excitedly as she handed her a small box.

Ella opened it cautiously, trying not to tear the paper, then squealed, "It's perfume! An' it's all the way from France too!"

"Well, I thought I better git ya some more since I used up so much of yer's."

Then Ella handed a small box to Dolly. "Here . . . open yer's now."

Dolly tore it open without worrying about saving the wrapping paper and laughed, "Oh! I got perfume too!"

"Well, I reckoned I better get ya some so ya would leave mine alone cause I been noticin' the bottle gettin' emptier an' emptier lately." Ella stood up and gave Dolly a tight squeeze.

"Now it's yer turn, Uncle Thomas." Dolly handed over a large box.

He opened it and pulled out a black hat with a feather in it. "My Lord, Girl! It's jus' what I needed!" He reached over and hugged her.

"Thanks fer gettin' em a new hat," Ella said, "I got so tired of lookin' at em in that battered ol' piece of felt that he's been wearin' fer years."

Uncle Thomas put the hat on his head then beamed. "Here's yer's from me, Dolly, now open it."

Dolly quickly unwrapped the present and held up a pair of pink satin ballerina slippers, knowing exactly what he had intended her to use them for. "Oh, Uncle! I kin use these! They'll work perfect!" She leaned over and kissed him on the cheek. "Thank you Uncle Thomas an' thank you too Ella. I love my presents."

I figured ya could put some rosin on the bottom of those slippers so ya won't slip off yer horse." He felt proud, knowing that he had chosen the appropriate gift for his beloved niece and that he had pleased her once again.

Uncle Thomas and Ella exchanged their gifts before Dolly served the rum punch. They lit the tree with a hundred candles that sent a brilliant golden sparkle over the room. The clock was about to strike midnight. They held their glasses high and toasted to bringing in Christmas morning.

"This was a magical Christmas Eve," Dolly thought as she slipped into her white linen nightgown. She climbed into the bed and pulled the covers up around her neck and instinctively began to think about Matt. She shifted positions, trying to get warm, and her thoughts drifted back to Jacob. He made her curious and she couldn't figure out what that attraction was. He wasn't at all her type but yet there was something about him. She remembered the haunting sweet odor of his breath and wondered about what was going through his mind when he was with her. She finally dozed off to sleep.

She dreamed that she was flying above the circus arena on Pronto's back. From high above the cheering crowd she looked down and saw Matt's face then fell to the ground. He ran over to help her up but when she stood up it was Jacob's face that she saw . . . not Matt's.

Dolly saw Jacob almost every day that week. She knew that he was falling in love with her. She tried everything to try to find the feelings for Jacob that she once had for Matt but couldn't. Matt had full lips. Jacob's were thin and rigid. Dolly couldn't imagine Jacob kissing her the way Matt did. But still . . . she wondered.

Two days before the year end Jacob called on Dolly again. "Come out, Dolly! Let's sit out on the porch."

"But it's so cold out there!"

"Well I thought you loved the snow and never worried about freezing your hind end off."

"Is it snowin' again?" Dolly ran to the window and peered out. "Oh Yeah! Let's do go on the porch! I'll get my wrap!"

As they sat on the porch swing together, Jacob slipped his arm around Dolly's shoulders and said, "Snuggle! I'll keep you warm."

This time Dolly was the one to blush. "I do love the snow, Jacob. There ain't nothin' purdier in the whole world . . . . Oh look! Icicles are formin' off the roof already. Ice crystals are so beautiful, don't ya think, Jacob?"

"You're eyes are like ice crystals . . . so pale . . . so blue . . . Yes, ice crystals are so beautiful," Jacob said without blushing.

Dolly thought it was strange that he said her eyes were like ice crystals. That's just what Uncle Thomas had once told her. That's how she decided that her circus name would be Dolly Crystal.

Jacob took another deep breath and said, "I've known you for quite some time, Dolly and now there's something I want to ask you."

The heavy white flakes were falling fast, covering the trees in the distance. She felt unsure about what was happening and said, "Yeah, Jacob? What?"

"Uh . . . I want you to know that . . . uh . . . I feel real strong about you and I'll be going away to college next fall . . . and . . . uh . . . you know that I'll be a good provider once I get my practice going. What . . . what I'm trying to say, Dolly, is . . . is that I'm in love with you and have been since the first day I laid eyes on you years ago. I'm asking you to marry me when I get back. There . . . I said it!"

"Oh Jacob . . . I don't know what to tell ya. I'm not sure how I feel about ya. I think I could fall in love with ya sometimes . . . but I jus' don't know. I'm flattered an' all. I . . . I'm sorry."

Jacob frowned, turned his face away from her then moved his arms back down. He slipped his hands into his pockets and turned back toward her, saying, "You're still in love with Matt Kilgore . . . is that it?"

"I . . . I don't know fer sure anymore."

"Jesus! What do I have to do to make you understand that he doesn't give a damn about you! Maybe it's time you heard the truth!"

"Heard what truth?"

"Dolly, you ought to know about what he once said about you." Jacob was beginning to sound jealous.

"What did he say about me, Jacob? Tell me."

"Well . . . Dolly . . . It's only right that you should know but you don't have to tell me if it's true or not because it won't change how I feel about you. Well . . . uh . . . he told all the boys back at school . . . a long time ago, about how you were raped by your uncle and he said that you were a wanton whore. He boasted that he took you into the woods after the hayride too."

Dolly stiffened and felt the blood rush to her head as she listened to what he was saying.

"Of course I didn't believe it Dolly. But it wouldn't make a difference even if I did believe it. I only wanted to punch him. In fact . . . I did just that! He wore a black eye for two weeks! Remember when you didn't see him for a long time after the hayride? Well, that was one of the reasons he stayed away. It wasn't just Sarah. Dolly. I . . . I still love you no matter what and I know you're not at all what he was calling you. You didn't go into the woods with him . . . did you?"

Stunned, her throat began to close. Then, like a volcano, her anger erupted and her voice cracked, "Yeah, Jacob . . . it's all true! "I guess I am a wanton whore!"

Jacob wrapped his arms around her and held her tightly. "I don't care about your past," he said. "You know that I treat you with nothing but respect. Dolly . . . I love you . . . I'm proposing marriage if you'll have me."

"Oh Jacob!" she cried, "What a way to propose to a girl!" She yanked away. "An' besides, I can't marry ya. I ain't good enough fer ya. I ain't good enough fer nobody!" she ran into the house and slammed the door behind her.

She ran up to her room and threw herself across the bed. Dolly couldn't imagine how any human being could be as cruel as Matt was. She promised herself that she would get revenge on Matt Kilgore one day.

Early the next morning Dolly felt sorry for the way she'd treated Jacob and couldn't bear for him to be angry with her, so she jumped onto Pronto's back and rode to his house on the other side of town to apologize. He lived just down the road from Matt in a big house with white columns on the front porch.

She knocked on the door and it opened right away. There stood Jacob, wearing his robe and holding a book under his arm.

"Why did you come to see me this morning, Dolly?" he asked as he stepped out onto the porch.

"Cause I wanna say I'm sorry fer the way I acted, Jacob. I'm flattered that ya want to marry me but I'm really all confused right now . . . that's all," she sighed. "Please try not to hate me too bad."

"I guess I understand . . . . I . . . I don't hate you but I'm not real happy about it. I wish you could forget him. He's not good enough for you. You know he doesn't love you like I do . . . in fact . . . he doesn't love you at all. You're just wasting your time thinking about him."

"But yer all wrong, Jacob. I hate Matt Kilgore. I jus' ain't too sure how I feel about ya yet . . . that's all."

He turned his face away and said, "What am I supposed to do? Wait around for you to change your mind? I just don't know . . . . maybe it's better if we don't see each other for a while."

Dolly became indignant then backed away and screeched, "That's a good idea! I'm sorry I came here!" Then ran back to her horse, screaming, "Ya better forgit all about me too, Jacob Turner!"

She jumped onto Pronto's back and rode off, kicking up a cloud of powdery snow behind her.

With her long skirt covering the tail end of her horse and her long red hair flowing in the wind as she rode away, Jacob watched. He stood at the door until she disappeared against the rising pink sun, knowing that she could never be tamed . . . knowing that he could never reach into her deep enough to win her heart.

CHAPTER 11

"Hurry up Dolly!" Uncle Thomas stood at the front door as he shouted up the stairs. "Me an' Ella's waitin'! Yer gonna make us late!"

Dolly appeared at the top of the stairs wearing an ivory satin gown. Uncle Thomas leaned his head to one side and smiled, "Good Lord, Girl! Yer the most beautiful thin' I ever seen!"

"Do I really have to go, Uncle? I don't really want to," she begged as she sadly gazed down at the tip of her shoe and dangled her foot reluctantly over the top step.

"It's the eve of the New Year. I ain't gonna go to no party without ya." The stern look in his eyes made Dolly obediently begin her descent down the stairs.

Dolly had never been to the Kilgore's mansion before. The entrance hall was bigger than any room in the house that she lived in and the chandelier was larger than she ever could imagine. She strained to produce a false hint of a smile as they entered the ballroom.

Matt's father moved over to greet them, followed by an old Black man holding a tray of filled champagne glasses. "It's good to see you here, Thomas. I'm so glad you brought your lovely wife and niece."

Uncle Thomas reached over and helped himself to a glass of champagne without offering one to Ella and Dolly. "This here's a might purdy house ya got an' it's real nice to be here."

Mr. Kilgore held out two glasses and said, "It's my pleasure to have you. Ladies, have some champagne." He looked at Ella but would not turn his eyes toward Dolly and she knew why. "My son, Matt, is not going to join us tonight but I'm sure you'll know everyone here. Oh . . . and Ladies, please forgive my servant for not serving you first. These Negroes sometimes just don't know any better."

Dolly resented him for talking about the old man like that and wanted desperately to get out of there. She realized that it was only a party for business reasons because Mr. Kilgore would not have normally invited people who were beneath his social stature to his home. She didn't like Mr. Kilgore but she kept a half smile on her face for the sake of her uncle.

Dolly's eyes combed the crowd of faces until she spotted Sarah Martin sitting next to Mrs. Kilgore chattering and laughing. Dolly's stare burned a path across the room until Sarah finally felt it and looked up. The two young women glared at each other for a moment then Sarah turned back to Mrs. Kilgore to whisper something into her ear.

Uncle Thomas led Ella off into a waltz and left Dolly standing there alone. Her discomfort became more extreme. She gulped down the champagne then reached for another glass from the old man's tray. Just as she held the glass to her lips she heard a voice from behind her.

"Dolly!" Abby called.

She turned around to meet her old friend's face and expecting to see Jacob by her side. "Abby, I'm so happy ya came." But there was no sign of Jacob. I was hopin' there would be more normal people like us here." She hesitated a moment before asking, "Where's Jacob tonight?"

"Oh, he didn't want to come. He didn't say why. I think something is bothering him but he won't tell me."

Dolly took a big gulp of her champagne and licked her lips. "Well . . . jus' git a load of this place will ya?"

"Oh it's magnificent isn't it, Dolly? I never realized that Matt lived in such luxury. And what a divine dress you're wearing. I love it. Where did you find it?" She examined the silky skirt by rubbing it between her index finger and thumb. "This is satin, isn't it?"

"Believe it or not, Abby, I got it second hand from Ella's sister up in Knoxville. She sent a box of dresses fer Ella." Dolly giggled and lowered her voice. "But she was too fat so she had to give em to me."

"I wish I knew her. She has exquisite taste." Abby was wearing a simple dark green dress and wore her hair in a plain bun. She never wore lip rouge or jewelry and how a woman could live with such an absence of vanity was beyond Dolly. She often felt the urge to hold Abby down, paint her face, curl her hair and get her into a red ruffled dress.

"Well, Abby . . . I might as well tell ya. Jacob wants to marry me an' I told him I couldn't. That's why he didn't want to come tonight."

Dolly waited to see if she would show any sign of jealousy or if she'd look surprised but instead Abby replied, "Oh, Dolly! He finally asked you?" She seemed to be happy about the news. "And you told him, No?"

"I . . . I'm jus' not sure . . . that's all. Sometimes I think there's somethin' there but . . . he is sweet an' all but I can't tell yet." Dolly grabbed Abby by the wrist. "Oh Look! It's Sarah Martin, an' she's comin' this way."

Within seconds Sarah was standing in front of Dolly and Abby. "Hello Abby." She smiled snobishly then turned to Dolly and said, "Who invited you to the party?"

"The same people who invited you."

"Well, Mr. Kilgore invited all of his factory workers for pure business reasons but I didn't know they were allowed to bring their trash with them."

Dolly, unable to control her anger, gritted her small white teeth together and glared. "Look who's callin' who trash! At least I never got pregnant an' killed my baby!"

Sarah's face turned crimson as she hatefully glared back. "Who told you that lie?"

"Matt did," Dolly answered with an arrogant tilt of the head.

Sarah's mouth fell open and her eyes grew wide. She drew her arm back getting ready to strike Dolly across the face when Abby's hand reached up and stopped her.

Abby yelled, "Hold on Girls! We're not having a brawl in here tonight." She turned to Sarah, "Only trash starts fights so back off and leave Dolly alone!"

Sarah furiously turned and stormed back over to Mrs Kilgore.

"Thanks fer stickin' up fer me, Abby," Dolly said. I was jus' about to knock er down."

"I wanted to knock her down myself."

"Did ya see the look she gave ya, Abby? She's scared now." Dolly wanted to laugh out loud and tried to hold it in but her cheeks began to puff out. Abby looked at Dolly then they both broke out into a loud laughter.

It wasn't long before Mrs. Kilgore approached Dolly. "I'm afraid I'm going to have to ask you to leave our home, Dolly."

"It would be my pleasure, Mrs. Kilgore, to leave this hellhole! I don't stay where I ain't welcome an' I don't stay where folks treat poor ol' Negroes like they was still slaves neither!" Dolly was trembling inside but held her head high.

Mrs. Kilgore's mouth fell open. "Why I never!"

"Abby stepped up and took Dolly's arm, "And it will also be my pleasure to leave, Mrs. Kilgore. I don't believe you Kilgores deserve our presence here."

Uncle Thomas, hearing the commotion, hobbled over to them, stumbling along the way with Ella right behind him. "Wait up Dolly! Where ya goin'?

"Mrs. Kilgore jus' asked me to leave an' Abby's leavin' too."

"Well, we ain't stayin' neither! Not where my family ain't welcome! Come on Ella!" Uncle Thomas turned to Mrs. Kilgore and said, "An' ya kin tell yer husband that the next time he has a party not to bother invitin' any of us factory workers cause we won't come. You folks are way too rude an'besides this kind of high-falootin' party is way too borin' fer us anyways. So now we'll bid ya goodnight!"

The four of them made their way to the front entry hall where the butler held the door opened for them to leave.

"My God! That was a relief to git outta there!" said Uncle Thomas. "Come on ladies . . . now it's time to go celebrate."

Gracie smiled when they came through the front door of her café. "Glad you folks could come. Sit down and I'll bring you something to eat. It's all on the house tonight!"

They sat down at the table and looked at each other solemnly for a moment, all thinking the same thing, then all at once they all began to laugh loud and hard.

"I never seen ya so steamed up before, Thomas. Did ya see Mrs. Kilgore's mouth pucker up when ya told her off? She didn't know what to say!" laughed Ella.

Thomas glanced across the tables. "Damn! There's Jacob sittin' over there all by hisself with his back to us. Dolly, why don't ya go over there an' tell em to join us."

Instead, Abby, knowing that Dolly felt uncomfortable about doing it, stood up and walked over to Jacob. "How would you like to join the Waffords and me?"

Jacob was surprised to see Abby. "I thought you went to the party."

"We did." Abby just smiled.

Jacob was soon sitting between Abby and Dolly at the table. He tried not to look at Dolly but his eyes kept wandering her way. She was so beautiful he could hardly focus on his thoughts.

The teakettle clock above the serving counter was about to strike midnight to signal the beginning of a new year. Uncle Thomas stood up and held his coffee cup high in the air, reciting, "Another year past an' another new year comin' . . . Ya gotta grab this minute cause the clock keeps runnin! Git ready cause it's almost the year eighteen hundred an' eighty-three!"

Jacob's eyes darted toward Dolly then back to Abby and reached over to give her a tight hug. He turned back to Dolly, feeling self-conscious, then hesitated.

"Hell, go on an' hug Dolly too. It's fine with me." Uncle Thomas laughed as he pulled a small jar of whiskey from his coat pocket.

Jacob leaned over and gave Dolly a quick hug then smiled back at Uncle Thomas.

"Gimme yer cup, Ella." Uncle Thomas poured some whiskey into her coffee and handed it back to her. "Who else wants some?"

Dolly held out her cup, "Go on Uncle . . . fill er up!"

"Here's to 1883!" shouted Ella as she held her coffee cup up then took a sip. She then leaned over and gave Thomas an uninhibited long passionate kiss on the lips.

"To 1883! May we all be blessed with good fortune this New Year and may Dolly never fall off of her horse again!" toasted Abby.

When it was time to leave Uncle Thomas yelled over to Gracie and in a slurred voice, "Good night purdy lady . . . an' we want to thank ya fer the best party we ever been to!"

Jacob stood first and pulled out Abby's chair, then Ella's and finally Dolly's chair.

They left together, singing in harmony to two different songs at once, as they went out the door. Arm and arm the five walked down the clay road together, stopping at Abby's house first. Jacob moved in between Thomas and Ella so that he would not have to hold Dolly's arm. Dolly couldn't stand it. She finally reached over and pulled his arm to make him walk beside her. She knew that was what he really wanted. He moved over but he pulled his arm loose. They finally stopped in front of Jacob's house and could still hear the noise from the Kilgore's party just up the road.

Jacob turned to Uncle Thomas and Ella and said, "I really had a nice time. Thank you for including me tonight."

Dolly was disappointed that Jacob did not say anything to her. She remained silent for the rest of the walk home but her uncle and Ella were too drunk to notice.

CHAPTER 12

"The Circus is comin' to town!" Uncle Thomas said when he came through the door.

Dolly's pale eyes lit up and she squealed, "Oh Uncle! When?"

He tossed his hat in the air. "In two weeks an' I'm takin' my girls to see it!"

She reached up and hugged him around the neck. "This is my chance. I'll go over there an' maybe I kin meet the owner an' try out fer the circus."

"Now hold on there . . . not so fast! I ain't seen ya ride in a long time. Are ya getting' better at it?"

"Oh yeah, Uncle. I kin do all sorts of stunts on my horse an', if I must say so myself, I'm purdy damn good!"

Dolly was so excited she could hardly wait. The pollen was thick in the air and the woods were spotted with dogwood blossoms. Jacob was still not speaking to her but she thought about him every day. Dolly couldn't help but think about Matt too. He was supposed to be coming home from college any day now. She wondered if she should tell him how much she hated him. The thought of it made her stomach tie in knots.

The morning the circus was starting to set up just outside of town, she mounted her horse and ran to watch. There were midgets and all kinds of unusual animals in cages. The equipment was being unpacked and the tent was going up. Dolly wandered around the grounds looking at all the strange people. There was a man taller than she had ever seen in her life walking beside a woman with a beard. Dolly couldn't help but to stare at the man with hair growing all over his face and hands. She felt embarrassed when he caught her but he smiled back at her, not seeming to mind her staring. There was an animal trainer practicing in an empty cage with his whip and a fat lady sitting on a stool mending costumes.

Dolly walked around to the back of the tent, where they kept the animals, and there stood a gigantic white horse tied to a post. She walked over to him and patted his nose saying, "Yer quite a handsome fella. Boy would I love to ride you." Just then a young slender dark-haired man approached her. She smiled at him and said, "I was just pettin' yer horse . . . hope ya don't mind".

"Oh . . . he's not mine. He belongs to Belle, who rides him in the show," he said with a smile on his lips.

"What do you do in the circus?" she asked.

"Oh, I walk the tightrope from sixty feet in the air without a net . . .," then modestly changing the subject he asked, "What's your name?"

"Dolly Wafford . . . what's yers?"

"I'm Steven Marsh but they all call me Sky Walker in the show," he answered.

"What about Belle? What does she do?" asked Dolly, being a bit self-conscious about sounding so inquisitive.

"Well . . . she rides this white horse and does tricks on his back. She's the star of the show." He didn't seem to mind all her questions.

"Oh, I kin do that too!" Dolly blurted out. "I kin do all sorts of tricks on my horse an' I'm good too . . . . I taught myself! I broke my leg once but I healed right up an' . . . an' I'd love to be in the circus someday." She knew that she was saying too much and decided to close her mouth.

Sky liked her boldness and honesty. "So you want to be in the circus, huh? Well, maybe you should talk to the boss . . . Mr. Phineas T. Barnum is right over there. He's the older man." He pointed to a silvered-haired man with low white eyebrows standing by the painted wagon talking to another man with a receding hairline and a beard.

"Well . . . jus' maybe I will!" Dolly was bursting with excitement.

She started over toward the silver-haired man when Sky Walker reached over and quickly grabbed her arm. "Wait! You can't just go up to Mr. Barnum like that! Let me talk to him first and maybe he'll want to see what you can do first," he laughed. "I'll talk to him in the morning. He's not in such a good mood today. Are you coming to the show tonight, Dolly?"

"Oh Yeah! I wouldn't miss it fer the world!" She started to walk away and turned again to say, "Oh! When will I see ya to know if he kin watch me on my horse?"

"Meet me in this very spot around ten in the morning," He nodded goodbye as he ran toward the tent.

Dolly stood for a while and watched the sign going up over the street. It read, "Barnum & London Circus proudly presents Belle Storm, the Queen of the Circus!" She sighed to herself, "One day that'll be me up on that sign." All the excitement took her mind off of Matt . . . and Jacob.

That evening Dolly was dressed and waiting at the front door, ready to leave and wringing her hands anxiously. "Hurry up Uncle Thomas! Come on Ella! Yer gonna make us late!"

"Well, come on girl . . . what er we waitin' fer! Let's go to the circus!" Uncle Thomas said as he finally made it to the bottom step with Ella right behind him.

Once they were seated Ella went to buy some peanuts. Dolly sat impatiently anticipating the first sound of the ringmaster's voice. It made Uncle Thomas happy to see Dolly so excited. He squeezed her hand hard when the music began.

The ringmaster walked out into the arena and through a his megaphone he shouted, "Welcome one and all to the Barnum and London Circus! We have clowns to make you laugh . . . we have daredevils to make your blood run cold! Tonight you will see Jumbo, the amazing giant elephant and we have the Queen of the Circus . . . Belle Storm, who will thrill you with her dangerous feats while riding her wonder horse, Star! And now, Ladies and Gentlemen, let the shoooow begin!"

Ella came back with the peanuts and sat down, offering them to Dolly first. But Dolly was too absorbed in all the excitement of the circus to notice Ella's offer. She sat in complete awe of everything that was going on in the ring.

The clowns came out first. Dolly recognized some of them from the day before. There were beautiful ladies wearing sparkling costumes and feathers on their heads, riding on elephants. A man walked out into the center ring with a whip and a chair. The cage rolled out and he went inside with two lions and one tiger, yelling and slashing the whip through the air. She felt sorry for the poor animals. They looked scared. Dolly thought to herself. "If that was me I'd make those tigers do whatever I wanted without a whip."

There was so much happening and too much to see all at once that she couldn't keep still in her seat. Jumbo, the giant elephant was dressed in red velvet with ostrich feathers and tassels on his head. "He ain't half as big as I thought. They musta exaggerated his size on the posters," Dolly said.

After the clowns and the trapeze artists, came Sky Walker to do his balancing tricks on the high rope. "That's the man I told ya about Uncle!" Dolly kept her eyes glued to him in amazement as he moved across the wire so high in the air. He must have been the bravest man she ever saw. The audience was silent until he reached the other end of the rope then broke out into a loud applause.

"And now, Introducing Bell Storm . . . the Queen of the Circus and her wonder horse, Star!" the ringmaster shouted. Everyone stood up and applauded as Belle rode out into the center ring, atop the giant white horse. Dolly gasped as she watched the bareback rider going in circles to the music then standing on the horses back. She stood on her hands while riding around the ring then moved back to a standing position and continued waving her arms.

After a few minutes Dolly's excitement faded. She said to Ella and her uncle, "Is that it? It's just like I could do when I was only fourteen!"

Belle performed a few more tricks but nothing new . . . and it was over. Dolly said sarcastically, "Hell, I kin do all that . . . only better. An' she didn't even do a single flip!"

"I thought she was purdy good myself," said Uncle Thomas. "Ya mean you kin do all that?"

"Yep. I told ya. I been practicin' fer a long time to git perfect . . . an' ya know what, Uncle? I'm gonna surprise the hell outta ya."

The next morning Dolly was dressed in her riding pants and standing in the very spot where she'd met Sky the day before. She fidgeted with the locket, sliding it back and forth over the chain and feeling anxious.

Sky was a few minutes late when he came up to her from behind. "It's all set Dolly. He wants to see you right now. So let's go . . . are you ready?"

"I . . . I jus' need to put on my ridin' slippers . . . wait jus' a minute! Jus', jus' wait!" She nervously pulled the pink ballerina slippers out of her shirt, smeared pine rosin on the soles then put them on her feet.

"Hurry . . . Mr. Barnum won't wait for ya," Sky yelled back at her as he started to walk.

Dolly hurried behind Sky as they headed toward the tent. When they were inside Dolly looked up and saw the man with the white hair sitting in the stands next to some other men and looking down at her.

Without hesitating, Dolly mounted Pronto and rode around the ring a few times, building up her speed. She was confident and it showed. Her long thick curls flew out behind her as she ran in the circle. She gracefully stood on Pronto's back and smiled up at Mr. Barnum then skillfully slid down the side of her horse touching her foot to the ground then back up again. "It's the best I kin do . . . it's the best I kin do," she repeated to herself as she was getting ready to do her triple death flip. "Please God . . . let me do this right."

Once back standing again she jumped high and flipped into a triple in mid air. "It was perfect." she murmured breathlessly when she heard everyone clapping and shouting.

"All right . . . stop! Get up here girl!" Mr. Barnum was signaling for her to come over to where he was sitting.

She obediently jumped down from her horse and ran up to steps. "Was I good?" she asked, trying to catch her breath and pulling her hair up off her neck.

"Yeah, you were good. Uh . . . How long have you been riding little lady?" The white haired man asked, "And who taught you to ride like that?"

"Since I was twelve . . . . an' I taught myself those tricks . . . an' I kin do some more too!" She lost her shyness, knowing that she was ten times better than Belle could ever hope to be.

Mr. Barnum leaned over and whispered to the other men next to him then turned to her and said, "Do you want to be in the circus?"

"Oh, more then anythin'! I been dreamin' 'bout this all my life! I kin go with ya right now . . . I kin start tonight." Dolly couldn't keep her mouth shut.

"Hold on girl!" he chuckled. "I only asked you if you wanted to be in the circus. I didn't say I'd hire you yet. What else can you do?"

She rambled on excitedly, "Oh I kin do just about anythin' on my horse I wanna do. I kin jump to the ground while he's still runnin' and jump back on and I kin even do a handstand on his back. I kin even tame wild critters too. Oh . . . an' I kin . . . ."

Mr. Barnum held his palm up to quiet her down. "Alright! Alright! You can be in my circus!" He leaned over and whispered in the other man's ear then looked up at Dolly and said with a smile, "And you can start tomorrow. Tell me little lady . . . what's your name?"

"Dolly . . . Dolly Wafford."

He smiled at the other man then turned back to Dolly. "We'll have to call you something else." He thought for a moment. "How about Dolly Ryder? Or what about Dolly Storm . . . you could be Belle's kid," he suggested.

"Well . . . Mr. I'm sorry Sir . . . I already thought of my circus name . . . how does Dolly Crystal sound to ya?" Dolly prayed he'd like it.

He scratched his balding head and said, "Crystal . . . uh, that seems to suit you. Dolly Crystal it is!" he agreed as he reached out and patted her shoulder. "You go with Sky and he'll fix you up with a costume and we'll see you tomorrow."

The other man moved closer and said, "Hello, Dolly Crystal and welcome aboard," as he shook her hand. "You were really something out in that ring. I might be joining P.T. in the near future. Oh, and by the way my name is Mr. Bailey . . . Mr. James Bailey."

"It's good to meet ya, Mr. James Bailey," she politely nodded. She jumped onto Pronto's back and said, "I guess I'll be seein' ya tomorrow evenin' then." She glanced up and spotted Uncle Thomas and Ella watching her from the stands on the far side. "Will ya please excuse me fer a minute? There's my uncle up there . . . I gotta go talk to em."

"Sure thing, Dolly. Go ahead."

Dolly rode over to where they were sitting and jumped down. Uncle Thomas had a smile that was a mile long and Ella's mouth was still opened wide. "Hey, you two! Ya never told me you was comin' to watch me. How'd me an' Pronto look in the arena?" Dolly yelled as she ran up to them.

Ella stood up and wrapped her arms around her while Thomas just looked at her and beamed.

"Why I jus' about shit my britches!" said Uncle Thomas. "I never believed you was that good!"

Dolly was happy that she had pleased them with her surprise but she needed to go see Sky. "I gotta go now but I'll see ya back at the house later."

"Go on an' do what ya gotta do now, Girl. I think I had enough surprises fer one day. Now go on," He said.

Uncle Thomas and Ella were both still grinning from ear to ear as she rode away.

She rode back to where Sky was and jumped down. "I'm startin' tomorrow night!"

"Welcome to the circus, Dolly. Let me show you where you're going to be." He led her to the wagon next to Belle's. "You pick out something you like and try it on, Dolly. I'll be right back," he said and left her in a hurry.

Dolly could hardly believe what was happening. Her first impulse was to tell Jacob but suddenly remembered that he still wasn't speaking to her.

CHAPTER 13

Dolly closed her scrapbook once more and sighed. Her mouth was dry for another beer but she had no money until her check arrived. She sat there unable to stand it and decided to ask Mike if she could charge her beer. He'd let her do it in the past and she always paid him back. Mike didn't like anyone to charge merchandise in his store but Dolly just had to ask. "Hello again Mike. Uh . . . do ya mind if I pay ya tomorrow if I git me another beer? My check comes in the mail tomorrow . . . ya know I'll pay ya back Mike." She licked her dry lips then wiped her mouth. Her red lip liner was almost gone but she was more concerned with having that beer.

"Aw, you know I don't like it when people can't pay cash," he said with a frustrating look on his face. "Well, go ahead and get one," he winced.

Dolly grabbed a bottle from the icebox. "I really appreciate it, Mike. Hey, kin ya throw a pack of Old Golds on my tab too?"

Mike smacked his lips in disgust as she yanked the pack from his hand. With her scrapbook under her arm, she walked out and went across the street to Joe's Bar.

It was still early and there was no one in the place. She sat down with the beer that she'd bought from Mike and gazed at the florescent lights flashing in the front window and said, "Hey Joe! Did ya know that the Barnum Circus used to be called the Barnum an' London Circus? Yep . . . before him an' Mr. Bailey got to be partners . . . but I never knew Mr. London. They was always changin' the name of that circus. Did I ever tell ya I was so famous people came from all over jus' to see me?" she chattered. "Why they knew my name clear across the Atlantic Ocean . . . In

France . . . an' London . . . all over! I was the best there ever was too. There wasn't nobody who could ride like I did or could tame wild animals the way I use to. Yesireee! I was quite somthin' back in those days, Joe!"

Joe was busy setting up for the night. "Oh . . . yeah, Dolly?" he answered in a disinterested but polite voice. "I don't remember hearing about that. Tell me about it," he said without looking up from behind the bar.

Dolly lit a cigarette and inhaled deeply as she watched the neon lights flashing off and on in the window. She picked a piece of tobacco off the tip of her tongue then began her story.

"Now . . . where was I?" she said. "Oh yeah . . . Mr. Barnum an' Mr. Bailey had to get rid of Belle Storm cause everybody came to see me perform . . . not her. When she left, they gave me er old dressin' room. It was actually a boxcar but I called it my dressin' room. They gave me Star to ride too, but I still rode Pronto everywhere I went. An' Belle, she took it real hard I heard cause she was the Queen fer a long time till I came along. An' they all said she kinda went crazy after she left the circus.

Well, I had to say goodbye to Uncle Thomas and Ella when we pulled out of Nashville. We only performed there fer that one week. I didn't think 'bout havin' to leave but I loved bein' in the circus so I stuck with Mr. Barnum.

I remember Uncle Thomas cryin' when he found out I was leavin' but he was happy fer me at the same time. He took me to the train station an' it was hard leavin' em cause I knew I'd miss em real bad fer a long time."

Dolly looked up at Joe behind the bar, taking one last draw on the cigarette before crushing it out, and noticed that he was cleaning the mirrors. She knew he wasn't listening to a word that she was saying so she paused. She took another sip of the warm beer that she was nursing and gazed out the window in front of her. She remembered the night of her first performance.

Dolly decided not to tell a soul about her offer to join the circus except Uncle Thomas and Ella. She wanted to surprise everyone who would be coming from Ridgetop. She'd especially hoped that Jacob would be there that evening.

She'd selected a pink silk costume dotted with white shimmering glass beads and wore her hair up in a tight knot with a pink rose over her ear. She'd spent over an hour painting her face with thick powder and rouge and drawing wide black lashes beneath her own until her face looked like that of a painted doll. She slipped on her pink ballerina slippers and mounted the tall white horse.

"Let's do it good, Star! Ya gotta do what I say Boy," she whispered into his ear as she patted the side of his neck. Dolly was nervous but tried not to show it as she waited for the ringmaster to introduce her.

"And noooow ladies and gentlemen," the ringmaster shouted, "the Barnum and London Circus proudly presents Miss Dolly Crystal and her wonder horse, Star!" That was her cue to ride out into the center ring. She took a deep breath and prayed, "Dear Lord, please make me do this good."

She heard the audience gasp as she entered the ring. It made her feel more confident as she comfortably picked up pace and stood on the horse's back. The crowd exploded into a loud applause.

"Oh, this won't be hard at all." Dolly said to herself, knowing that she had impressed them before she even got started. She skillfully slid down to one side and touched the sawdust floor with her toes then back and to the other side as the horse pranced in a circle. From a standing position she bent over and flipped around, facing back, then bent down and did a handstand on the horse's hind end.

Dolly confidently performed every one of her tricks and saved her triple death flip for last. She began to feel slightly nervous. While she was going into her triple she suddenly realized that she had misjudged and was only able to fit two somersaults in. She felt her face turn red from embarrassment but when the crowd cheered and whistled the embarrassment quickly vanished. She looked out at her audience and smiled.

"They loved me!" Dolly squealed to Sky Walker when the show was over. "I was nervous at first but I ain't nervous nomore.

I made one mistake when I couldn't do my triple but that don't matter . . . they thought I was good anyways."

"You were wonderful, Dolly Crystal. This circus is lucky to have you aboard." Sky was pleased with her act but also seemed disinterested. "I'll talk more with ya later . . . I gotta go . . . I'm late."

"That's funny," Dolly mumbled as he disappeared. "I ain't never seen him with a girl yet. It's awful strange how he keeps runnin' off in a hurry all the time." She didn't give it another thought after that.

On her way back to her boxcar she spotted Matt standing in front of her wagon and all at once felt her legs almost give out beneath her. She stood about twenty feet away from him with her mouth gaping wide open as he moved toward her. "What in the hell are ya doin' here?" She blurted out hatefully.

"I . . . I only wanted to tell you that I saw you in the show tonight," he said in a defensive tone as he walked up to her. "And I was thoroughly surprised. I didn't expect to being seeing you in the circus. I had no idea you could ride like that."

"Well, there's a whole lot ya don't know 'bout me, Matt Kilgore!" she snapped back.

Making no attempt to get any closer to her, he said, "You don't have to yell, Dolly. I just wanted to say hello to you since I'm only going to be home for a week."

"I could care less how long yer home fer! Ya got some nerve even talkin' to me after all ya said 'bout me to everbody so git yer dumb ass outta my way!"

Just then Sarah Martin stepped out from behind one of the wagons and stood next to Matt, which only fueled the fire of Dolly's fury. Without saying another word, Dolly darted past them and ran into her wagon.

She furiously yanked off her costume and put on a silk robe that she'd found hanging behind the door. She threw herself onto the sofa and buried her face in a pillow and screamed.

The door flew open and there stood Abby and Jacob.

"My God!" screeched Dolly. "This is a damn nightmare! First I see Matt an' Sarah together an' now I see you two come bargin' in!"

Abby's mouth dropped open but Jacob seemed unaffected.

Dolly stood up and cleared her throat. "I . . . I'm sorry, I didn't mean that . . . I didn't mean fer it to come out that way. I'm sorry. Please close the door an' sit down a minute." She picked up her handkerchief and blew her nose hard.

Abby stepped over and put her arms around Dolly. "We know you didn't mean it, Dolly. We saw Matt and Sarah heading this way. That's why Jacob and I ran over here. We knew you'd be upset."

Jacob didn't say a word. He stood by the door feeling like an unwelcome intruder as Dolly and Abby carried on hugging each other and whispering about Matt Kilgore.

Abby and Dolly finally unlocked their embrace to sit down. Jacob sat on the straight-back chair by the door with his arms folded and his legs crossed, feeling self conscious, while the girls continued talking.

"Dolly, why in the world didn't you ever tell me that you could do all those amazing tricks? And how come you never told me that you were going to join the circus? How exciting this must be for you. My gosh, am I ever shocked with what I saw tonight. We just came into Nashville to see the circus and there you were out in the arena. I'm flabbergasted!" Abby said all in one breath.

Abby's excitement made Dolly forget about Matt. "We're leavin' fer New Orleans in one week. Uncle Thomas an' Ella don't know yet cause I jus' found out tonight. Oh Abby, I'm scared. I'm happy but I'm scared. I never been away from Uncle Thomas before."

"Oh he's going to be happy for you, Dolly. You have nothing to be afraid of. You'll be fine on your own. You know how to take care of yourself. With your talent you'll be the biggest star in the circus one day. But I'll miss you when you're gone." Abby gave her a hearty hug.

Dolly nervously folded the handkerchief into a tiny ball, then unfolded it again. "Kin I ride home with ya tonight? It's a long way by myself an' besides, I kin leave Pronto here fer the night.

In fact, Pronto ain't even goin' back home at all," she laughed nervously.

They all rode back together in Jacobs's buggy. Dolly caught Jacob's eyes staring at her several times as she sat on the other side of Abby talking. She jealously wondered why Jacob and Abby were together that evening.

They finally reached Ridgetop at two in the morning. Jacob stopped to let Abby off first, since her house was on the way, and rode straight to Dolly's house, not saying a word.

"Jacob . . . How come ya ain't talkin' tonight?" Dolly asked.

"You know why, Dolly. We're not supposed to be seeing each other. Remember?"

"Yeah, but that don't mean we can't talk to each other an' be civil."

In the moonlight Dolly could see tears glistening in his eyes when she looked up at the side of his face. "Jacob . . . I didn't mean to hurt ya. I think the world of ya but I don't think I ever got Matt outta my head . . . . not really . . . . even though right now I despise em."

"I don't think you know what you want." Jacob pulled up in front of the house then said, "Goodbye, Dolly."

"Will I see ya later, Jacob?" she asked humbly as she stepped down and turned around.

He glared back at her, not answering. Dolly stormed into the house before he could see her cry.

The following afternoon Uncle Thomas took a day off from work and drove Dolly back to Nashville.

As they began their journey into Nashville Dolly's mind was filled with Matt again. She knew that someday she would get her revenge for all the pain that he'd caused her. She'd be patient. The day would come and she would make him sorry. Jacob would be sorry too.

Uncle Thomas broke the silence and said, "Well, it looks to

me that me an' Ella, we'll finally have the place to ourselves an' ya won't be 'round botherin' us no more."

"Oh I know yer gonna miss me cause ya ain't gonna have nobody to lie to."

"Whata ya mean? I never lie!"

"Yer foot," Dolly laughed. "Ya kin never tell the truth 'bout yer foot!"

"Well, I been meanin' to tell ya fer a long time. The truth that is. Maintaining a serious expression he said, "It happened when I was asleep one night."

"How could ya lose yer foot when you was sleepin'?"

"Well, jus' before I went to bed that night I spotted this big ol' cougar out in the back of the house. He was glarin' in through the window at me with his big shinin' eyes so I made sure the door was shut tight before I got in the bed. When I went to sleep I dreamed 'bout that cougar chasin' me but he had big ol' horns on his head! Well, he finally caught me an' chewed off my foot an' ate it. An' when I woke up it turned out not to be a dream after all cause there was blood everwhere. I looked an' the door was still shut an' there wasn't no windows broken an' that's when I discovered my foot was missin'! An' that's when I knew that cougar musta been the devil hisself!"

"Well, thank ya fer tellin' me the truth . . . finally!" Dolly laughed.

Along the way Dolly told him all about the plans to go to New Orleans.

"Then we go to who-knows-where after that," she said sadly as she held onto his arm.

Uncle Thomas was happy for her just like Abby said he'd be. "This is what ya always wanted, Dolly an' I'm glad fer ya," he said with a gentle squeeze to her arm. "But ya jus' better behave when yer gone. An' ya better come back an' see me whenever ya can. Ya hear?"

"Ya know I will, Uncle. I promise." Dolly meant what she said but wondered when she'd ever see him again.

"Well, Girl. Here's where we say goodbye. Give me a hug."

"I promise I'll come to see ya first chance I git. I love ya, Uncle," she said as she hugged him tight.

Jacob never came to say Goodbye during the following days before the circus left Nashville. He would be going off to college in Boston by August and Dolly wondered when she'd ever see him again. Even though Dolly's thoughts were consumed by her new circus career she still caught herself thinking about him more and more.

CHAPTER 14

Dolly heard Joe's voice saying, "No customers so far. That hurricane is supposed to start hitting here tonight and it's not a big one but it's moving fast. I'm not gonna bother boarding up the windows." He walked over to Dolly's table and placed another cold beer in front of her. "This one's on the house. I'm closing early tonight."

"Thanks, Joe. Hey . . . don't ya wanna hear more of my story?" She looked up at him expecting him to ignore her.

"Sure, Dolly. Let me hear more about your circus days." Joe smiled at her. He was a tall, good-looking man in his fifties, with dark eyes and streaks of gray around his temples. He was the only person, besides the two little girls, who was nice to her.

She couldn't wait to get on with her story. There was so much to talk about. She took a few big swigs of beer until the bottle was half empty. "I can't remember where I was . . . oh yeah," she continued.

"We took off to New Orleans to do the next show. I was amazed how fast Mr. Barnum and Mr. Bailey had everybody workin' to set up the circus an' it took hardly no time at all. After the tent was set up an' everybody was ready we put on the best show ever that first night. There was newspaper reporters everywhere takin' my picture an' everbody swarmed aroun' me like I was the queen bee.

That's where I met Jack Wade, who I despise . . . but I'll tell ya 'bout that later. He was one of the reporters from the newspaper. When I finished my act an' was back in my dressin' room, there he was . . . as bold as a man could git . . . sittin' in a chair in my boxcar . . . waitin' fer me. I said to em, "What in the hell are ya doin' in my dressin' room?"

An' he says to me, "Miss Crystal . . . I just wanted to meet you in person. Can I talk with you for a minute or so?"

Well, he was a nice lookin' man so of course I said, "Yeah, I got a minute fer ya."

He started askin' me all sorts of questions 'bout where I came from an' how long I was with the circus an' I gave em all truthful answers. He took some pictures of me sittin' in front of my dressin' table an' then asked me to go eat dinner with em so we could talk more. I went with him to Pete's Salt Wagon where they served seafood. Well, bein' from Georgia an' not getting' it too much it sure was good. Well Sir, we kinda started goin' out together purdy regular the whole two weeks we were in New Orleans. He liked me a lot an' made sure my picture was plastered all over the newspapers. He said he could make me famous.

I even told em 'bout Uncle Ernest an' what happened back when I was a kid. What a big mistake that was! It was all the whiskey I drank that made me tell so much an' he knew it. But I'll tell ya 'bout that later. Anyways, I was on my way to bein' famous an' I trusted that newspaper reporter to do it fer me.

Work didn't seem like work to me. It was fun ridin' on Star an' purdy soon nothin' mattered much except havin' fun. I was a real flirt with the men. They all liked me an' I'd tease em all.

I thought 'bout Uncle Thomas all the time. Of course I missed him real bad but it felt good not to have to answer to nobody fer a change . . . besides I was way past seventeen by then.

Grant, one of the midget clowns came up to me sayin', "Hey, did ya hear about Belle? They say she went crazy an' shot her own head off. Guess she got depressed after you took her job away from her, Dolly."

I didn't like the way he put it but it was probably the truth but I didn't feel any grief fer the woman . . . after all I hardly even knew her.

I got a letter from Abby that Jacob's father died jus' before he went away to college in Boston. I remember I felt real bad cause I really liked his father a lot. Her letter made me think a lot 'bout Jacob an' I sure did miss em." The old woman paused long enough to take a few more generous slugs of beer and light another cigarette.

Joe was busy behind the bar putting bottles up and taping the mirror. "Yeah? So go on."

"We went from New Orleans out to California. We had our own train too. In fact I had my own boxcar. Did I tell ya that already, Joe? Well anyways I said goodbye to Jack an' hoped I'd see em again one day.

First stop was San Francisco. Damn! What a wild place that was! There was so much to see an' do it made my heart race. I was Dolly Crystal . . . Queen of the Circus . . . an' I had any man I wanted right at my fingertips. I got more attention then anyone else in the circus an' I was startin' to make a lotta money too.

After we finished up in California we went on to St. Louis. Mr. Bailey wanted to go back East again to Boston next. That's where Jacob was goin' to college. By then it was almost a year since I seen em an' I looked forward to gettin' together with him again so I sent a telegram to say that I was on my way right after we left St. Louis.

When we finally got to Boston we was settin' up fer the first night an' Jacob came up an' surprised me. When I saw em my heart flickered. He hugged me real hard an' I had to hold my breath cause I couldn't breathe.

I wanted to impress em so I showed em how high on the hog I was livin'. I had the nicest boxcar of all an' it was right next to the dining car too. It was painted pink an' it had my picture on the side ridin' on Star . . . an' Jacob was impressed.

He really did look good to me. He got handsomer evertime I saw em. He told me he was studyin' real hard at medicine an' he was makin' good grades at school. I was so proud of Jacob. He said to me, "I've got to get back to my class now but I'll come tonight and watch you perform. We'll go to dinner after that."

I looked up at him an' I could smell his breath that smelt like cucumbers an' sugar an' felt the urge to kiss em but I didn't. I simply told him that I'd do my best out there that night an' couldn't hardly wait to see em after the show."

Old Dolly had to stop there. She held the bottle of beer to her lips to take a sip but it was empty. "Hey Joe! Do ya mind givin' me another Schlitz an' I kin pay ya fer it tomorrow?" Joe was so busy working that he didn't hear her. She said again, "Hey Joe! Another one please!"

"Oh . . . sure, Dolly." He walked around the bar and placed a bottle in front of her.

"Yer not listenin' to a word are ya." Dolly did not get an answer. It was like she wasn't there. "Hell, it don't matter anyways."

CHAPTER 15

She remembered that night well. She could still see Jacob's adoring face out in the crowd watching her from the stands as she rode around the ring. She was getting ready for one of her stunts on Star's back when she thought about how much she had missed Jacob. She had been thinking more about him than she had Matt. The only time she thought about Matt was when she tried to think of a way to get her revenge. That's when she realized that it was Jacob she was in love with.

Jacob watched in awe without taking his eyes off of her for a second until her act was over and she was out of sight.

Dolly ran to her dressing room to change out of her costume, feeling that something wonderful was about to happen. She hurriedly slipped into one of her favorite dresses, let her hair down and dotted her earlobes with expensive perfume.

She heard a knock on the door just as she was about to step out of it. She opened the flimsy door and smiled down at Jacob's face. "Well, come on in Jacob . . . I was just about to go lookin' fer ya."

"You were wonderful out there tonight, Dolly. I remember when you once told me that you'd be in the circus someday but I had no idea that you'd turn out to be the star of the show so soon. What you've accomplished in only a year is more than most people could never have in a lifetime." He sat down on the one chair in the room and looked around. Dolly's dressing room was filled with bouquets of flowers and smelled like perfume. "Looks like Little Dolly Wafford has done pretty well for herself. And now she's the Queen of the Barnum and Bailey Circus."

"Yep. I guess I did do what I said I would." She reached for his hand and said, "I'm real sorry 'bout yer father dyin' an all."

He looked up at her, squeezing her hand. "Thank you, Dolly. My father was a great man."

"How'd he die?"

"Heart attack. My mother didn't take his death well because we weren't prepared. It was so sudden. It happened just a week before I went off to college."

"It's been an awful long time since we seen each other ain't it?"

"Yes, Dolly, too long. Remember the last time I asked you to marry me? Well, I want you to know that offer still stands. I still want you for my wife."

"Jacob, yer crazy! Now look at me. Do ya think I could be a wife of a doctor?" Her heart was pounding but determined to play hard-to-get, she said, "I'm flattered an' all but . . ."

Suddenly he stood up and pulled her close in his arms then kissed her hard. Dolly was too shocked to respond. It was not like Jacob to be so bold.

"There. That's all you needed to help you make up your mind," he said confidently as he stepped back.

Dolly stood with her mouth wide open, not able to speak. His lips were soft. Not rigid like she'd always imagined they'd be. She loved the way his lips felt. She loved the way he kissed her.

"Don't say no again, Dolly. I want you to think about it. There are plenty of other women out there who would jump at the chance to marry me . . . but I want you . . . no one else. And I'll have you, damn it! Even if it takes the rest of my life to win your love!" He reached for her again and kissed her even harder.

This time Dolly kissed him back. After several long passion-filled kisses, she took a breath. "Oh, Jacob, I guess I loved ya all the time an' didn't even know it." Then she pulled away. "But I don't know where I'm gonna be when ya finally git outta college. How could we ever git married?"

"It doesn't matter where you are. I'll come find you." He kissed her eyelid and stroked her cheek with the back of his hand. "I'm so painfully in love with you." He kissed her again lightly and said, "Ever since we were kids I've loved you. I've always loved only you . . . every day and every minute . . . I've dreamed of making love to you all my life."

Goose bumps covered Dolly's legs as he continued kissing her. She loved everything about him. The taste of his sweet mouth, the strength of his masculine arms but most of all she loved the honest and sincere love that he had for her.

Jacob kissed her again on the tip of her nose then glanced at his pocketwatch. "Damn, I promised to take you to dinner."

"I ain't hungry Jacob. I don't wanna go to dinner. Not jus' yet. Kin we jus' stay here fer a while an' talk?" Dolly's pale crystal blue eyes melted into his as she began to play with the top button on the front of her dress until came undone.

He pressed his body hard against hers, making her tremble all over. He whispered his sweet breath into her mouth, "Dolly, please say you'll marry me." His lips softly met her's again. "We don't have to wait. We can be married and no one has to know." He kissed her hard and guided her onto the bed. Pushing her red curls away from her face, he said, "I love you. I always have and I always will. Please say you'll marry me."

"Oh Jacob . . . Yeah, I wanna marry ya!"

He fumbled with the buttons on his pants. "I can't wait . . . I want you now," he breathed heavily into her ear.

Dolly stood up and shamelessly stepped out of her dress. She loosened her corset until it fell to the floor then she pulled down her bloomers and kicked them across the room. She stood naked in front of him for a moment, inviting his eyes to explore every detail of her slim white body, before she fell back onto the bed next to him.

Jacob rolled over on top of her and looked into her eyes as he gently slid his erection into the soft wetness between her legs. Slowly and deliberately he moved. "Oh Lord . . . I can't believe we're really doing this," he moaned as he slowly plunged deeper inside. "Say it again. Say you'll marry me again . . . now . . . or I'll stop," he breathlessly threatened with his devilish grin.

"Oh Jacob, ya know I will. I love you too."

"Oh Dolly . . . This feels better than I've ever dreamed." He kissed her neck then then moved up and kissed each of her eyelids. "I'm getting ready to explode." With a distorted face he groaned long and loud. The look on his face and the sound of his moans excited her and she moaned out loud along with him.

Jacob looked down at her as the sweat dripped from his chin onto her face. "My God, I never realized . . . . I never thought it would be this wonderful."

She gently bit his finger and then kissed it. "How many girls have ya done this with before, Jacob?"

"Only one."

Dolly stiffened. "Yeah? Who?"

"Her name was Dolly Wafford but it was only in a dream that we made love. Oh, Dolly . . . I never wanted anyone but you . . . and you know that." Jacob ran his hand lightly up and down her inner thigh then rolled over onto his back.

She turned over, propped up onto her elbows and began toying with the hair on his chest. "Well . . . I'll be damned. Hey . . . I never knew ya had this much hair before, Jacob."

"You've just never seen me naked before," he said in a husky relaxed voice.

Before they were rested Jacob was back on top of her again. They repeated their lovemaking several times before he finally panted, "No more! I can't! No more!"

She loved the way he explored her body from head to toe and the way he woke her every hour to make love again and again.

The morning light came into the tiny boxcar through the one small window at the foot of the bed. Dolly opened her eyes and rolled over to watch Jacob's face as he slept. It felt good to wake up next to him. She thought about all the years that he was in love with her and it made her shiver.

"Good morning," he yawned with half-opened eyes.

"Good mornin'. I guess we wore each other out didn't we." Dolly was wide awake. "I'm feelin' sort of hungry."

"I'm hungry too . . . for you!" He said as he rolled over on top of her again.

When they were finished Dolly moaned, "I'm so sore, Jacob. I don't think I kin do this anymore fer a while.

He enjoyed hearing what Dolly had just told him and it made him smile. He loved looking at her. Her face was pink from his whiskers and her lips were puffed up. She was so beautiful with her long tangled hair and her wild pale blue eyes.

She sat up and reached for her riding pants. "Let's go eat. I'm starvin' to death!"

Breakfast was served in the main tent. Everyone had begun eating by the time Dolly and Jacob walked in.

"Ya almost missed breakfast, Dolly!" Mike, the giant yelled. "Ya better get some before I eat what's left!" he joked.

Jacob pulled back a chair for Dolly at the large table and walked over to the food. Within moments breakfast was on the table and Jacob sat down. They started packing the eggs and sausage into their mouths so fast that they had to laugh at themselves.

"My God, we better slow down or somebody's gonna choke," Dolly mumbled with a mouthful.

"So where do you want to get married?" Jacob asked.

"Oh, I don't care . . . jus' as long as we do it." Dolly took another bite of her biscuit and held it in her mouth without chewing. Then her eyes darted around the tent at the circus people she was now working with. They were odd, she thought. There was Flo, the bearded lady, Grant, the loveable midget, Sweet Mike, the giant, Ted the lion tamer, Sky, the tightrope walker and of course Mr. Barnum . . . . She loved them all. This was her life and she loved it. If she were married she would have to give it all up. She tried to think of a way to be married and stay in the circus. She laid her fork down and chewed on a dry biscuit.

"What are you thinking about, Dolly?"

"I don't know . . . . I reckon I'm jus' tryin' to figure a way . . . a way to be married to ya but not have to leave the circus . . . I don't know . . . what do you suggest?"

"I'd say you'd have to give it up. That's all." Jacob took a sip of milk and wiped his mouth with the back of his hand. He wasn't prepared for what she was about to say.

"How could I give it up, Jacob? How kin I give up my friends an' my career? I been wantin' fer this all my life . . . ya know that! What do I do?" She picked up her fork and stabbed at a piece of ham.

"Marry me . . . that's what! I'll make you happy. You don't need the circus. You hardly know these people and besides that they are all freaks anyway."

Dolly mashed some egg into her fork and thought before saying in a whiney voice, "They ain't freaks an' besides . . . I worked too hard to get where I am." All at once she felt anger beginning to stir inside. "Oh Jacob, ya know I love ya more then anythin' but I jus' can't give it all up . . . Not now! How could ya expect me to?" She slammed her fork back onto the plate.

"Then I guess you don't want to get married do you! You love the circus more than you love me! I wish you could make up your mind, Dolly!"

"I have made up my mind!"

"Then you won't marry me?"

"I didn't say I wouldn't marry ya, Jacob. Jus' not right now. Besides . . . ya gotta finish college first."

"I can't take this anymore. You're so damn fickle! You're like a merry-go-round! My head's spinning enough already! Maybe it's best that we don't see each other again . . . then . . . just maybe I could get over you!" Jacob stood up and threw on his coat.

In a muffled breath, Dolly mumbled sarcastically, "Oh hell . . . here we go again."

Jacob was just about to say something but when he looked down at Dolly's face . . . the face that he'd adored for so long, the fury left him. His eyes softened as he pleaded for the last time. "Please marry me . . . I'll wait until you're ready." He placed his index finger over her lips and whispered, "Shhh! Don't say a word right now. Think about it. Think about me while I'm gone." Then he turned and walked away.

CHAPTER 16

Old Dolly sat savoring every detail of that memory of her first night with Jacob until her thoughts were interrupted by the loud weather report coming from the radio that Joe had just turned on. "Do ya have to play it so damn loud?" Dolly shouted over the noise. "I was gettin' ready to finish tellin' ya my story."

Joe walked back and turned the radio down. "Sorry Dolly, I thought you were through. Go on." He began wiping the radio with the dirty rag.

"Well . . . Let's see . . . Oh yeah . . ." Dolly went on. "Well I had a fiancée named Jacob. Me an' him was supposed to git married, but I would've had to quit the circus an' I jus' couldn't, so he got real upset at me an' left. I tried to forgit 'bout Jacob cause I didn't wanna give up the circus an' I cried over em a lot.

Oh, how I loved bein' famous . . . I loved the circus more then anything. I used to go back to where they kept the lions an' tigers an' talk to em. They got to where they knew me. I'd sneak em some leftovers an' they'd come right up to the bars an' let me pet em. Big Jack was the biggest lion but he was the sweetest of all. When Ted, the lion tamer, used to do his act with Big Jack I used to git mad at the way he treated that poor lion. He used to hit em with a whip to make him do tricks. That would piss me off cause I knew all those animals needed was a little kindness. Anyways, I got to be friends with those cats. It wasn't too long after that, Mr.Barnum let me try to work with em. That Big Jack was a ferocious lookin' beast too . . . but he was jus' a big ol' pussy cat to me. Of course we never told Ted about it. That is till I got purdy good at it an' one day I showed Mr. Barnum how I had a better way with animals then Ted did an' he let me try my act out fer em. Why there was nothin' to it. I jus' looked right into their eyes an' they'd do exactly what I told em all to do. I'd use the whip jus' fer appearance sake an' crack it in the air. But Big Jack an' the rest of the cats knew I would never hit em with it.

I got to be better than Ted after a while an' I took over that act too. Ted had to leave but he went right to work fer the Ringlin' Brothers. I did my bareback ridin' act an' then I'd go straight to the cages and do the lion tamin' act. I truly became the Queen of the Circus. Yep . . . I was the best they ever had!

A couple of years went by . . . I think it was around 1887 er so, the year Mr. Bailey joined us, that my horse, Pronto, got real sick with some disease that only horses git an' they couldn't make em no better. Mr. Bailey was afraid the other horses would catch it so he said to me, "I'm sorry Dolly, but we gotta have him put down." I loved that ol' horse too. He was all the family I had left. I remember sittin' on the ground an' holdin' his head jus' 'fore he died. He was smart an' knew who I was. That horse told me goodbye in his own way by rockin' his head on my lap. He even had tears in his eyes. Oh, I cried fer months over that damn animal . . . . you'd a thunk he was my brother instead of my horse.

We traveled all over the place . . . from one big town to the next an' I never heard from Jacob fer a long time. Mr. Bailey got mad at Mr. Barnum an' left to do his own circus . . . I never got the whole story what the blow-up was all about. They was always disagreein' about somethin'.

That year Jumbo got killed by a train too . . . the poor thing. He got crushed between two trains . . . our circus train an' some other train that was comin' down the track. I could hear this big loud boom an' I ran out an saw him jus' layin' there . . . not movin'. Well Mr. Barnum got real upset cause he paid ten thousand dollars fer that elephant . . . but I only felt sorry fer that poor elephant.

I musta been about twenty-one but I was the best anybody ever seen an' Mr. Barnum knew it. I was the only one in the world who knew how to do the triple death flip an' also tame wild cats. I never learned nothin' from nobody neither. That death flip was a dangerous stunt cause I had to jump real high to get in a triple somersault an' be able to land back on my feet on the horses' back . . . an' he'd been runnin' real fast an' sometimes I'd even jump through fire. Oh . . . ya shoulda seen me. I made all the people in the audience stand up an' gasp. Then when I'd do my lion tamin' act there wasn't a person sittin' down in the whole place. I made em all nervous when I'd accidentally-on-purpose drop my whip an' bend over with my back facin' Big Jack to pick it up again.

I had all the liquor I could drink too. Sometimes I even performed better after a few drinks. An' I wore all these sparkly outfits with matchin' slippers . . . Yesireeeeebob! I was quite a dish back in those days an' I made more money then anybody else in the circus.

Finally Mr. Bailey came back an' joined us again . . . I guess they mended their differences but anyways we went to callin' it Barnum & Bailey's Greatest Show on Earth . . . an' was bigger an' better then ever. Seems like they was always changin' the name of the circus . . . from Barnum to Barnum an'London to Barnum an' Bailey . . . an' of course much later they was bought up by the Ringlin' brothers . . . but that was after P.T. died.

I heard from my friend, Abby, that Jacob got a job at a hospital in New York. He wasn't a surgeon yet but close to it. I really loved em too. I was real sorry I lost em but I woulda lost the circus if I got married.

My Uncle Thomas wrote an' told me he quit his job at the glass factory cause Mr. Kilgore kept sayin' bad thin's 'bout me. He told me not to worry cause he could git another job . . . but later on he found out nobody wanted em cause he was getting' too old. Him an' his wife, Ella, they was havin' a real hard time too an' had to move to a boardin' house. Well, when I got wind of that I felt purdy bad. Here I was makin' all that money an' they was so poor so I sent em a bunch of money to buy a new house. I didn't get a chance to even to see it though cause I was too busy travelin' all over the place. I told em to pick out a house bigger and better then the Kilgore's . . . and they did! It was the biggest house in Ridgetop too! Well, I started sendin' em all the money I had since I never needed it cause all I ever bought was clothes an' liquor with it anyways.

My uncle wrote an' told me thank you an' they was real happy in that big house. They even got a butler an' a maid an' Mrs. Kilgore was tryin' to butter-up to Ella all the time cause she liked rich people. Well, the worm turned an' Ella started snubbin' Mrs. Kilgore. It sure made me feel good to know that the Kilgores was finally jealous of my uncle an' Ella. It did my soul good to know I could help em like I did.

Jus' a few years later, around end of 1890, just before we was to go back down to Atlanta, I got a telegram that Uncle Thomas was real sick so I took off back to Ridgetop to see em right away. I felt bad cause I didn't go visit him fer all those years. I jus' never had the time off. In fact I broke my promise to him about behavin' myself cause I never behaved back in those days. An' the other promise was to come see him whenever I could . . . I never did that neither. You kin imagine how guilty I felt about it.

When I got to Ridgetop Uncle Thomas didn't even know who I was at first. He had a stroke an' couldn't talk er move. Ella, she looked old an' tired. I guess she was gittin' up past er mid-thirties by then but she looked a lot older then she was. Right after he died she said to me, "Uncle Thomas wanted ya to have this Dolly," an' she handed me a letter. She told me he wrote it just after he had his first stroke an' I never even knew he had one before that last one. I was cryin' when I opened it. Inside was the photograph of him an' my daddy an' Ernest that he used to keep on his dresser. I kept that letter all these years here in my scrapbook. Here, I'll read it to ya."

> "My Dearest Dolly,
>
> I'm writin' this letter before I get too sick an' die on ya. I want to tell ya how I really lost my foot. It was way back before ya was born, in 1829, when I was working at the paper mill up north of Atlanta. There was this Injun I worked with loadin' logs. His name was Eagle Claw. Me an' him, we got along pretty good, even if he was an Injun, till one day we had a fight over a girl. She was the one I wanted to marry but he loved 'er too. I fergot to tell ya she was an Injun too.

We got in a fight right there at the mill one day an' he told me that one of us had to die. Well, I agreed to meet em fer a fight to the end that night. He pulled a knife on me but I jumped away before he could get the thing into my gut. I pushed em in the creek an' started beatin' up on em an' made em drop his knife in the water. I liked the man. In fact he was my very best friend an' I didn't want to kill em. But his proud Injun blood made em fight real mean. It turned out he had a hatchet too. He pulled it out of his shirt an' came back at me. I jumped out of the water an' he came chasin' me. I tripped and fell an' he threw that hatchet an' it chopped my foot clean off. It felt real strange seein' my foot layin' there on the ground unattached to my leg. Blood was gushin' everywhere an' I jus' grabbed my foot up an' tried to put it back on but it hurt like like hell an' I got real scared. Eagle Claw was coming at me again with a big rock all ready to smash in my head an' I had no choice but to grab that same hatchet that just cut off my foot an' sling it at his face. It landed right in his forehead deep between his eyes. Well, ol' Claw Foot jus' stood there fer a minute an' held his hand out to me before he fell down. I went over to em an' he looked up at me an' said, "You are my friend, Tom." I reached down an' took his hand then his eyes closed. I felt bad about em but I needed to get help before I bled to death. I crawled up to the back side of the mill an' hollered out loud til somebody came out to help. I was holding' on to my foot hopin' somebody could get it back on again. I went delirious in the hospital an' they said I wouldn't let go of my foot until it was white and stiff an' started stinkin'. That injun girl didn't want me back after that. And that's the truth Dolly. I wanted ya to know this. I never wanted to tell ya I killed a man but I don't want to die with a lie layin' on my chest. An' Dolly, I want ya to know that you was more like my daughter then my niece. I think ya knew that anyways.

Truly Yours Forever,
Uncle Thomas"

Joe looked up and said, "That's some story, Dolly."

"Yep, it was jus' like em too! Ya shoulda heard some of the tales he told me about his missin' foot. Guess he didn't want me to think bad about em but I think he was real brave. He had a certain way 'bout em too that ya jus' couldn't explain. An' sure, I'd catch em in a lie er two but that man never complained er fussed an' he always knew how to make me laugh. Oh he was a very special man. He thought he was jus' an ordinary man, but I knew he wasn't. Yesiree . . . there ain't never gonna be another one like my Uncle Thomas." She wiped the corner of her eye and lit another cigarette. "Well, I read that letter over and over again right after my poor ol' uncle died. I remember cryin' harder then I ever did in my life. He was all the family I had . . . him an' Pronto . . . an' now they was both gone.

Years later Ella went to live with er sister, Margaret, up in Knoxville an' I didn't see her again fer a long time."

Dolly noticed Joe wiping the counters and knew that he had lost interest again so she paused and crushed out her cigarette. "Ya got anything to eat around this place, Joe?"

"There's some peanuts back here. Want some?" He walked over with the small bowl.

"Yep. My stomach's been a growlin' since I got here," she said as she threw a few peanuts into her mouth then washed them down with her beer. She gazed at Uncle Thomas's letter and drifted back to the day her beloved uncle died.

When Dolly pulled up in front of that huge white mansion Ella came running out. "Dolly! Oh I'm so glad yer here! He's been hangin' on fer ya." She threw her arms around Dolly and said, "It don't look too good. The stroke was bad an' he can't even talk."

Dolly followed Ella upstairs.

"He's in there," Ella said as she pointed to a wide sliding door.

"Uncle Thomas? Are ya awake'?" Dolly tiptoed into his room. He was peacefully sleeping. The hat that she'd given him for Christmas long ago was hanging on the bedpost at the foot of the bed. His face was pale and his thin hair was snow white.

She sat on a chair beside his bed and reached for his boney hand. His fingernails had grown very long and his wrists were very thin. Her uncle had always been a sturdy man, even though he lacked one foot and it made her ache inside to see him so frail.

"Uncle? Kin ya hear me? His eyes slowly opened but he could not speak. Dolly held his hand to her cheek and said, "Oh, Uncle Thomas, I know ya can't answer me er talk to me but I want ya to know I'm here an' I love ya so much. I jus' don't know how I'm gonna git along without ya." Her eyes swelled with tears but she did not try to hide them. "I'm so ashamed cause I never came to see ya like I promised I would an' I didn't really behave like ya told me to neither. Do ya forgive me, Uncle?"

Dolly noticed the tears in his deep-set eyes as she felt a weak squeeze from his hand then closed his eyes again. "I know ya forgive me . . . . I know ya love me too. Thank ya . . . oh, thank ya so much fer lovin' me. Ya know how I love ya back, don't ya?" She leaned down and kissed his forehead, knowing it wouldn't be long before he was gone. "I don't know if you kin hear me but I rekon it's gettin' time fer ya to leave soon an' be with the good Lord. You'll see Daddy again . . . an' yer mama. Oh I'll miss ya so much, Uncle. Oh . . . I'll miss ya so much but you kin jus' go anytime ya want now. Jus' don't worry 'bout me an' Ella cause we're gonna be jus' fine."

Ella came into the room with a tray. "Ya want hot tea, Dolly?"

"I don't think I do, Ella. Thank ya anyways," she said, not looking away from her uncle's face.

Ella put down the tray and sat on the edge of the bed and took her husband's hand. "Yer uncle's been so good to me an' I can't stand the thought of losin' em. What am I gonna do without em?" Her bottom lids filled with tears.

Dolly sat on the other side of the bed and took his other hand. His eyes opened and he looked at her. The two women sat beside him without saying a word. Each holding his hand while his gaze was focused on Dolly.

An hour passed. Ella moved over to the chair feeling exhausted and fell asleep.

"Yer so cold, Uncle. Do ya need another blanket? She went to the cedar chest and pulled out a heavy quilt then pulled it up around his shoulders. She noticed his face had lost all color and it was darker on one side than the other. She sat back down beside him and reached for his hand again. It was stiff and cold. His eyes were still on her but his tears had dried up.

"Wake up, Ella . . . . he's gone."

Dolly never knew exactly how much he'd heard her say to him that day. She only hoped that he had felt her love to take with him.

The old woman wiped a tear away and yelled, "Hey Joe! Are ya gonna listen to me er not!" She popped another few peanuts into her mouth and chewed until she felt something hard then spit it out into her hand. She looked down and saw an orange-brown tooth in the palm of her hand. "Aw shit, there goes another one."

"Another what," asked Joe.

"Another . . . another peanut I dropped on the floor," she lied, sliding her tooth in her cigarette pack. "Ya got a napkin?"

Joe passed her a couple of napkins then set back to work. Dolly stuffed a napkin into her mouth to absorb the little bit of blood. She could hear the wind roaring outside. Joe was still paying no attention to Dolly but she didn't look up to notice. She pulled out the napkin and said, "Oh yeah . . . where was I again?"

"After Uncle Thomas died we had the biggest an' fanciest funeral anybody ever seen. Of course Ella was really upset. She cried fer months. Well . . . I guess I did too . . . but only when I was alone at night. Seems all I had left was the circus cats an' Star, my horse. Everybody thought I was just this happy-go-lucky thin' but deep inside I was very lonely an' sad.

I'll never forgit the time Big Jack turned on me. I guess he was in a bad mood that day cause I didn't do nothin' any different when I was doin' my act with him. When I bent over to pick up the whip, that I accidentally-on-purpose dropped, he lunged at my arm an' almost tore it off. I bled like a chicken with its' head cut off. It took over two hundred stitches to sew me back up again but it didn't keep me outta that cage. I went right back in jus' days after it happened. I glared at Big Jack an' he never tried to hurt me again . . . but I never trusted him again after that."

Joe's loud voice drowned out Dolly's story, "Dolly . . . I'm sorry but I gotta close up now. Maybe you outta go on home for the night. The winds are getting strong out there."

Dolly peered outside, wondering where the time had gone, and it was getting dark. The palm trees by the Lighthouse Grocery were bending almost to the ground. She knew that Joe hadn't listened to a word of her story but it felt good to tell it anyway because it took her back in time . . . back when she felt so alive. She slowly got up and stumbled out through the door.

The rain pounded hard against her face and the forceful wind almost blew her over. She tucked the scrapbook down into the front of her dress and held it closed tight against her bosom until she finally made it around to the back and stepped inside her tiny room.

CHAPTER 17

Old Dolly reached up under the skirted sink for her usual can of soup and opened it. She spotted another roach scurrying across the floor as she reached for the pot.

Feeling very tired, she took her cup of soup then sat on the bed and gazed at the walls until she spied Mr. Barnum's face staring back at her.

"I tried to tell Mr.Bailey he was makin' a big mistake but he didn't listen to me, P.T. I know ya woulda kept me on if ya didn't go an' die on us."

After swallowing the last noodle from the bottom of the cup, she stayed on the bed staring at the walls for a long time. A jabbing pain hit her in the chest forcing her to lie back. She closed her eyes, allowing her thoughts to drift back again.

Dolly Crystal, the queen, was on top of the world. Her twenty-four years had gifted her with more fame and beauty than most people only dream about.

"Mr Bailey says we're hittin' Nashville next," Sky told her. "He said they're all planning a huge reception for you there. I guess all your friends from Ridgetop will be comin' to greet you."

Dolly's first thoughts were of Matt Kilgore. Even after all those years she still loathed him and felt the burning thirst for revenge as strong as ever. She could never forget him until she satisfied that craving. She had to see him just one more time.

Dolly picked up her mail and found a letter from Jacob on top. She hadn't seen him in five years and was almost afraid to open it. She left the mail office and headed back to her boxcar. She couldn't resist ripping it open before she reached her room.

"Dearest Dolly,

I am now legally a doctor. I graduated last Saturday. I wish you could have been there to share my happiness with me.

It took a lot of courage for me to write this letter, Dolly. I've not forgotten our night together. In fact that's all I think about every night when I close my eyes. I can still see your eyes and smell your hair, even after all these years.

I'm sorry for not coming to say goodbye but I was so hurt and angry because you chose the circus over marrying me. I acted foolishly.

I'm writing this letter because I must see you again. I promise I won't harass you this time. I hear that the circus will be in New York City this March twenty-third. That's two months away. Please meet me at Tarrantini's Café on Fifth Avenue right after the first show. I'll be waiting. I miss you, Dolly. Please write to me.

Love Always,
Jacob."

Dolly had just enough time before the show to quickly write a short note to Jacob, telling him that she would look forward to meeting him in New York and mailed it.

She could hardly wait to see Jacob again but her thoughts returned to Matt.

It was only a few days later when Dolly stepped down off the circus train in Nashville to the sound of the crowd's cheering. People crowded around her, holding out pictures and magazines, begging for her autograph. There was a sign stretched across the road that read, "Welcome Home Queen Dolly," flags were waving everywhere. The school's marching band was playing "Hail to the Queen" as she made her way through the sea of familiar faces with her searching eyes. Matt's was not amongst them, nor did she see Abby's.

As she made her way through the crowd and spotted Sarah Martin standing off in the distance in front of the coffee shop.

Dolly moved toward her, knowing that Sarah was watching her with envy. As Dolly approached her she could see that Sarah's eyes were moving from Dolly's head to her feet. Sarah did not look as pretty as she once did and her clothes were not as nice as Dolly's.

"Hello Sarah," Dolly smiled.

"Hello," Sarah responded without returning a smile. "How are you, Dolly?"

"Oh life's never been better." Dolly was surprised that she felt no jealousy or hard feelings for the way Sarah had once treated her. "An' I hope life's treatin' you good too, Sarah."

"Things are just fine, Dolly, as if you really cared. Why you finally made it to the top didn't you? What did you have to do to get there? Did you do favors for the men to get what you wanted?" Sarah had a look about her face that revealed hard times. There were dark circles under her eyes and she had gained too much weight, making her appear to be older than her years. Her dull hair was pinned up in a simple bun on top and she wasn't wearing lip color.

"Why that ain't a nice thing to say, Sarah. Maybe yer jus' jealous . . . but I really don't want ya to be. I don't have any hard feelin's fer you no more."

Sarah just stood with her mouth drooping and looked at Dolly, realizing that there was no competing with her anymore. Dolly was dressed in splendid clothes and was much more beautiful now than she was. Dolly's talent and fame made Sarah feel shabby and at a loss for the usual sharp words that made her feel superior. She hung her head and walked away, feeling defeated.

Dolly felt a warm satisfaction in knowing that Sarah was actually jealous of her but at the same time she felt pity for her. Dolly remembered all the cruel words that Sarah had said to her and the way she snubbed her years ago but still, she could not hate Sarah.

"Mr. Barnum, I wanna to take a short trip into Ridgetop . . .

to take care of some unfinished business. Do ya think it's alright since we ain't gonna start till tomorrow night?" Dolly asked.

"Just make certain you're back in Nashville on time, Dolly . . . that's all . . . it's fine with me. I'll let you use my royal coach and driver." Mr. Barnum turned to one of the men standing behind him and said, "Miles, take Miss Crystal where she wants to go but have her back no later than midnight tonight."

"Yes sir, Mr. Barnum," the man said. "Are you ready to leave now Miss Crystal?"

Dolly left immediately for Ridgetop. There was no time to waste.

"Please wait here fer me, Miles." She stepped down from the yellow and red painted circus coach wearing a red-laced bustled dress with a small ostrich feathered hat with a matching parasol. Her diamond necklace and earrings glistened in the afternoon sunlight as she gracefully glided down Main Street. She looked like the queen that she was.

The whole town gathered around when they spotted her, begging for her autograph and shouting, "There she is! It's Dolly Crystal!" Many of them had known her as plain little Dolly Wafford but now gazed upon her with envy. Some were afraid to approach her and some were jealous but most everyone saw her as royalty.

She made her way across the street to the old café where she once worked while all admiring eyes followed her. She walked in and sat down at a table.

Gracie came over to her, not recognizing her and said, "Ma'am, what can I get for ya today."

"Gracie? Don't ya know who in the hell I am?'

"Why Dolly! Is it really you? I've been hearin' so much about ya!"

"Gracie . . . I don't have much time here. Could ya tell me where Matt Kilgore is?" she asked impatiently.

"Oh yeah . . . Matt. He's runnin' the glass factory. His father retired few years back an' oh . . . and he got married to . . . uh . . . Sarah. Yeah, he married Sarah Martin."

Dolly's pale eyes widened with surprise. "Thank you, Gracie an' it was real nice seein' ya again. I'm sorry I ain't able to stay an' visit with ya but I'm sorta in a hurry. I'll see ya next time I come to town," she said as she headed for the door.

She could feel her face burning as she marched toward the glass factory where Matt worked. The more she thought about it the less it bothered her that he and Sarah had gotten married. "They deserve each other," she thought.

She barged through the reception room and through the door that read, "Matthew Kilgore, President."

There sat Matt behind a large desk with his back turned and looking out the window. A sudden jolt hit her in the pit of her stomach when she saw the back of his blond head, then eased when she remembered her anger. She stepped closer and said, "I jus' had to see ya again Matt."

Without turning around in his chair, he recognized her voice right away. He stood up and turned around with a startled look on his face. "Dolly! What on earth are you doing here?"

Dolly fluttered her long eyelashes and lied, "Ain't ya glad to see me, Matt? I jus' wanted to say hello." Fully aware of her flawless beauty, she moved even closer to make certain his eyes could explore her in more detail. "Yeah Matt, I guess I jus couldn't git ya outta my mind . . . even after all these years." She examined the toe of her shoe and said, "I only wanted to stop to tell ya that I'm gonna be performin' in Nashville tomorrow night an' wondered if maybe you could come see me." She lowered her eyes, trying to appear bashful and added, "I been thinkin' a lot about ya Matt."

He gulped out loud, not believing his ears. "Dolly . . . I had no idea that you would even remember. Why look at you. You're famous and you're perfectly beautiful. You could have any man you wanted. Why would you still want to see me?"

"That's cause I never stopped lovin' ya Matt Kilgore," she answered as she struck a theatrical pose by touching her cheek with her gloved hand. Inside, the fire of intense hatred for him raged but she knew that if she could contoll her temper he would take the bait.

"I've thought a lot about you too, Dolly. I came to see your act quite a number of times. You were in Chattanooga twice and I took a trip to Philadelphia once just to see you. I know you never saw me out in the crowd and I figured you forgot all about me. I was going to . . ." Matt continued to chatter nervously.

"An' now yer a married man," Dolly interrupted. She twirled her fingers around her small lace handerchief. "Oh, an' how is yer wife . . . uh . . . Sarah . . . . ain't that right?" She noticed that Matt had sweat on his upper lip and his hands were shaking.

"Oh . . . yeah . . . Sarah . . . she's just fine. I only married her because you were gone. She . . . she's shopping in Nashville today and we have a little girl . . . . we . . . we named her Katherine and she . . . she's one year old now. My mother's taking care of her right now . . .", he continued to ramble on . . . . just like Dolly used to do.

It did her heart good to see him squirm. "Maybe you could bring yer little girl to the circus sometime to see me an' I do hope you an' Sarah will remain very happy together."

"Yes . . . yes, we are happy. And I know my little girl would love to come see you and maybe, well . . . I definitely would love to . . .," he stopped, realizing that he was chattering senselessly.

Well Matt, I jus' wanted to stop by an' see ya, that's all." She cupped her small gloved hand over the doorknob and slowly turned it. "I really gotta git goin' now so I'll bid ya farewell." She stepped through the door and began her casual stroll down the hall.

"Wait! Dolly! When will I see you again? Where are you going to be tomorrow . . .," Matt's voice trailed off into silence as she walked through the hall and back out to the street.

Without looking back, Dolly walked straight toward the coach, knowing that Matt would be following right behind her.

"Kin we git on back to Nashville now, Miles?" she asked the driver, who had just finished watering the horses.

"Why yes, Miss Crystal," he answered as he helped Dolly to climb back into the coach.

Matt came running down the street after her. "Dolly! Wait! I need to talk to you!"

The driver looked over. "Should I wait Miss Crystal?"

"Yeah, wait."

Matt ran up, opened the door and climbed in beside her. "Dolly Wafford, I've waited for you too long to let you get away from me again. Driver!" He shouted. "Take us for a ride toward Franklin!"

Her plan was working. She felt the twinge of stinging hatred as he sat next to her.

"Will that be all right with you, Miss Crystal?" asked Miles.

"Yep. Jus' take us where he says."

Matt took her hand and looked into her eyes as the coach started to move. He cleared his throat and said, "We're going back to the spot where we first made love."

"This is crazy, Matt. What in the hell are we doin'? Yer a married man now." She snatched her hand away.

"I want to be alone with you one more time. Oh Dolly, you know I never stopped loving you. It was just that my family wanted me to marry Sarah."

"Go on," she said, clutching the small black beaded purse that her uncle had given her, tightly with both hands on her lap.

"I never got you out of my mind, Dolly. I should have not listened to my father and married you instead of Sarah. I've missed you all these years and would have written you a letter but I never knew where to send it."

"Well, Matt . . . I missed you too." she said as she slid her hand to his lap, only inches from his crotch, teasing him and knowing that she was accomplishing what she'd set out to do.

"Oh Dolly . . . Please let me make love to you . . . here . . . right now, in this coach," he pleaded as they rode out of town.

"No Matt, not here. Jus' wait." She had him in her palms and it felt good to see him beg. She gently squeezed the damp bulge in the front of his pants.

"You have to let me, Dolly. Please," he begged.

"But yer married to Sarah now."

"I'll get a divorce. I'll marry you if you want me to," Matt's voice trembled.

Dolly knew that he was lying again just to get what he wanted. Her voice grew cold and calloused as she raised her chin and said, "That's outta the question, Matt. Ya got a kid now so let's jus' leave it like it is."

"What's happened to you, Dolly? You seem so different all of a sudden."

She'd finally gotten the exact amount of revenge she needed to satisfy her. It had gone far enough and now it was time to back off and get rid of him . . . for good. Dolly's sweetness vanished as she clenched her jaws and said, "I think I changed my mind about ya, Matt. Now that I got to see ya it jus' don't seem as intense as I thought it would. I think it's all my success that makes ya look so small an' unimportant to me now. Now I think it's time we git back . . . don't you?" She confidently squeezed his hard dripping penis one last time, making certain that he had reached the peak of throbbing arousal then suddenly pulled her hand away.

A puzzled look crossed Matt's sweating face as he said, "I don't understand you, Dolly. Why are you doing this? You said you loved me."

She felt her anger about to explode then suddenly had to release what she had harbored inside for so long. "Do ya really think I could still love you? Do ya really think I'd lower myself to yer level? Yer nothin' but a scoundrel an' I wouldn't be caught dead with the likes of ya! Ya disgust me with yer lyin' and cheatin' ways, Matt Kilgore! Why, Ya ain't even good enough fer Sarah an' ya certainly ain't good enough fer me . . . an' ya never was!"

Matt's cheeks began to puff and his eyes narrowed into an evil squint as he all of a sudden realized what she was doing to him.

Even knowing that she'd won she could not resist continuing with her attack. She felt the blood rush to her face and said, "Yer pathetic an' I wouldn't make love to ya if ya paid me!"

Matt lashed back, "You think you're some kind of queen or something? Why you're still nothing but a tease and a low class whore! I'm not going to let you get away with this, Dolly!"

Turning on him like an angry lioness, she screamed, "I am a queen an' yer the whore . . . not me! Ya always lied to git what ya wanted. Well . . . I jus' think ya used up all yer lies . . . cause ain't nobody believes ya no more an' now ya kin go to hell!" With her teeth clenched and her eyes scrunched half closed, she snarled, "I despise you, Matt Kilgore!"

"Why you fucking bitch!" He lunged toward her, grabbing her hands and holding them tightly together. With his other hand he reached into his pants. "Now we'll see who's not good enough for who!"

Dolly's thoughts suddenly flashed back to Uncle Ernest and saw his face in Matt's.

He pushed her back and threw all his weight on top of her, raising her skirt to her waist and tearing her bloomers apart at the crotch.

"Git offa me ya son-of-a-bitch!" Dolly screamed as she tried to fight him off. "Miles! Miles! Stop! Stop an' help me!"

The driver was partly deaf and could not hear her over the loud clomping of the horses' feet on the rocky road.

Matt forced his large hardness into her and began gyrating violently while he held her hands down tight. He relieved himself within seconds . . . then it was over.

"You disgust me . . . ya bastard! I'll kill ya fer this!" She reached into her beaded purse for a small metal nail file and jabbed him in the arm with it.

Matt snatched the file from her hand and tossed it out the window. "Not if I kill you first, you whore!"

For the first time Dolly's anger turned into terror. She threw the door open and jumped out of the coach onto the side of the road. The driver saw her fall and came to a halt.

"Please help me! He's tryin' to kill me!" She had landed with her bare knees onto the granite rocks and as she stood up she felt the warm blood running down her legs beneath her long red dress.

Matt jumped out of the coach and glared at her before running off into the woods.

As the driver climbed down to help Dolly back into the coach he spotted the torn pieces of her bloomers lying on the ground. "Why didn't you call for help?" he asked.

"I did! Ya jus' never heard me!" She started to cry. "Kin we jus' leave now, Miles?"

Dolly cried all the way back to Nashville. Her plan had backfired and Matt won again. Dolly could never tell a living soul about what had just happened and she'd never see Matt Kilgore again.

It was dark before they arrived in Nashville. The driver took her straight to the circus grounds and helped her down from the coach.

"Dolly!" yelled Sky Walker, running over to her, "How was your trip?"

Ignoring him, she quickly ran toward her boxcar.

"Dolly, come back here. Are you all right?"

"Jus' leave me be," she said as she stepped into her dressing room and slammed the door.

Dolly's performance the following evening was as brilliant as ever. Not wanting to talk to anyone after the show, she went directly back to her dressing room to the whiskey bottle. She poured one glass after another until she found herself in the spinning world where she could forget everything.

Over the days that passed most everyone who in the circus noticed a difference in Dolly. She was no longer talkative and friendly.

Mistaking shock for snobbery, Mike, the giant said to Mr. Barnum, "Looks like Dolly's turned into a real queen. She won't talk to anyone in a decent tone and acts like she's better than the rest of us."

Mr. Barnum knew what was wrong with Dolly because Miles had told him what happened. He could not argue and said nothing.

CHAPTER 18

March came and it was time to meet Jacob in New York. She'd missed him but dreaded seeing him at the same time. She was afraid to face him for fear that he'd know. But how could he possibly know unless Matt told him, and Dolly knew that he would never to admit to it because it would ruin his marriage to Sarah. Dolly still had it in the back of her mind that somehow Jacob would find out.

Dolly got through her act as usual without a flaw and hurried to change so she could go meet Jacob at the Tarrantini's Café on Fifth Avenue.

She dressed modestly in a tailored brown dress and wore a simple felt hat. She looked plain but respectable. She preferred her flashy clothes but for this occasion she felt that she had made the appropriate choice.

Jacob was sitting at a table just inside the café window. "Dolly!" He stood up and hugged her, "You look absolutely wonderful! But it looks like you've lost weight."

"Oh, hell, Jacob. I've always been skinny. Did ya forgit already?" she laughed as she slid into her chair.

He stammered, "I . . . I didn't mean to say you were skinny . . . just beautiful."

"Ya look purdy good yerself, Jacob . . . with yer nails all shiny and that expensive suit ya got on. I never seen ya lookin' so handsome." Dolly knew that the biggest mistake in her life was when she let him go so long ago and she did not want to lose him again.

The talk was small and polite as they ordered and began their lunch. Dolly had three glasses of wine with her food and soon began to loosen up.

"So how many patients of yer's died so far?" she joked nervously.

"Not one yet." Jacob didn't like Dolly's joke but he smiled anyway, knowing that she was only feeling the wine. He noticed the dark circles under her eyes but said nothing.

She giggled nervously as she slurped down the last glass of wine, "Well, Jacob . . . It sure is nice to see ya after all these years . . . again! Here it is, 1891 an' stittin' here together. I didn't think I'd see ya again an' I was so happy when I got yer letter." She had to stop herself from saying too much.

When they finished eating Jacob said, "Take a stroll with me, Dolly."

She stood up to smooth her skirt and almost lost her balance. "That sounds like a good idea . . . Where ya takin' me?"

"Window shopping. I might even buy you something," Jacob laughed as he took her arm and led her out through the front door.

"I want ya to buy that . . . an' that! Oh yeah . . . an' this here too!" Dolly giggled as she staggered along pointing to everything she saw in the storefront windows.

Jacob swung her around by the arm and said, "Anything you want, Dolly. If you really need a stove or a pair of men's boots I'll buy them for you." Jacob hugged her, lifting her off her feet then putting her back down.

"Nope . . . I don't really need em but I would like somethin' else," she said as she strutted ahead of him. "Jus' buy me another drink an' I'll be happy!"

They sighted the Essex Hotel and Pub just ahead and Jacob said, "Come on, Dolly. I'll buy you that drink if you want it."

Dolly was thirsty for some liquor and anxiously walked inside with him. Music filled the room as they sat at a small table against the wall and ordered whiskey.

As soon as the drinks made it to the table she gulped down half of the glass and wiped her mouth. "So how do we start from here, Jacob?"

"I don't know . . . so many years gone by . . . It's hard. All I know is that you're still the only one for me. I never even looked at one girl at college. They guys all thought I was . . . you know, peculiar."

Dolly had to laugh. "They thought ya perferred boys to girls?" Her blue eyes lit up, making her look like the young girl Jacob knew so long ago, "I think that's funnier then hell, Jacob. Hey look! My glass is empty already an' I'm ready fer another!"

"I never saw you drink so much before, Dolly," He said as he signaled for the waiter.

"Oh Yeah, I drink lots these days. It makes me feel happy."

"Are you happy, Dolly?" Jacob reached for her hand. "Do you think about me at all? Do you remember what I told you five years ago about waiting for you to change your mind about leaving the circus and marrying me? I make a lot of money now, Dolly. When my father died I inherited a fortune. I could buy you your own circus now if you wanted it."

"I'm sorry to hear about yer father, Jacob, but . . . well, maybe we should jus' take it slow fer now . . . . don't ya think?" Dolly almost sounded sober.

Jacob shrugged his shoulders. "If you say so."

Jacob truly turned out to be a beautiful man, she thought. She noticed the chain from his gold pocketwatch and a large diamond on his finger. "So yer rich now, huh?" she smiled.

"Yep." He took her hand and examined her diamond ring and said, "Looks like you've done pretty well yourself."

They held their hands on the table to compare which diamond was larger. Dolly's was slightly bigger. They both laughed at the same time. That broke the ice for them then after one more drink she started to relax.

Dolly still felt the magic with him as she caught a whiff of cucumbers and sugar on his breath again. His haunting dark green eyes seemed to pierce so deeply that she feared he'd read her guilty mind. She had to focus on wiping all thoughts of Matt completely away.

Several drinks later the sun had disappeared and they were feeling a warm glow.

Jacob stood up and asked, "Would you care to dance?"

"I ain't danced in so long. In fact you were the last person I danced with at Ella's birthday party. Remember that, Jacob?"

"No . . . it was Matt you last danced with . . . not me."

Dolly felt tense for a moment when she heard his name come from Jacob's lips.

He took her hand and said, "Dolly, you are the most exciting girl I've ever known. Those crystal blue eyes of yours have always been filled with a wildness I could never tame." As he swayed with her on the small dance floor he whispered into her ear, "I don't suppose we'll ever get married . . . will we, Dolly?" Jacob kissed her on the nose and said, "Will I just have to settle for this for the rest of my life and grab every chance I can get to be with you?" He held her closer and whispered, "Do you know how much I love you still?"

That sweet breath again. Dolly felt the tickling warmness from the drinks she'd had and without thinking first, she blurted out, "Jacob, I ain't had a moment that I felt happy since I last saw ya. I been in love with ya since I don't know when an' I wanna marry ya!"

Taken by surprise, Jacob's eyes widened. "About time! I better marry you before you get too old for me." He stopped for a moment then asked, "Are you sure it's not just the whiskey?"

"Yeah . . . I'm sure. I never been more positive in all my life."

He excused himself by nodding and said, "I'll be back in a few minutes . . . now don't go away." He left her stranded in the middle of the dance floor.

Dolly walked over to the table and sat back down. She thought about all the years she'd been in love with Jacob and all the times she regretted losing him. "I ain't gonna lose em again . . . ever," she said to herself as she sat gazing toward the door, waiting to see him walk through it again. She took off her felt hat and put it on the table then smoothed her hair to make sure it was still up in place and waited.

Jacob returned to the table and sat back down. "How would you like to go upstairs and look around?"

Dolly's pale eyes grew round. "Look 'round at what?"

"You'll see." He stood up and pulled her chair out then grabbed her hat and said, "Just come with me, Dolly."

He led her up two flights of stairs and walked ahead of her, playfully pointing out the details in the décor along the long hallway. "And here is a genuine hand carved wooden door. You will note that the door has an imported crystal doorknob . . . and . . . Oh! Here is my favorite door, also with an imported crystal doorknob. Just look at this beautifully shaped keyhole." Then he bent over to examine it.

Dolly laughed, beginning to feel more sober. "Come on, Jacob . . . quit bein' so silly. Yer makin' too much noise. Are you drunk? Let's go back downstairs."

He turned around and held up a key then inserted it into the door and opened it. "Come on in, Dolly Crystal."

Before she could took a step he swept her up and carried her inside, kicking the door closed with his foot, and headed straight to the bed.

Dolly's hat fell to the floor as he tossed her onto the bed. She looked up at him and said, "We ain't even married yet!"

Jacob had to laugh. "Dolly, did you forget already that we've made love before?"

She looked at the bed and cringed. Her conscience was too filled with shame to want to make love with him. "Ya know, Jacob . . . I never been in a hotel room before in my life. We always stay in wagons an' boats an' boxcars."

"Well . . . I'll introduce you to a lot of things you never did in your life. I'll buy you your own hotel. I'll buy you a house bigger than the Astor's mansion down the block. You can have anything I have, Dolly." He looked down at the front of his pants and said, "But I hope you ask for something else first."

He flopped down beside her. "I can hardly believe I'm here with you again, Dolly. You have no idea how often I think about our last night we had together." He turned to face her and slowly moved his mouth closer until his lips met hers.

As they kissed, Dolly knew that the fire they had for each other was hotter than ever before. "Jacob . . . oh, Jacob . . . my darlin' Jacob. I loved ya fer so long. I never even thought of bein' with no other man." Dolly had to stop when she suddenly pictured Matt's angry eyes glaring hatefully at her just before running off into the woods two months earlier. It made her feel dirty. Hot tears began to work up toward her eyes. She sniffed the salty liquid to the back of her throat and swallowed hard.

"What's wrong with you, Dolly?" Jacob's eyes were filled with deep concern.

"Oh . . . I . . . I was jus' thinkin' how happy I am this very minute," her lie slipped out, "I jus' want fer ya to hold me fer a while. Kin ya do that jus' fer a bit . . . till I git used to bein'with ya again?"

Jacob saw that she was trembling and pulled her tightly into his arms. "Oh, Dolly . . . I'm trembling inside too." He stroked her soft cheek with his lips.

Paralyzed with shame, Dolly was afraid to move or say anything. "Oh, how could I tell em? He would hate me an' I couldn't bear to lose em again," she thought.

Jacob held her for a long time, smoothing back her long hair and kissing her nose gently. "I remember the first time I met you."

"Yeah . . . in front of the church when we was twelve."

"And you were trying to get me to say something to you . . . but I was scared of girls back then."

"Ya didn't even have the courage to look at me back then," she faked a laugh but felt like crying.

"You know, Dolly? We've been alone in this room for almost an hour and we haven't made love. Are you going to tell me what's bothering you?"

Consumed with guilt, Dolly could no longer stand it. She had to escape. "Kin we jus' go out fer a while, Jacob?" she asked in a quivering voice, trying hard to hide the deep secret that tormented her.

"If you'd like . . . . but tell me what's troubling you!" Jacob was beginning to show concern. This wasn't like the Dolly Wafford he knew.

"Nothin' Jacob. I jus' don't feel real good . . . that's all." Dolly got up and smoothed her hair then picked her brown felt hat up off the floor and put it back on.

Jacob wanted desperately to make love to her but had no idea what was going through her mind. "Dolly," Jacob gulped, "It's just that . . . . It's . . ." He stopped.

"It's jus' what, Jacob?"

"It's just that I thought you wanted to make love with me. I'd never ask you to do anything you didn't want to but if you would just . . .," he paused, "Could we stay a while longer?"

Dolly didn't want sex. She wanted nothing to do with it. She couldn't. Not after what she had been through. Suddenly she was overwhelmed with anger. Matt and Ernest both had used her for sex. She would not be used again.

"I . . . I'm so sorry Jacob!" She burst into tears and ran out the door, down the stairs and out to the street.

Jacob slipped into his shoes and ran after her. "Dolly! Dolly! Wait up!"

He spotted her turning the corner and picked up speed, almost knocking a woman over on the way.

When he caught up with her, he reached out and grabbed her by the shoulders. "Tell me! Tell me now! What's the matter?"

She let her guard down and began to sob, "Oh, Jacob . . . . ya won't want me when I tell ya what happened."

"I'll always want you! Now tell me . . . what happened!" Jacob began to feel scared. "Let's go sit down and talk."

They walked over to the park and sat on a bench in the dark.

"I don't know where to start." She slid her feet back and forth on the grass as if she were getting ready to spring up and run.

Jacob could feel that she was shaking all over and put his arm aound her shoulders. "Tell me, Dolly."

"Well, remember how Matt Kilgore hurt me so bad? All these years I hated him but I jus' had to try to get him back fer what he did to me. I went to see him a while back but all I intended to do was tease em an' cause em to feel the wantin' . . . then leave em like he did me. I never meant fer it to git so bad," She confessed.

"What did you do, Dolly?"

"It ain't what I did . . . it's what he did to me!" She sobbed harder.

"Damn it Dolly, just get it out!" He said sharply as he felt the old jealousy striking back like a bolt of lightning.

"I can't tell ya!" She stood up and started to run.

Jacob ran after her again. He tackled her down onto the grass and held her down tight. "Shhh! It's all right! It's all going to be all right!"

"He raped me, Jacob!" she exploded, " . . . Jus' like Uncle Ernest did! Oh, dear God, it hurts so bad inside . . . I'm so ashamed!" Dolly buried her face in the wet grass and cried loud and hard as Jacob continued to hold on to her.

"I'll kill that no-good-son-of-a-bitch!"

"Oh please! Oh please don't go talkin' like that!" she sobbed.

Jacob realized that she had already been through enough. He offered a comforting smile and said gently, "Dolly, I love you . . . I still want you for wife." He held her close, stroking her hair, then rolled her over and kissed each eye, saying, "My poor Dolly . . . My poor precious Dolly."

At that moment a policeman, who had heard the voice of a woman crying, came running over to them, blowing his whistle and shouting, "Police! Police!" Jacob was still lying on top of Dolly on the dark ground. "Get away from that girl! Get off her! Now, I said!" He held up a pistol and shot it into the air.

Jacob jumped up, pulling Dolly up to her feet with him. "We weren't doing anything, Sir!" he exclaimed. "It's just that she's upset . . . I . . . I was trying to help her.

"Sounded to me like she was being attacked!" The policeman said as he held his lantern up to Dolly's face. Dolly stiffened up and wiped her face with both hands then held her chin up and stared back into the light of the lantern. "Are you all right young lady? Hey! I've seen you before. Oh, I know who ya are! Ain't you that circus queen, Dolly Crystal?"

"Yeah, that's me." Dolly answered solemnly as she stood up straight and adjusted her hat.

"I almost didn't recognize ya in that dress cause usually you wear real fancy stuff . . . don't ya? Uh . . . do ya mind autographing somethin' for me?" he asked excitedly then motioned for Dolly to step into the light of the street lamp and reached into his pocket.

"Here . . . hold this for a minute." Barrel first, he handed his pistol to Dolly, without thinking. He fumbled to pull a piece of paper from his coat pocket and held it under her nose. It was a picture of Dolly standing on top of Star's back that looked like a page from a magazine. He handed it to her along with an ink pen and quickly retrieved his pistol from her hand with an embarrassing grin. "Ya know . . . I've taken my wife an' kids to see ya three times so far," he chattered on while Dolly signed her name. "I think that death-flip through the ring of fire ya do is really amazin'. An' watchin' you in that cage with all those lions . . . doing all those incredible tricks . . . why, I think you're really something, Dolly."

She hurriedly signed the magazine page and held it out with the ink pen. "Thank you."

"Oh, thanks for the autograph. Wait till the kids see this!" He tipped his hat.

"It's my pleasure." Dolly felt numb.

Jacob and Dolly walked back to the hotel and fell back onto the bed, both exhausted.

"Can you believe what that officer did? What a stupid ass he was . . . handing his pistol to you like that. It makes you wonder how safe we are with a police department full of guys like him. My Lord . . . what a night!" Jacob yawned, "Let's just get some sleep, Dolly." Still fully dressed, he rolled over and pulled her close to him and closed his eyes.

Dolly watched his sleeping face just like she once did years before. She loved him now even more. So much more that she ached inside. She adored him even more for being so understanding and forgiving her so easily without question. His anger was toward Matt, not her. She pulled the covers up around his neck, rested her head on his pillow and drifted off to sleep.

They awoke to the sound of horses clattering feet, carriage wheels squeaking and people chattering on the city streets below. Dolly turned her face up toward Jacob's inviting a passionate kiss before making love.

"That was just as good, if not better, than the first time," Jacob said as they finished their third round of lovemaking. "We're getting married and that's that!"

"Yeah, I'm ready to give it all up fer ya now. I jus' promised Mr. Barnum that I'd finish out the next two cities. How does June the twelfth sound to ya? I had that date picked out when I first got yer letter."

During their two weeks together in New York, Jacob came to watch Dolly perform every night and every night Dolly could hardly wait to see him after the show. During her act she knew that Jacob's eyes were following her every move and tingled from the excitement of knowing how hungry he was to get her alone again. He inspired her to perform like never before.

"Alright, Star . . . slow . . . slow . . .," she softly spoke into the horses ear before swinging her feet up to his back. "We gotta be perfect fer Jacob. Now Boy, I want ya to keep this pace." She stood on his back and rode around the arena twice before the flaming hoop was placed in her path. Just before she reached the flames she leaped high into the air and did a triple somersault through the ring of fire, landing back onto her feet with ease. "Good Boy!" she said as the crowd cheered and whistled. She caught a glimpse of Jacob standing and cheering along with everyone else. She was happier than she'd ever been in her life, she thought as she caught his eyes watching her with adoration.

After Dolly finished her act she rode to the back of the tent where she slid down from her horse. She motioned for Grant to give her a hand with Star. "Do ya mind puttin' Star up fer me? I'm kinda in a hurry to git outta here," she said, looking down at the tiny man.

"Don't mind at all. I'd do anything for you, Your Majesty," he teased as he bowed down to her.

"Grant, yer so full of shit!" Dolly said as she jokingly thumped the top of his head with her small fist.

"Aren't ya gonna do your lion act tonight, Dolly?" Grant asked.

"I'm skippin' it. Tell Mr. Bailey to fill in with another act fer me. I gotta run!" Dolly darted away.

She ran to her dressing room and tore off her short pink costume and slid into a silk robe. Still out of breath and sitting at her dressing mirror, she caught Jacob's reflection as he stepped through the doorway. Without turning around she said, "What took ya so long?"

Jacob walked up behind her, still looking at her face in the mirror, and put his hands on her shoulders. "I'm glad you didn't go into that cage tonight. It scares me to see you in there with all those vicious animals."

"Oh, they ain't vicious. Ol' Big Jack is gentle as a lamb, now that I straightened his ass out fer bitin' me once."

Did I ever tell you how beautiful you are, Dolly? And did I ever tell you how deeply I'm in love with you?"

"No, Jacob. Tell me." Dolly dotted perfume behind her ears and rearranged the curls on her forehead.

He yanked her to her feet and kissed her long and hard. Dolly felt his hands move from her tiny waist down to her buttocks. "Oh, Dolly . . . If we continue like this I'll be worn out old man by the time I'm thirty . . . then you'll have to do all the work." He picked her up into his arms and carried her over to the bed.

"I can't wait to be Mrs. Jacob Harvey Turner," Dolly smiled, "Even if I do end up killin' ya from too much love makin' . . . at least I'll have good memories."

Jacob quickly peeled off all of his clothes while Dolly slipped out of her robe then struggled with her corset in a lying position.

As she pulled off her bloomers and laid back she whispered, "Come on Jacob . . . do it to me . . . now," she begged.

He stood naked for a moment looking down at her. She reached up and took his hand and pulled him down on top of her.

He slid himself into her soft wetness and his mouth pressed against hers. He gyrated and wriggled deeper and deeper until he could go no further. He paused and took a deep breath. "Oh Dolly, you feel so good. I don't want this to end."

Dolly was so aroused she moved her hips in a circular motion, wanting more and craving the violent thrusts he was about to deliver.

Jacob could hold back no longer. He began to pump and move with her. As his mouth moved down to her breast she jerked convulsively and groaned out loud. Jacob became so excited by her release that he stiffened and shuddered with her.

A warm relaxing glow filled their sweating bodies as they lay there in each other's arms.

"Dolly . . . I never dreamed of being this gloriously happy. I've loved you all my life, I love you now and I'll love you always. You belong to me from now on."

"We're invited to a party, Dolly." Jacob told her the next evening after the show.

"Who's party an' when?"

"I told some of my colleagues about you and they all want to meet you so they are having a party in your honor tomorrow night."

"In my honor?"

"Yes, in your honor. They all want to meet the queen."

"Well now ya got me all in a whirl. What dress am I gonna wear!"

The following evening Jacob came into Dolly's dressing room and caught her going through her wardrobe. "You have plenty of time to get dressed." He took her by the arm and led her toward the bed.

She yanked her arm away and said, "I wanna start gettin' dressed now, Jacob!"

"We'll get ready after we make love." He pulled her back onto the bed.

When the lovemaking ended, Dolly asked, "Do ya mind goin' back to yer hotel now? I need some time to work on myself . . . in privacy! I wanna look my best so you kin be proud of me."

"I'd be proud of you if you wore a nightshirt," he said as he kissed her goodbye.

Dolly put on her burgundy satin gown and pulled her gold locket out over the lace that hugged her neck. She fussed with her hair and managed to pin it up, leaving loose tendrils of curls on the sides. She applied her lip color and doused perfume on her neck and wrists then glanced at her reflection and said, "Ya look purdy as a picture, Dolly Crystal."

Jacob pounded on the door. "Are you ready, Darling?"

"Jus' a minute!" she grabbed her black beaded purse just as Jacob was opening the door.

He gasped when he walked in and saw her. "I'll have to keep my eye on you tonight or Dr. Schweigart will want to steal you away from me."

Jacob and Dolly walked up the sixteen steps leading to the front entrance of the large brick house. The butler, with a stone-like expression, opened the door and said, "Please come in," as he made an inviting motion with his hand.

The entry hall was brightly lit by a huge crystal chandelier and there was a wide staircase leading down to the main room. Arm and arm, as they began their decent, the butler announced, "Presenting Doctor Jacob Turner and Miss Dolly Crystal."

The music stopped and everyone in the room looked up. It made Dolly feel almost like she was in the arena again. She took another step then tripped over her long dress. She started to fall but Jacob quickly grabbed her and steadied her back to her feet. Dolly felt her face turn hot as everyone in the room applauded her.

Her embarrassment vanished by the time they reached the bottom step.

"I never been in such a big house before in my life. Oh ain't this place jus' somethin', Jacob?"

"Welcome, Jacob," said an older man as he approached them. "Please introduce us." He glanced over at Dolly and raised his brows in an evil arch.

The music began as Jacob said, "Dolly, I'd like to introduce Doctor Schweigart, the director of the hospital." He turned to Doctor Schweigart and said, "My fiancée, Miss Dolly Crystal."

"Mighty nice to meet ya," said Dolly as the doctor kissed her hand. She felt a sudden thirst for alcohol. "What do ya have to drink?"

"I'll get you a drink, Dolly," said Jacob as he squeezed her hand. "I'll be right back."

"So you're the famous queen of the circus. Or I should say, the famous Dolly Wafford that Jacob has been rambling on so much about over the years. I've seen your pictures in all the papers. How does it feel to have the whole world adoring you?"

"It's really been grand, Doc, but I'm more excited 'bout bein' Mrs. Jacob H. Turner then anythin'."

Doctor Schweigart placed his hand on hers and said, "Would you care to dance, Dolly?"

"Oh . . . I'd be delighted, Doc."

Dolly's eyes searched the room for Jacob as she followed the Dr. Schweigart out into the middle of the ballroom for a waltz.

As he twirled her around to the music, he said, "There have been many young women just dying for Jacob's attention but he never seemed interested. I thought it was because he was so devoted to his work but now I see why he never gave the other young girls a second thought. You're every bit as beautiful as he said you were."

"Ya mean in all the years ya knew em he only talked 'bout me an' no other girls?"

"No other girls . . . only you. He's a very ambitious young man. He seems to get what he goes after."

"Oh yeah Doc, he is cause he finally got me."

"Yes, and you got him. Did you know that Jacob is the best surgeon in his field? He's well respected and tremendously admired by his colleagues. Dolly, I suppose you know that you're about to marry a great man, don't you?"

"May I cut it?" Dolly heard from behind, after dancing for less than a minute. There stood Jacob with a glass in his hand. He held it to her lips as she took a sip then set it on a side table. Jacob held her small waist and led her to the middle of the floor.

Dolly soon noticed that not many others were dancing but instead standing around, watching them.

"Everbody's lookin' at us, Jacob."

"That's because you're the most beautiful thing in this room. I can't even keep my eyes off you."

When the short waltz was over every man in the room swarmed around Dolly until she lost sight of Jacob.

"May I get you another?" a tall handsome man said as he took the empty glass from Dolly's hand.

Dolly was impressed with the ambassadors from all over the world, famous scientists and prominate political figures who knew Jacob but it hadn't dawned on her that they also knew Dolly Crystal, Queen of the Circus as well.

She spotted a familiar woman sitting in a chair by the staircase. She stared at her for a moment until the woman looked at Dolly. She quickly excused herself and excitedly headed toward her. "Abby? Abby!" she squealed, "Is that you?"

"Dolly! Oh Dolly, how wonderful to see you!" Abby stood up and ran over to hug Dolly around the neck. "It's been so long. Oh, let me look at you! I've missed you so!"

"Well look at you all fancied up in that red dress! An' Abby, ya even got on lip rouge! I never thought I'd ever see the day!"

Abby blushed. "Well, you always told me I dressed too plain so I thought I'd take your advice and liven myself up a bit." Abby took Dolly's hands and said, "I'm so happy for you and Jacob. He told me that you and he were getting married in June."

Dolly wondered why Jacob had not mentioned that Abby was in New York. "When did ya git here, Abby?"

"I live here, Dolly. In fact . . . not too far from Jacob."

Dolly felt the old twinge of jealousy hit her again. "Why, Jacob never told me."

"He wanted it to be a surprise."

"Well he's always full of surprises ain't he?

"Oh, and I'm so sorry to hear about your uncle. I know how much you loved him. I didn't come to the funeral because I didn't get word until too late. I hope you'll forgive me for not being there with you."

"That's fine, Abby. I know you was busy. And yeah, I did love em more then ya know an' life jus' ain't as good without em. But I still take care of Ella an' I send er money ever month."

"That's very generous of you, Dolly. I hear Ella is the best-dressed woman in Ridgetop now. But how can you afford it?"

"Oh, I make more money then I kin spend."

"Dolly . . . I'd like you to meet my husband, Larry," Abby said as a handsome young man approached them and took her by the arm.

"Oh my Lord! Abby, yer so full of surprises this evenin'! How do ya do, Larry."

"Larry, this is Dolly Wafford . . . I mean Crystal, my very closest friend I told you about," Abby said as she locked her arm around Dolly's.

Jacob appeared. "I see you found Abby. She looks wonderful doesn't she? Oh, and she's a doctor now too."

"Why Abby," Dolly said, "I'm so proud of ya. I don't know of too many lady doctors. Why in the world didn't ya tell me about . . ."

Abby interrupted, "Oh you always knew I'd be a doctor one day. Now tell me about you, Dolly."

"Well, there ain't much to tell really. I jus' joined the circus an' well, you remember. An' we been travelin' all over ever since."

Jacob said, "If you'll excuse me I have to go see Dr. Schweigart for a minute. Come with me, Larry. He wants to meet you."

Abby pulled Dolly back down to the chairs, "There's so much we need to talk about."

"Good Lord . . . it's good to see ya again, Abby. So yer Doctor Mitchell now. I thought 'bout ya. I know I never wrote but they keep me so busy."

"I know, Dolly . . . same here . . . . but I'm Doctor Solomon. Remember? I'm married."

"I'm so happy fer ya Abby . . . as long as he's good to ya."

"Oh, Larry is wonderful. I met him during my internship at the hospital. He's a surgeon like Jacob." Abby's eyes bounced back and forth, making sure no one was near and whispered, "Did you hear about Sarah's father?"

"Nope. What?"

"Well . . . her mother died two years ago and her father became too depressed to work. He sold his store to Matt's father for peanuts and he gave it to Matt. They took advantage of him and now the poor man has nothing. Sarah helps him out some but they say her marriage to Matt's not going to last. I wonder what she'll do. I couldn't imagine Sarah being poor. Could you?"

"Well, I would say that she's gettin' what she deserves. Why ain't the marriage workin' out? How do ya know?"

"Everybody knows. I went back home last month and everyone was talking about how Matt runs around with every girl in town. They even have a little girl. Isn't that sad?"

Dolly felt uncomfortable talking about Matt. "Abby . . . I gotta go find Jacob. I wanna dance. I'll talk to ya again later."

Dolly danced every dance and guzzled down six more drinks until she felt drunk. Jacob noticed that Dolly's laugh was too loud and she was slurring her words but he wanted her to have a good time so he didn't say anything. He watched her as she staggered over to see Abby again.

"This here's some party ain't it, Abby?"

"Yes, it is," said Abby as she guided Dolly back down to the chair, "But you have to be careful with your drinking. Why, I've seen you stumble twice and almost fall."

"Well, wouldn't that a hoot!" shouted Dolly, "The queen fallin' down again! Ha! Well, I been handlin'liquor purdy damn good fer a long time now an' I ain't fell down once!" She stood up and twirled around.

Abby thought Dolly was obnoxious but still loved her in spite of her drunkenness.

"Do you want to dance, Dolly? asked an older distinguished-looking man with gray hair.

"Oh, sure do!" She fell into his arms, barely able to stand.

Instead of leading her out to dance, the man put his hands on Dolly's waist and guided her over to Jacob. With a disgusted look on his face he said, "Dr. Turner, maybe you'd like to dance with your fiancé'. I don't believe she's quite up to dancing with me tonight."

"An' yer full of shit!" Dolly slurred, "I kin dance with whoever I want! An' if I say so myself, I'm purdy damn good!"

"I think it's time to go, Darling," said Jacob with an

embarrassing grin, "Come, Dolly, let's say goodnight to Abby and Larry and Dr. Schweigart."

During the ride back to the circus grounds Dolly felt so happy that she started to sing at the top of her lungs, "The sun's so hot I froze to death . . . Suzanna don't ya cry!"

Jacob thought she was cute. There was a childlike quality about her that he adored but he was worried about her uncontrollable drinking. The gray-haired man she had insulted that evening was the mayor of New York City. Jacob knew that she would have to stop drinking so much because it would affect his career.

The two weeks went by too fast for both of them. Jacob asked Dolly to cut down on the drinking and she agreed to to do it. They discussed wedding plans and their future together. Dolly knew that she would not change her mind this time. Their bond was stronger than ever before but all too soon it was time to say goodbye.

"I'll meet you in Ridgetop on June, the eleventh," said Jacob as he helped her onto the steps at the train.

"We can't see each other the day before our weddin', Jacob. What's wrong with you anyways!"

"Oh yeah . . . almost forgot. Well then, I'll see you when you come marching up that isle. Jacob kissed her goodbye and as she stepped into the train and said, "After our wedding we'll never have to say goodbye again."

As the circus train headed south, Mr. Barnum asked Dolly to join him for dinner in the dining car to discuss her leaving the circus.

"Ain't ya feelin' well, P.T.?" asked Dolly as she took a bite of of her fried catfish.

"Why do you ask, Dolly?"

"Ya don't look good to me. Ya look pale an' yer eyes er all glassy. Maybe ya been worryin' too much about this damn circus.

I think what ya need is some rest. When was the last time ya took off an' enjoyed yerself anyways?"

"Come to think of it, Dolly, maybe you're right. I'm going home in the morning for a while," said Mr. Barnum as he lifted his fork with a trembling hand.

Dolly was concerned about him. She had grown to love and admire the old man for all the kindness he had always shown her. "That'll be good. Then maybe when ya come back ya might feel like yerself again." She wiped her mouth with the back of her hand and glanced over at Ted's table where he was sipping on a glass of wine. She watched for a moment, salivating, as the wine meeting Ted's lips before she turned her head back to face Mr. Barnum.

"So what's this about you getting married and deserting us?"

"Oh, he's so wonderful, P.T.! I knew em all my life too. Did ya notice I ain't been drinkin' lately? I quit . . . fer Jacob. An' fer good too. Oh, I jus' know I'm doin' the right thin' by marryin' em." Dolly reached for Mr. Barnum's hand, "But it'll still be sad fer me to leave this circus. It's jus' 'bout all I ever knew. I'm gonna miss it . . . an' I'll miss you more then anythin'."

"We'll hate not having you here . . . you know that. Of course, because you're leaving, I plan to lose a little money but I only hope you're happy. Take my advice. Do everything and anything that makes you happy while you're still young enough cause when you get to be my age it's not so easy."

The following evening, after going to bed, Dolly dreamed that she was holding a bottle of scotch with no opening at the top. She bit into the glass but her front teeth broke off. She smashed the bottle against the edge of her dressing table but it would not break. When Jacob suddenly entered the room and caught her she was wearing her wedding gown but it was black. She gave Jacob a toothless smile as she hid the bottle behind her back but he only glared back at her. His glare turned into a blank stare and when she touched him he fell straight back onto the floor like he was made of wood. She leaned over to help him up but he was cold and stiff. She kissed his lips but he did not kiss her back. When she pulled away, his face suddenly became Ernest's face. It startled her and she awoke in a cold sweat.

"Damn, I need a drink right now," she muttered. The early morning sun barely cast enough light to see around her dressing room. She gazed up and spotted a small spider crawling across the ceiling of her boxcar. It's shadow made it appear larger than it was. "This is gonna be much harder then I thought it was. Hell, I might as well jus' git up an' git dressed.

She heard a commotion going on in the dining car next door. She got up, threw on her satin robe and hurried over where breakfast was being served. Everyone was there and they were talking about Mr. Barnum. She listened closely.

"Yeah, he died right in his bed alright. I haven't heard what happened to him yet. Have you heard anything?" The voice belonged to Flo.

Dolly moved over to her. "Flo! What are you all talkin' 'bout?"

"Mr. Barnum. They found him in his bed this morning . . . dead!" she answered as she nervously smoothed her beard down with both hands. "Nobody knows why he died just yet."

Dolly walked back to her boxcar without saying a word. She couldn't believe it. She'd just had dinner with him. How would the circus survive without him? "At least he went home to die an' that was a good thin'," she thought. When reality finally sank in, Dolly cried for poor Mr. Barnum.

All the newspapers ran front-page stories about Mr. P. T. Barnum's death. Dolly read that he was world famous for having said, "There's a sucker born every minute" but she knew different. She knew that it was really Mr. Hannum who said it first. In fact Mr. Barnum thought it was very funny and joked about getting all the recognition for having created the well-known phrase. He knew that Mr. Hannum was outraged by it. There had been a lawsuit going on for years over which circus had the original Cardiff Giant, which was a big hoax anyway. Each accused the other of having a fake. It turned out that Mr.Barnum had the carved fake but Mr. Hannum, who thought he had the real McCoy, had a fake too.

Dolly knew that he was a shrewd businessman and maybe not always the most honest but he was certainly the smartest and the toughest of all. She knew the sweet, fatherly side of him that no others did. She knew that she would miss him terribly.

"How come you didn't go to the funeral, Dolly?" asked Sky.

"Cause I had to buy a weddin' gown. An' besides, I don't like seein' nobody dead. That's why."

"Thousands of people came to show their respects, including Mr. Hannum. I tell ya . . . he had some nerve showing up at P.T.'s funeral."

"Well, P.T.'s dead so it don't matter to him no more."

CHAPTER 19

St. Augustine, Florida was next and Dolly looked forward to seeing the St. Johns River where Uncle Thomas grew up. Mr. Barnum had always wanted to go there too.

Mr. Bailey was not quite as likeable as Mr. Barnum was but Dolly seemed to get along with him. He was now the new owner of the circus but she knew that he would not be as good as Mr. Barnum was.

On the way down to Florida Dolly wrote a letter to Jacob every day. She had to go to the circus mail office to pick up her mail but she would get clumps of it every week. She sorted it out and read only what she received from Jacob.

> "Dearest Dolly,
>
> I am truly sorry to hear about Mr. Barnum. I know you thought a great deal of him and will miss him very much.
>
> June twelfth seems so far away. I can't think of anything but you. Please be safe with those wild cats of yours. I don't want anything to happen to you. I worry. I'm sorry this letter is so short but I'm in a rush because they need me at the hospital. I'll be happy when you are safe in my arms again. I'm waiting.
>
> Love,
>
> Jacob."

Dolly woke up feeling tired after her Sunday night performance. It had been a long hard week and she needed some time alone so she decided to take a walk over to see the river.

She stood on the bank and gazed across the St. John's River to the other side where she used to live. "My Lord, that was a long time ago," she thought. The sun was high and it was hot. She slapped a mosquito on her arm and wiped the spot of blood away with her finger. Her memories of St. Augustine were not happy ones. Her thoughts drifted to Valdosta when she was abandoned and how hard it was to find food. She remembered picking blackberrys until her hands bled and sneaking in with the pigs to eat their slop. She thought about the day she went home and her mother was gone. Being so young at the time she never realized how abnormal it was for a mother not to feel love for her own daughter. She knew her father loved her but she never knew him. Uncle Thomas was the first person she could remember ever putting their arms around her.

Her thoughts shifted back to St. Augustine and she imagined seeing Uncle Thomas on the river in a fishing boat waving to her. She smiled, thinking about how he had always joked about his missing foot. If anyone else had lost their foot they wouldn't have laughed about it like he did. He was a happy man because he knew not to cry about things he could not change.

She squated down and swirled her arm in the water. A big frog jumped out onto the bank next to her and sat there looking at her. "Hello little fella. Did I scare ya?" She slowly reached over and stroked his head and he closed his eyes. "I'm leavin' now so you kin have her spot back if ya want." She stood up but he did not budge.

Dolly went back to her dressing room feeling very relaxed. She climbed into bed and slept the rest of the day, dreaming about Jacob.

Three days before the wedding Dolly packed her trunks with everything she owned and looked forward to leaving the next day. She'd miss the circus and all of her friends but being with Jacob was more important to her. She wanted to be Mrs. Jacob Turner more than anything.

That evening she was going to do her final performance. Dolly boasted to everyone that she was going to marry a successful doctor and have lots of babies. She knew that she'd made the right choice but it was hard to believe that she was really leaving the circus. She had planned to give her best performance ever before bidding farewell.

The next morning she opened her mail from Jacob. There was one letter from his mother but she wanted to read Jacob's first.

"My Darling Dolly,

It won't be long now and we will never have to be apart again. I miss you every minute of every day and can hardly concentrate on my work. I'm so in love with you, Dolly. I feel upside down inside and it's wonderful.

My mother has taken care of all the wedding arrangements, since you are so busy, and she is very excited. I hope you're excited too.

After we become Dr. and Mrs. Jacob Turner I plan to make you pregnant with my first son, Jacob Harvey Turner Junior. I hope you want as many children as I do.

We'll grow old together and have a big family and lots of grandchildren. I want at least six babies and twenty grandchildren. Can you handle that?

People will say, "There goes old Doc Turner with his lovely old wife, Mrs. Dolly Turner. They make such a nice old couple, don't they? And they still are very much in love after sixty-five years, which is not like old people at all.

Now that I have made you chuckle I can be more serious now. I dream of you at night and you're in my thoughts all day. I wish you could be here with me now. I need to make love to you again soon . . . and again after that . . . and again after that.

I can barely wait to see you at the altar in your wedding gown. I know you will be the most beautiful bride ever. Kiss your hand and brush it against your face for me. That's my kiss to you. I must end this letter here as I am needed at the hospital soon but I will mail this on the way.

This should be the last letter I'll write to you, since I will be seeing you directly after you receive it. I love you with all my heart. Please never stop loving me.

Anxiously waiting for you,

Jacob"

Once she read his letter at least twice she opened the envelope from Jacob's mother. She read it once. Then in disbelief, she read it again, feeling her head spin until she heard herself screaming, "Dear God! No!" Then she let out a shriek from the bottom of her lungs.

Sky heard her and ran over to her boxcar. He pounded on the door, yelling, "Dolly! Open up!"

She didn't answer and he knew something was terribly wrong so he pushed the door open and saw her sitting on the floor. He quickly stepped over and knelt beside her. She had a frozen expression on her face with the letter clutched in both hands pressed against her chest.

Sky took her by the shoulders and shook her hard. "Dolly! Dolly! Are you all right? Damn it! Tell me!"

She looked at Sky and started screaming. She threw her head against the floor and continued to scream uncontrollably, still clutching the letter.

Sky pried the letter from her hand and read it.

> "My Dearest Dolly,
>
> I'm so sorry to have to tell you this. You best be sitting down. It's difficult for me to even write this letter but I must tell you what happened to my son, since he was planning to marry you.
>
> Yesterday Jacob went to visit his friend, Matt Kilgore, at his house. He did not come back home. This morning they found both, Jacob and Matt, in the Kilgore's back yard, dead from gunshot wounds to the head.
>
> Sarah Kilgore told me today that she witnessed Jacob threatening to shoot Matt. She saw Matt shoot Jacob first then turned his gun to his own head.
>
> I don't understand why they were fighting and I guess we will never know.
>
> We are having funeral services on Friday, the tenth. I know you plan to be here on the eleventh. Abby plans to meet you at the station. I do hope this letter reaches you in time.

My Dear, once again I am sorry. I do hope you will be all right. Please come soon.

With Kindest Regards and Deep Sympathy,

Mrs. Elvira Turner"

Sky noted the dates. It was the day of the funeral. His heart went out for Dolly as she wept in his arms.

Dolly dressed while still in a daze and caught the first train to Nashville that afternoon.

By the time she arrived Jacob's funeral was over but she wanted to visit the cemetery to see his grave.

Abby met her at the train station in her father's wagon. "I'll ride you over to the church where Jacob is buried if you want me to," said Abby.

"If ya don't mind . . . I'd rather go alone. Kin I use yer horse when we git to yer house?" Dolly wiped her nose with the back of her hand.

Abby handed her the reins and jumped off the wagon when they reached her house. Dolly got out and unhitched the horse then mounted his bare back, wearing a black dress and veil, and rode off to the church cemetery alone.

She approached Jacob's grave slowly and looked down at the freshly overturned earth.

"Oh . . . Jacob!" she sobbed. "Ya can't die yet! What about our weddin'!" Dolly dropped to her knees and began to claw into the loose soil with her bare hands trying to get to him. "Why did ya go an' do a thing like that, Jacob? Yer a damn idiot fer lettin' Matt shoot ya first! What am I gonna do now? Oh Please, please, Jacob. Come back . . . I need ya!" she continued to scream at him as she dug.

The sun was beginning to disappear behind the mountains and Dolly had wept until she was drained of all her tears. She sat on Jacob's grave staring blankly at the sky.

"Dolly?" Mrs. Turner placed her hand on her shoulder and

calmly said, ""Dolly, you can't stay out here all night. You better come home with me now."

Dolly looked up with her tear-streaked face and cried, "Oh Mrs. Turner, I love em so much. I can't jus' leave em here alone."

Jacob's mother took Dolly's arm to help her up and noticed the black dirt under her fingernails and her arms covered with dirt up to her elbows. She looked at Jacob's grave and saw the hole that was three feet deep. "Let's go now Dolly."

Dolly rode home with her with Abby's horse following on a lead.

When she stepped through the door she felt everything begin to spin and fainted in the entrance hall.

When she woke up she realized that she was in Jacob's bed. Overwhelmed with grief she wailed, "Where are ya, Jacob? Come back to me." She could smell his sweet odor as she buried her face into the pillow.

Mrs. Turner was standing beside the bed with Abby. Dolly looked up and saw that their eyes were filled with tears too. They sat on the bed with Dolly and wept with her.

"Jacob wanted you to have this." Mrs. Turner handed her a small box as she wiped her eyes. "We'll leave you alone and let you open it."

After Mrs. Turner and Abby left the room Dolly slowly opened the small box. It was her diamond engagement ring. She sobbed hard as she slipped it onto her finger. "Thank you, Jacob . . . ."

She lifted her face to the ceiling and prayed out loud, "Dear God, please take good care of em fer me." She reached into her bag and pulled out a bottle of scotch. As she brought the bottle to her lips she said, "Here's to ya Jacob!" Then took several big gulps.

The following morning Dolly dressed and started downstairs. The smell of bacon frying filled the whole downstairs as she made her way to the kitchen. The cook was scurrying around while Jacob's mother was sitting alone at the table nursing a cup of tea.

"Kin I join ya?" Dolly asked.

"Of course, Dear. Please . . . sit down."

Dolly could see that Mrs. Turner had been crying and felt sorry for her. "Mrs. Turner . . . I know how bad ya miss Jacob . . . I miss him too. I can't believe this is really happenin', kin you?" Dolly sat down and picked up her napkin.

"I can't believe it either," said Jacob's mother as she wiped a tear away. "Dolly . . . Dear . . . I want you to stay here and live with me."

"Oh, no . . . I couldn't . . . . I gotta go back to work fer Mr. Bailey. He can't hardly git along without me . . . an' besides . . . I love the circus . . . only second to Jacob of course."

Dolly turned the engagement ring around and around on her left finger as she tried to picture him at the jewelry counter picking it out. Mrs. Turner's eyes met hers and the sting of tears touched them both at once. Dolly began to feel light-headed again.

Just then the back door flew open. "Dolly? Mrs. Turner? Is it all right if I come in? I stopped by to say goodbye." Abby stood in the doorway wearing one of her usual dull gray dresses that finally seemed to fit the occasion.

Dolly stood up to hug her but then felt her legs give out beneath her as the room began to dim. She sank to the floor at Abby's feet.

"Dolly!" cried Jacob's mother, "Are you all right, Dear? She threw herself onto the floor and knelt down beside her.

"She just fainted. She'll be fine," said Abby, as she stooped and pulled Dolly's bottom lid down. "Looks like she may just be run down." Abby could smell the whiskey on her.

"The poor child. She's been through so much. I suggested that she stay here to live with me. I know Jacob would have liked that," said Mrs. Turner.

Dolly's eyes slowly opened. "What happened?"

"Oh, I just wanted to say goodbye and you passed out," said Abby. "When was the last time you actually ate food?"

"Don't remember . . . days ago I guess."

Abby and Mrs. Turner helped to pull Dolly back to her feet. "I'm gonna be jus' fine. Maybe I better eat this delicious breakfast Mrs. Turner's cook made fer me. Then I'll be jus' fine. Really."

"Well, Dolly, I've a train to catch so I must say goodbye. Where will you be?" Abby bent down to kiss her lightly on the cheek.

"Back at the circus . . . where I belong," answered Dolly, pushing her red ringlets back away from her face. "It's jus' the best thing I kin think of right now."

"Goodbye, my Dear," said Jacob's mother as she hugged Abby.

"I'll miss you both. I'll write." And Abby was gone.

That was the last time Dolly would ever see her good friend.

CHAPTER 20

Dolly rejoined the circus right away. Mr. Bailey was happy to have her back again but he was not aware of what he would soon have to deal with.

Dolly went right back to work but she was too stricken with grief to face her nights alone. She began drinking heavily more each night to escape the pain of her tragic loss. She would barely stay sober long enough to skillfully perform her act then return to her dressing room to pour a drink.

She began to feel sick to her stomach every morning. In the weeks that passed Dolly knew that she was pregnant. She had gained weight and her breasts were swollen and tender. She suspected that it was Jacob's child but had to confirm it with a doctor, but one she'd never seen before.

She wasn't sure if she was happy or sad about it but she was, indeed, pregnant.

The doctor came back into the room and said, "Yes, Mrs. Turner, you are pregnant. You're about four months along now."

She thought for a moment then said, "Four months? Doc, could ya be mistaken? Maybe I'm only two months pregnant instead?"

"No." He shook his head. "At least four months. I'm certain of it."

"This can't be!" Dolly ran out and down the street crying.

"Look! It's Dolly Crystal!" She heard a voice shout as she ran by. A man and a woman with several small children chased after her calling, "Dolly Crystal! Wait!"

Dolly dodged them and ran into the bookstore on the corner. She hid behind the shelves of books and slid to the floor sobbing.

She couldn't tell a soul that she was going to have Matt Kilgore's baby. She stayed locked in her dressing room for days. Alone and scared, the only relief she found was in a bottle of scotch.

"Well . . . I ain't gonna keep the little Kilgore bastard," she said to herself as she poured her fifth drink. "I hate ya fer bein' inside of me, ya little . . ." Then her anger turned into desperation. All of a sudden she felt helpless. "What am I gonna do now, Jacob?"

Dolly concentrated on her more dangerous stunts in hopes of losing the baby but nothing seemed to have an affect the strong life growing inside her. She tried to think of some way out. She barely wanted to live herself, let along bring another life into the world . . . especially one conceived out of hate and not love.

She tried to hide her middle, as it began to swell, by picking out the costumes that concealed it best. Not a soul would she tell . . . especially not Mr. Bailey.

She increased her drinking, in hopes that it might abort and continued to abuse her body in every way that she could imagine. She took unnecessary chances every time she spun in the air doing her famous somersaults just to see if she'd fall. Nothing seemed to work. She carelessly dared Big Jack to come at her again. She wanted him to tear the baby out of her.

"What are you trying to do, Dolly? Kill yourself?" asked Sky. "You nearly let that lion tear you to pieces out there tonight!"

"So what if he did. Who would care?" she said as she sat on the edge of her bed twirling her handerchief around her fingers.

"I would . . . that's who."

"Well, Sky, ya jus' don't know what I'm feelin'. Maybe I don't wanna live no more! What do ya think about that!"

Sky put his arms around her and said, "If anything happened to you I don't know what I'd do. I love ya like you were my own flesh and blood sister. Don't ya know that? I want you to try. Try to get over Jacob's death. I know how much you loved him but you're still young. You have a whole wonderful world out there to explore before you go thinking about killing yourself."

Dolly wanted to tell him everything but she couldn't. She couldn't say a word to anyone about this baby. At least not yet. "I appreciate yer concern, Sky, but how do ya git over somebody ya loved so hard fer so long so fast? I kin hardly think er eat er sleep. I miss Jacob so much it feels like my heart was jus' tore right outta me."

"Just take it easy from now on. Promise? I have enough worries of my own to have to worry about you killing yourself. No . . . I take that back. It didn't come out sounding right. What I meant was that I'm just scared for you, Dolly. Listen, if you need help just come get me. We'll talk. I'll help you and you'll get through this in time, you'll see." He hugged her and left.

Dolly loved Sky too but it didn't help much. She still didn't care whether she lived or died anymore.

She became worse over the following weeks. The depression and the alcohol caused Dolly to become hateful toward everyone she worked with, including Sky. She began having temper tantrums when things were not going her way. The unborn child clung to its' life regardless of what Dolly tried to do. She became more miserable and more determined to get rid of it. Even her largest costumes started to get too tight. Dolly didn't know how to stop the baby from coming. This was going to ruin her career.

One evening she examined her thickening middle in the mirror. It was so obvious. Her navel was protruding and her breasts were swollen. Oh, how she hated Matt Kilgore. She hated this thing growing inside of her. She hated the world she lived in and everyone in it. Oh, how she desperately needed Jacob to be with her. Why did he have to leave her.

There was a knock at Dolly's door. She opened it and Mr. Bailey stepped inside.

"What do ya need Billy Boy, a drink? I got one fer ya if ya want it." She staggered over and sat on the edge of her bed.

"No, a drink is not want I came for, Dolly. I came to talk to you."

"Well, spit it out Billy Boy," she slurred.

"You've been acting awfully funny. I know you lost Jacob but it's something else. Are you gonna tell me what's troubling you?"

"Ya wanna know what's troublin' me? I'll tell ya what's troublin' me. Jacob's dead and I'm gonna have a baby only the baby ain't his. It belongs to someone who I detested with all my heart. That's what troublin' me!" she blurted out without thinking about whom she was telling. "I can't stop it. What am I gonna do? I'm pregnant! I'm so damn pregnant!" She threw herself onto the bed and burst into tears.

Mr. Bailey said, "I know it, Dolly. Everybody knows it. Why your belly's as big as a watermelon. What in the hell are we gonna do now? Everybody knows you're not married. How are we going to keep it out of the newspapers and how in the hell could parents bring their children to see you."

Dolly got up and poured a glass of whiskey then fell back onto the bed, facing the ceiling. "I guess it's over fer me . . . huh?" Her eyeliner was smudged, accentuating the dark circles under her eyes. She was pale and drawn and her fingernails were chewed to the point that there was dried black blood under the stubs that were left.

Mr. Bailey, disgusted with the way she looked and tired of her being drunk all the time said to her, "Girl . . . I don't know what else to say. I'm a business man. You understand."

"So yer lettin' me go. Is that it?"

"I have to, Dolly. I have to think about what's best for my circus."

"It's Mr. Barnum's circus . . . not yers! An' he'd never let me go!"

"It's my circus now. P.T. is dead . . . I'm sorry." Mr. Bailey tried to sound compassionate to compensate for his harshness.

"But where am I supposed to go? I aint got no money saved. An' how kin I feed this baby?" She screamed out loud, "Oh Lord! How could ya do this to me!"

Mr. Bailey didn't answer. He gave her a digusted look and left.

Dolly lay there, not knowing what her next step would be.

After a few mintues Mr. Bailey appeared back at the doorway. "Damn it! You're too valuable to lose. There's nobody that can do what you can do, Dolly. I want you to go . . . but I need you. I'll see if I can figure out a way to help."

Two days later Dolly was packed. Mr. Bailey was sending her to a private home in Boston where they would take care of her until the baby was born then help to find a home for it. She would then return to the circus saying that she had been very ill. It would work. Dolly knew it would.

"But Boston of all places!" she thought. That was where Jacob went to College, where he lived . . . and where he thought about her. She would see Jacob wherever she looked but she decided to do her best to get through the months of waiting just so she could get rid of the baby.

Sky took her to the train. "It'll all work out. You'll be back soon and everything will be back to normal."

"It'll never be normal fer me again. Not without Jacob in my life. But yer sweet fer tryin' to make me feel good."

She kissed Sky goodby and got on the train.

She sat next to a fat lady dressed in a nurse's uniform. Dolly pulled out a flask of whiskey and took a generous slug.

"Excuse me, Miss," said the nurse, "It's not good to drink alcohol when you are expecting. It might harm the baby. When are you having it?"

"Oh I ain't expectin'. I jus' look like I am."

"Honey, you can't fool a nurse. I see it. Why are you hiding it?"

"I don't believe it's none of yer concern, Miss. An' I ain't havin' no baby so jus' forgit talkin' about it." She took another big swig from her flask.

Insulted, the nurse turned her head toward the window and did not say another word to Dolly during the train ride to Boston.

When Dolly arrived at the home the housemother took her directly to her room. She was served chicken soup and milk on a tray but she was too tired to eat and fell asleep.

The morning light filtered through the sheer curtains in her room. Her room was much nicer than she'd expected it to be. There was a wingback chair facing the window with a small table and lantern next to it and the walls were papered in a soft foral pattern that matched her quilt. There was a brass bell on the table by her bed along with a pen and paper.

There was a light knock at the door and a fat nurse stepped in. "How are we feeling this morning?"

Dolly suddenly sat up and said, "Why yer the same nurse I met on the train!"

"Well I'll be! It's the rude young lady with the flask!" She shook her head. "I guess we're gonna have to learn to get along now aren't we, Miss Crystal, since I'm the only midwife in this home."

"I guess ya know now I was lyin' about bein' pregnant," Dolly smiled. "What's yer name nurse?"

"Nurse Rosemary Stringretter . . . but I'm called Rosie." She couldn't help but to laugh. "If this isn't a coincidence. I came from the Boston Hospital and this is my first day here."

"If ya came from Boston what was ya doin' on the train to Boston?"

"A friend of mine from NewYork met me in Jacksonville for my father's funeral."

"I'm real sorry yer father died . . . an' I'm glad yer my nurse, Rosie.

In the beginning Rosie liked Dolly. She thought she was funny and charming but over the following weeks she observed Dolly's hateful side. Dolly told her how she had become pregnant, how she hated the baby and tried to kill it. Rosie cared for Dolly in a very professional manner but had no respect for her.

After the baby was born Dolly did not want to look at him.

"Don't you even want to see what he looks like?" asked Rosie.

"No. Jus' git it outta here!" She was afraid that she would see Matt in his face. She felt nothing but relief from having the small mass of life that she hated for nine months removed from her body.

Rosie said, "There's a couple right her in Boston who want him. Are you sure you won't change your mind?"

"Hell no!" Dolly cupped her face in her hands and cried, "Oh Rosie, I jus' don't want em cause of who his father is. I know it ain't the baby's fault. Can't ya understand? I can't have no baby cause then my career would be over. Besides, he'll be better off with somebody else."

Rosie had to agree.

CHAPTER 21

Dolly selfishly moved back into the full swing of the circus without giving her baby son a second thought. Hating the world, she began to drink more than ever. If she couldn't have Jacob and Uncle Thomas, she thought ruthlessly, at least she'd have her reign as the Queen.

Her pictures appeared in magazines and newspapers all over the world and she was soon on top again, becoming more famous than ever.

She continued sending most of her money to Ella and keeping just enough to buy liquor.

Salt Lake City was the next stop.

Sky seemed to be the only person left in the circus to still care about Dolly but often when he went to see her she'd slam the door in his face. He realized that her that actions were only because of her heavy drinking. He'd seen all the suffering she'd been through and understood why she was the way she was. He knew that she was still giving all her money to her step-aunt and admired her for it. Sky would not give up on Dolly and even after being abused by her he stuck by her side.

He came to see Dolly with a letter in his hand. "I thought I'd pick this up for you since you never check your mail anymore."

"So what!" She snatched the letter from his hand and tore it opened right away. All of a sudden her face changed. "Oh, it's from Abby. Sky, I got a letter from my best friend, Abby." She began to read out loud.

> "Dearest Dolly,
>
> I miss you dreadfully but I'm afraid that I'll miss you even more because my husband, Larry, and I are moving

to Europe. I will not be able to see you before we leave, so I must say goodbye in this letter. I do not know when, or even if, we are ever coming back.

I will be working at the hospital for the orphans in England. I may never gain wealth there but this is what I have always dreamed of. I'll write when I can. Maybe when you come to England I'll see you.

I would have written sooner but I had to attend a funeral in Florida and have been busy ever since trying to catch up on work.

And Dolly, I want you to know that I do not believe all the stories I read about you in the newspapers. I know you better than anyone does. You will always be my most treasured friend.

Abby"

Sky wrapped his arms around Dolly when he saw the tears.

"She's movin' so far away, Sky. I'll probably never see er again." Then, like night turning into day, her voice changed and she bellowed, "I need a Goddamn drink!"

Sky truly loved Dolly and his heart went out to her every time she would shed a tear. He couldn't bear to see her in so much pain. "Come on now, Dolly. There are still some good folks around here who love you." He smiled and pulled her chin up with his finger. "Now don't go saying there's nobody left. What about Ella? And what about me! What am I . . . a damn tent pole? And don't worry. You'll see Abby when we go to England again."

"Jus' hand me that bottle of scotch over there."

Sky reached over for the bottle and handed it to her. "Drink all you want but it's not going to bring back Abby . . . or Jacob.

That following evening in Salt Lake City, Dolly thought she recognized Jacob's face in the crowd during her performance. But when she looked at him for the second time he smiled back and then she knew it wasn't him.

Her mind began playing tricks on her the more she drank.

She felt that the alcohol was the only thing left to give her peace of mind. Being drunk all the time also took her away from reality. Maybe Sky was wrong. Maybe the drinking would bring Jacob back again.

Slipping into her own private world, trying to bring Jacob back, she re-read his letters over and over again until she could feel his presence in the room.

Her days were spent behind dark red curtains that blocked the sunlight from her life. She no longer had a desire to see the brightness of the morning sunrise that she had always loved so much. She resented other people when she'd hear them chattering and laughing outside her window. She resented seeing other people happy because it reminded her of how happy she and Jacob were.

At times she was afraid that she would forget what his face looked like. The alcohol helped her see his face more clearly. The drunker she got the closer he moved in.

"Oh Jacob . . . where are ya? I need ya with me. Dear God, please let this all be a dream."

Jacob's letters became so wrinkled and torn that she could barely make out the handwriting but she knew them all by heart.

One afternoon Dolly slipped over to the mail office. She hadn't checked her mail in months and was hoping for another letter from Abby but she found a letter from Ella instead and tore it open.

> "Dear Dolly,
>
> So many years gone by and I miss ya awfully. I read about Jacob in the newspaper and I am so sorry. I felt purdy awful myself when yer Uncle Thomas died. I miss him real bad still.
>
> I guess I shoulda told ya sooner but I jus' sold the house an' moved up to live with my sister, Margaret an' er husband, George. I got plenty of money so ya don't have to keep on supportin' me now.

There's a little boy I met named Daniel. He lives out in the country on a farm. His father is my sister's brother-in-law. Anyways, the little boy only has one leg. He was born that way. I gave yer Uncle's horse, Pete, to em. Daniel loves Pete as much as you did.

Margaret ain't been feelin' well lately. She's gettin' so thin I worry 'bout er. Her husband, George, treats er mean an' sometimes I think I wanna kill em.

Now I have some good news fer ya. The Good Lord knows ya need some good news so here it is.

Yer Uncle Ernest finally did it. He killed hisself jus' 'bout three weeks ago. He ended up doin' it with a gun. They said it was very bloody an' he suffered fer days before he died. He was really depressed since ya stabbed em an' he was in that wheelchair fer so long an' he was bound to do it sooner er later. They said first he shot hisself in the head but the bullet jus' went in an' out again without killin' em. Then he shot his chest but it went through em too without doin' nothin'. Somebody heard the shots an' came jus' in time to see him shoot again but he missed. They said he was spittin' up blood an' in real bad pain fer days before he finally died. I thought you'd enjoy hearin' that.

Please write when ya can.
As Always, Ella"

Ella was the only person left in her life who loved her unconditionally and wondered if she'd ever see her again. Dolly clung to the thin thread of reality for a moment. What would she do with all that money now that Ella didn't need it? Dolly had no use for money other than to buy liquor so she decided to continue giving it all to Ella. She thought about Ernest again and felt a perverted comfort in hearing about the way he died. "He musta been in real agony," she smiled.

CHAPTER 22

After drinking all day she was still able to perform in the arena as well as ever but she could no longer feel the excitement or hear the cheers from the crowd. Her passion for the circus faded as she routinely did her triple death-flips without feeling. Each day she moved, like a vampire, from her dark dressing room to the arena after the sunlight was gone then back to her room again.

Sky picked up Dolly's fan mail and brought it to her every evening. She only searched through it for a letter from Jacob but never opened her mail.

The private euphoric world that she'd created became more real to her each day. It was only a matter of time before he would be back from the grave and she knew she was getting closer to the place where she and Jacob could be together again.

One evening while having dinner in her room she poured two glasses of wine and set one across the table for Jacob.

"Jacob, when are ya comin' to git me? Ya said we was getting' married now where the hell are ya? I want ya to show yerself now!"

As she held the glass of wine to her lips she felt a cool breeze then caught a whiff of cucumbers and sugar. She stared at the empty chair across from her until she finally watched it move. "Jacob, is that you? Are ya there?"

His image appeared amidst a soft luminous glow as he stood with his hands on back of the empty chair. "Did you call me, Darling?"

"Oh Jacob, I knew you'd come back! Oh is that really you?"

He sat down and picked up his glass. "Yes, Darling. It's really me," he smiled. "Here's to us, Dolly. I'm here now and we'll never be apart again," His green eyes pierced through her heart like a spear. He took a sip then stood up and walked over to her. He put his hands around her neck and kissed the top of her head.

Dolly stood up and threw her arms around him. She kissed his warm soft lips long and hard before his image slowly faded away.

She often found Jacob standing in her room or across the table from her at dinner. She spotted him in the crowd during her performances and sometimes he'd walked with her back to her boxcar.

She spoke to Jacob frequently while others were present, never aware of what they were saying about her. Jacob began to stay with her for longer periods until he was there for good.

"You still amaze me, Dolly. You've become a true queen," Jacob said while lying in bed beside her. "And there's no other person in this world who could even dream of having your talent."

"Ya really think that, Jacob?"

"I know that." He rolled over and kissed her cheek. "I'm on Star's back with you every minute you're in that ring. Did you know that? I hold you tight when I think you might fall. I'm also in the cage with you and Big Jack but I can't control what he's thinking and I worry that I may not be able to stop him if he ever decides to go after you again."

"Hell, Jacob. Ya worry too much. I'm jus' fine in there with that old worn out cat. He's getting' so old he ain't hardly got no teeth left to bite with. Now roll over an' go to sleep. I gotta get up early this afternoon."

Over the months she began to argue with everyone until she got her way, knowing that she was the most important act in the circus. Jacob said that she was a true queen and now she believed it. Eventually they began to avoid her because she was crazy but it didn't matter to Dolly because she had Jacob.

"Did you see the newspaper today Dolly?" Mr. Bailey yelled as he threw the paper on her lap.

Sitting in front of her mirror admiring herself, she said, "No . . . why?" She held the paper up to read it. On the front page was her picture but it didn't flatter her. "Those damn reporters! Why in the hell did they take that picture of me when I didn't even know? Why look at it! I look awful!" She laid the paper back down onto her dressing table and went back to fussing with her hair.

"Well read it!"

"Okay, okay, Billy Boy!" She picked up the paper and began to read.

> "Dolly Crystal, Queen of the Barnham & Bailey Circus was intoxicated during her performance last Wednesday night. She insulted her fans by screaming curse words at the crowd for making her lose her concentration. She has been noted to be under the influence of alcohol on a daily basis.
>
> Parents of small children left during the middle of Dolly Crystal's act on several occasions.
>
> It was also discovered that, even though Miss Crystal had never been married, gave birth to a baby boy and gave him up for adoption, not being sure who the father was.
>
> Her promiscuous behavior lately has her fans in a state of shock. Some say that it was brought on because, as a child, her own uncle repeatedly raped her. It has also been stated that Miss Crystal once attempted to murder her uncle.
>
> This may be her excuse but we can no longer trust her to perform in front of our children. She is found to be offensive and immoral.
>
> Mr. James Bailey said that she was very difficult to work with but she was the most talented bareback rider and lion tamer in the world and he had to keep her on because she brought in high revenue for the show. He said that he did not know how much longer he could do it."

Dolly threw the paper across the room in a rage. "Those sons-a-bitches! Where did they hear all this shit!" She took a large gulp of whiskey then stood up raising her arms high over her head with her fists clenched tightly. "I'm gonna git whoever wrote that! How dare them!" She glared at Mr. Bailey; "Why in the hell did ya say what ya did about me, Mr. Bailey?"

Mr. Bailey could no longer stand the sight of her. "Because it was true," he answered before walking out, leaving Dolly alone.

"Oh, Jacob . . . What'll I do now?" she said, staring at the wall until Jacob appeared.

"I told you that you drink too much."

"How do ya think they found out 'bout me? Who coulda wrote all that stuff?"

"Don't think about it right now. I'm here. Think about me while we are making love and I'll make you forget what you read in the paper. Now come on, let's go to bed now."

Over the following weeks there were numerous articles written about Dolly Crystal's drinking and loose morals. Her dark secrets were exposed to the world. Giving her illegitimate child away, being raped and trying to kill her uncle and now they were saying that Dolly Crystal was going insane.

Her fans became fewer with each passing week. During Dolly's performance in the arena people booed and hissed. She only became angrier and her behavior worsened. She shouted obscenities back at the crowd but they could not hear what she was saying.

"I finally found out who wrote that first article about you, Dolly," said Sky one evening after the show. "Do you remember Jack Wade with the Daily Star back in New Orleans?"

"Why that bastard! An' I went an' told em everything an' he said he wouldn't write about it! How did he know 'bout the baby anyways?" Her teeth clenched as she slammed her fist down on her dressing table.

"Well, why on earth would you tell a reporter all about your dark past?"

"Cause I didn't know no better . . . that's why! Jack Wade better never show his face 'round me again er I'll kill em! Er maybe I'll jus' git Jacob to kill him fer me!"

"Jacob's dead, Dolly."

"Maybe so, but he ain't dead to me cause I see em every night an' we even make love. In fact I think he's here now." She smiled and looked past Sky's face and said, "Oh we was jus' talkin' about ya darlin'." She kept silent for a moment then answered, "Yep. He's leavin' right now. Ain't ya Sky?"

Sky didn't know what to say so he just nodded goodnight and left.

Dolly turned to Jacob and said, "Oh what a fool I was to tell em everythin'. I hate Jack Wade! I hate Matt! I hate all men . . . . except you, Jacob," Dolly cried. "I don't know what happened. Everythin's jus' fallin' apart. Kin ya jus' put yer arms around me?"

"There, there now Dolly," Jacob said as he held her tight and gently kissed her brow. "You still have me."

Dolly was unbearable to be around. She was never sober and complained about everything from the music to her costumes.

Mr. Bailey wanted to let her go right away but could not find anyone to replace her. Besides, he knew that she was the best. He hoped that it would all blow over and soon the public would forget the scandal. He decided to keep her on for a while longer hoping things would change.

Dolly's craziness never interfered with her performance. Mr. Bailey was amazed that she could perform so brilliantly once she reached the center ring. Knowing he could not afford to lose her, he humored her the best he knew how just to keep her working.

CHAPTER 23

Mr. Bailey was right. After only six months there was no more mention about Dolly's torrid past in the newspapers and not one more scandal surfaced. Her drunkenness never showed as she continued her brilliant performances in the ring and in the cages, doing her triple death-flips through the ring of fire and daring Big Jack to attack her. Her audience now saw her purely as Dolly Crystal, the Queen of the Barnum & Bailey Circus and they adored her once again.

Several years passed and nothing seemed to change in Dolly's routine. She was happy only when she was with Jacob but she could not see him in the arena, even though he'd told her that he was with her all the time. She could not bring herself to smile while performing so she started painting her lips with an artificial red curl that created the illusion of a smile for the audience. But as soon as she'd leave the ring her smile would melt away with the red paint . . . until she could be with Jacob again.

Hiding from the daylight, she became so pale that she had to apply more rouge than ever before. Little did her audience know that behind the mask of face powder and red rouge Dolly had drawn skin and dark pockets below her eyes.

"You look terrible, Darling," Jacob said one evening as they were in bed. "You really need to stop drinking so much. I don't want you see you die young like I did."

"I jus' can't. I don't like bein' aroun' people no more, Jacob . . . only you. An' the liquor makes it easier fer me. Do ya understand?"

"I understand everything about you. I've known you my whole life . . . and even after my life. I seriously worry about you though. Please try to take better care of yourself . . . for me, Dolly. And for God's sakes watch it with Big Jack. It makes me nervous thinking about you in that cage with such a huge beast."

"Oh hell, Jacob. Ya worry 'bout everythin' I do. I been takin' purdy damn good care of myself fer the past thirty years an' if ya don't trust me now ya ain't never gonna trust me. Mr Barnum says I'm good. He trusts me in that cage with Big Jack."

"Well, Mr. Barnum doesn't love you like I do."

Dolly looked up into his dark green eyes and said, "Let's make love now, Jacob."

The next morning when Dolly awoke, Jacob was gone. His side of the bed was rumpled but the door was still locked from the inside. "I wonder where he goes in the daytime. I don't like it when he leaves me alone," she yawned. She rolled over and tried to go back to sleep.

"Dolly? Wake up."

She turned over and saw Jacob standing over her. "What fer? I don't do my act till tonight."

"I have something for you."

"What is it, Jacob?"

"Hold out your left hand." As Dolly extended her left hand to him he kissed it then slipped the diamond engagement ring on her finger. "I want you to wear this."

"I fergot all about this ring. I hid it. How'd ya find it? It sure is sparkly ain't it?"

"I have to leave for a while now, Darling. I'll see you this evening after the show and we'll make love again all night.

There were times when Dolly would try to see herself as others saw her. She didn't want to be crazy anymore but she knew for as long as she hung on to Jacob she could never act normal again. She remembered what she had said to Uncle Thomas just before he died. She knew that she was keeping Jacob away from the Lord and began to feel sad for him. It was time to allow him leave. It would be hard, she thought, but she'd work on it.

Gradually Dolly began going outside during the day. Though she still drank just as much, the color was beginning to come back to her face. She decided that she wanted to live in the real world. That is, if she could find it again.

She could not give up the alcohol, even though she tried and eventually decided that it was hopeless. She gave up trying to quit but she did try to improve her behavior. She made an effort to be nice but even that was hard to do. People irritated her. She was still the queen but somehow managed to humble herself from time to time.

Jacob began to visit Dolly less and less. Most of the time she was too drunk to see him. The few times he did come she tried to say goodbye but couldn't.

One night she woke up and watched Jacob's sleeping face next to her in bed. Her heart ached for him. She wanted him to find peace. "Wake up, Jacob!" she yelled, "I want ya to go away now! Go on up to Heaven where ya belong. I don't want ya here no more cause everybody's callin' me crazy cause of you!"

Jacob's eyes filled with sadness as he answered, "If that's what you want, Dolly. I'll go now. I'll love you always and I'll be waiting for you." His face faded away into the pillow.

Dolly sobbed, "Goodbye Jacob . . . my love."

Weeks passed and Jacob never returned. Dolly was feeling so alone and desperately needed someone to talk to so she went over to see Sky.

She crossed the grounds and went straight to his boxcar and pounded on the door. "Hey Sky! Ya in here?" She threw the door open and stepped inside. She peered around for a moment then decided that he was probably in the bed.

"Hey! Git up!" She peeked into the back compartment where Sky slept and saw Grant, the midget clown, next to him in the bed, naked. "My God Sky! What in the hell er you two doin'? All these years an' I never knew . . ."

Sky hurriedly jumped out of the bed and threw on his robe while Grant covered himself with the blanket. "Why don't you knock, Dolly!"

"Well ya don't have to git so mad."

"And it's none of your business what Grant and I do!"

Dolly's blue crystal eyes began to sparkle with tears. "I was jus' lookin' fer some company . . . that's all."

"I'm sorry, Dolly," said Sky. I didn't mean to yell at you."

Grant got up from the bed with the blanket wrapped around his middle and walked over to Dolly and hugged her. "What's wrong, Your Majesty? Is there anything we can do to help?"

"Oh, Grant . . . yer so sweet an' Sky . . . so er you. I don't care if you two do what ya do. It's me. I'm all messed up inside," she sobbed as she twisted the diamond engagement ring around on her finger. "I got nobody . . . Jacob's gone . . . an' I mean he's really gone. I'm jus' so lonely . . . that's all."

"Aw, Dolly, you poor thing," Sky said.

"Mr. Bailey can't stand me no more cause I'm no good. I gave my baby away . . . I'm a whore an' I hate who I am. What am I gonna do? I wanna try to get normal but it's hard cause I'm so all alone an' I can't even see myself no more!"

Sky stepped up to Dolly and put his arms around her. "Dolly, we love you but you've got to stop drinking so much. It's killing you . . . and it kills us to see you this way."

"And you have to stop talking to Jacob. Everybody thinks you've lost you mind," said Grant.

"Jacob's gone now . . . fer good. I made em go," she said as her eyes filled with tears.

"Forive us," said Sky. We didn't mean to make you feel bad."

Dolly wiped her eyes with the sleeve of her robe and smiled. "Well, if ya want to make me happy . . . then tell me what two men do to each other in the bed. I never could figure it out. If there ain't no place to put it then what do ya do?"

Sky had to laugh. "Okay, Dolly! I'll tell you. We use our mouths."

"Oh . . . how disgustin'!" Dolly stepped away from Sky. "I never heard of such a dirty thing in all my life!" Then she grinned and said, "Kin I watch you two fer a spell? I got nothin' better to do an' I might git educated."

They all laughed.

"Dolly, you know we'd do anything for you . . . but not that!" Sky brushed his dark hair back from his face and looked down at Grant and laughed again, only harder.

"Well . . . at least come cheer me up an' have a drink with me," begged Dolly with a twinkle in her eyes.

Sky and Grant both still thought the world of her and knew there was a strong soul beneath all that craziness. Sky nodded and said, "That, we can do! Mind you . . . we don't like to see you drink so much . . . but let's go over to your place."

CHAPTER 24

It was January of 1897. Jacob never returned again but Dolly was still bitter and drank herself to sleep each night.

Mr. Bailey made an announcement that there were plans in progress to take the Barnum & Bailey Circus to Europe for an extended stay. The plans were to tour there for about three years.

"Did ya hear?" asked Sky. "We're going to England first then we're going to tour all of Europe. You can see your friend, Abby again."

"Yeah . . . I heard," answered Dolly as she finished tying her pink slippers.

"Mr. Bailey said we'll be gone two . . . maybe even three years. I think this will be really good for the circus. They'll love us over there . . . don't you think?"

She was beginning to feel excitement about going. It would be good to see Abby and it would be a good chance for her to start all over again. She would quit drinking and become an even bigger star than she was. "Oh yeah! I'm really lookin' forward to it, Sky. An' I'm givin' up the liquor too!"

After Dolly's performance that evening she ran to her dressing room, desperately craving a drink. She reached for the bottle and held it to her lips then paused. Her mouth was dry and she was trembling. "Why, I ain't gonna do it." She put the bottle down on the table and sat back. "This is my big chance to make it up to everbody an' start a new life without bein' drunk all the time." She'd decided to get rid of the bottle when she heard a knock at her door. She opened the door and her face lit up, "Well come on in Mr. Bailey!"

He stepped inside with a solemn look on his face and said, "Dolly . . . I don't know how to start." He smoothed his hair back and took a deep breath before saying, "I'm letting you go and Dolly, this time I won't change my mind."

"What are ya tellin' me, Mr. Bailey? I ain't goin' to Europe with ya? I thought I was valuable to ya!"

"True, you're the best thing that ever happened to this circus but at the same time you are the worst person to work with. You are spoiled and half the time you don't even know where you are or even who the hell you are. I don't want to be burdened with your grotesque behavior anymore. I've had enough."

"But I'm tryin' to quit drinkin'! I'll get straight again, I promise!"

"No, Dolly. It's too late. I want you out of here by tomorrow."

His sharp words sliced through her heart like a razor. Feeling like a cornered snake her fear turned to venomous fury. "An' you kin go to hell! I'll go someplace else! The Ringlin' Brothers will snatch me up in a heart beat . . . an' you'll be sorry ya lost me, Billy Boy! An' I hope this circus falls apart after I'm gone. Why yer the meanest, most hateful son-of-a-bitch I ever met in my life!" she screamed as she shoved him out the door.

The next morning Dolly angrily tore her costumes off the hooks and threw them into her trunk. She kicked a table over then threw herself onto the bed. "I hate em! I hate em!" she screamed as she pounded her fists into the bed. "Oh God! Don't take it away from me! I'm sorry! I'll do better . . . I promise!" But she knew it was too late. She grabbed her bottle of whiskey and poured down as much as she could hold.

An hour later Sky came into Dolly's dressing room. "Dolly, I just found out we're leaving in a week."

"I ain't goin', Sky."

"What do you mean you ain't goin'?"

"Ol' Billy Boy jus' let me go! He said I was grotesque!"

Sky wasn't surprised. "Well, what do you have planned? Do you know where you'll go?"

"Oh, don't ya worry yer cute little head off about me. I'm Dolly Crystal . . . Queen of the Circus! I won't have no trouble at all!" she slurred while slinging her things into her trunk.

"Well Dolly, the reason I'm asking is that I just overheard one of the Ringlings saying to Mr. Bailey that he wouldn't touch you with a ten-foot pole. I didn't know Mr. Bailey let you go though. I really am sorry for you Dolly."

"I can't believe they don't want me! Why I'm the best there ever was! What'll I do, Sky?"

"You should have enough money. Maybe you could start your own circus."

"Hell, Sky, why I ain't got that much money! Remember? I was sendin' most of it to Ella fer years. An' the rest of it, I guess I jus' musta pissed it away cause I ain't got much left."

"I wish I could help you, Dolly." He hugged her goodbye and opened the door.

"Before ya go, Sky . . . I jus want to thank ya fer getting' me in the circus in the first place. I don't think I ever told ya thank you . . . did I?" Her nose was red and her eye makeup was smudged. She blew her nose in her handkerchief then gave him a half smile.

He took Dolly's hand, kissed it and looked into her pale crystal eyes. "I'll miss you Queen Dolly." Just before walking out he turned to her and said, "You were the best."

Dolly was devastated. If the Ringling Brothers didn't want her, nobody would want any part of her either. It was over and she knew it.

She finished packing her clothes, costumes and jewelry, which was all she had left to show for all the years of her success. She came across the red scarf that Matt Kilgore had given her so long ago. It made her think of Matt but only the good memories of him so she decided to keep it and stuffed it into her trunk along with all her other memories. She looked around her dressing room. It had been her home for so many years.

Dolly was determined not to cry. She sucked the salty tears to the back of her throat and swallowed hard. She stuffed her photographs of Uncle Thomas, which she had planned to put into a scrapbook someday, into her separate carrying bag. She took the handle of the heavy trunk and dragged it down the steps, closing the door behind her. She stopped and looked at the engagement ring on her left hand then slid it off her finger and dropped it into her bag. Snow began to fall as she made her way to the train station.

As Dolly neared the ticket booth, she had no idea where she was going. She'd heard that the Astor's mansion in New York had been converted to a brand new hotel, called the Waldorf Astoria. "It would be nice to stay there", she thought. "They say that it's elegant enough for royalty." She reached the ticket booth and said, "Give me a ticket to Miami. I'm goin' where it's warm."

CHAPTER 25

With very little money Dolly knew she'd have to be very careful with what was left. She had to rent the cheapest place she could find. Now she understood how Belle Storm must have felt before she committed suicide.

She found a small efficiency in the heart of Miami. At first she felt lost. She had no friends in Miami to help her but she knew she'd find a way to survive. There was no time to waste feeling sorry for herself so she decided to make the best out of what she had. She was thankful she had her beautiful clothes and still had her good looks because she knew they were the only tools she'd need.

"Alright, Dolly Crystal! It's time to git on with yer life!" she announced to her reflection in the mirror. "Let's see . . . what kin I wear today." She pulled out the red dress she'd worn the day Matt raped her. It was still her most beautiful dress but she could not bring herself to put it on. She squeezed into her bright blue dress with black lace. "It's perfect!" she said as she sat down to her make-up table.

She strutted up and down Flagler Street, hoping someone would recognize her. She had no problem getting all the attention she was looking for. She was stopped by young and old alike and asked to sign her autograph. Because she knew how to charm the men, she was approached by them as well, even the ones who did not recognize her as Dolly Crystal, Queen of the Circus. Dolly was delighted and felt almost happy at times.

"Well hello Pretty Lady," said a tall, well-dressed young man passing her on the street.

Dolly smiled at him and replied, "Well hello there yerself!"

It didn't take too much effort on Dolly's part to get him interested in her. He invited her to his hotel and she went. After a few drinks she found herself in his bed.

Dolly did not feel shame. She needed a man to love her. When he was finished satisfying himself with her he handed her some money.

"What's this fer?" she asked.

"It's for you. You know . . . your services."

Dolly took the money and left.

"That wasn't so hard," she thought. "At least now I know where to git some money when I need it."

Now Dolly had dual reasons for strolling up and down Flagler Street. Most people still recognized her as the old circus queen, which fed her starving ego. She could have any man she wanted, even if it was only for a brief hour within the four walls of a hotel room.

She bought a scrapbook and every night, while getting drunk, she pasted pictures in it until it was a complete story of her life. She mounted the letter from Uncle Thomas on the front page along with a picture of herself sitting on Pronto. This scrapbook became her most prized possession.

Over the following few years Dolly's beautiful clothes began to fade and look outdated. Her gloves became soiled and her shoes were worn out but she continued to wear them, never noticing how shabby she appeared to others. Even in her shabbiness she could still attract the men she needed.

She decided to sell all of her jewelry because she needed the money. The only two pieces she kept were the heart-shaped locket she wore that Uncle Thomas had given her and the diamond engagement ring from Jacob. She went through the money fast, spending most of it on whiskey and did not pay her rent. She had to move again.

She found an even cheaper apartment near the Miami River and moved in with the few possessions she owned, which were her old circus costumes, her pink ballerina slippers and her scrapbook. But she stayed long enough for the rent to come due. After that she continued moving from one place to another, dodging the rent just to keep from parting with the money she needed for her whiskey.

One day when she was low on whiskey she toyed with the idea of selling the diamond ring that Jacob had given her. She tried to remember where she'd hidden it and searched through all of her belongings over and over again. "No, I can't sell it. What in the world was I thinkin'?" she said to herself. As poor as she was, she decided that even if she could find it she would never sell her most precious keepsake from Jacob. But she feared it was lost forever.

Summer of 1907 Dolly moved again to small room near Bay Front Park.

One afternoon she took her beer and walked out to the pier to watch the birds. The sky was blue and the ocean breeze felt cool against her sweaty skin. She saw a sea gull fly into a pole and fall to the pier. She went over, picked it up and held it in both hands. "Aw, ya poor thing. Knocked the daylights outta ya, huh?" She reached over with one hand and took a sip of her beer. "Well, I'll fix ya right up."

Dolly looked up and spotted an old woman in a tattered dress watching her with the bird. She said to the old woman, "Well, what do ya know! It's little wing is broke right in two!" Dolly looked up at the strange woman again as she cradled the injured bird in her hands. "Don't I know ya from someplace? Can't say from where but I know yer eyes . . . . do ya know who I am?"

"Yep. Yer Dolly Crystal . . . the Queen of the Barnum and Bailey Circus," said the shabby old woman with a grin.

Dolly could hardly believe her ears. Someone actually did remember her after all. "How did ya recognize me?"

"I also know ya as Dolly Wafford." The old woman stared at

her. Ya don't know who I am, do ya Dolly? Why don't ya take a close look." The woman stared directly into Dolly's eyes.

Dolly recognized the bulging brown eyes. "Ella? Ella, is that you?" Dolly gently placed the sea gull down on the bench. "My God! I never thought I'd ever see ya again!"

"Yep . . . It's me, Dolly! I almost didn't recognize you at first neither!"

"What in the hell happened to ya, Ella? Ya look so poor! I thought you was livin' high on the hog in Knoxville an' all. How did ya git here in Miami . . . an' how'd ya find me?"

"Well . . . first of all I'd like to give ya a hug." Ella reached out with her arms out.

"It's so good to see ya again, Ella." Dolly embraced her.

As Ella's arms wrapped around her middle, she smiled and said, "Ya don't have that tiny little waist no more, do ya Girl."

"Must be all that noodle soup I eat! Well . . . ain't ya gonna tell me about how ya got here?"

Ella scratched the back of her neck. "It's really jus' a mess what I been through. Ya never answered my letters so I reckon ya didn't know what happened. Remember I was livin' with my sister, Margaret an' her husband George? Well . . . anyways she died last year. Her husband, George, got married again only a month after she was dead an' then he told me I had to leave my sister's house. I didn't have noplace to go so I got a job at the hotel cleanin' rooms fer a while. They let me live there for free but it burned down only jus' months after I started. I lost everythin' an' then got arthritis real bad an' found out my heart ain't too good so I can't do that kind of work no more . . . so I floated around fer a while an' last month I decided to come down here."

"What happened to all yer money?"

"Well . . . George, he lost his job an' wanted to start his own newspaper an' call it the Whitmore News. He asked me fer money to git it goin' an' since I was livin' with em I gave em' all I had. An' later on he started makin' lots of money but he never did pay me back. I asked em fer it after Margaret died but he told me it was all invested an' he couldn't give it to me."

"Why that no-good-son-of-a-bitch! Ya mean he literally kicked ya out an' kept everythin' that belonged to you an' yer sister an' married somebody else?"

"Yeah, that's exactly how it happened. But it's okay now cause I found out his business is failin' an' he's losin' everythin'. His new wife, who didn't love em anyways, jus' left em an' he's really havin' a hard time. That's all I need to feel good 'bout it all."

"I hope he gets poorer then us!"

"I think that jus' might happen, Dolly," Ella smiled. "I'm jus' glad I came down her to Miami an' run across you!"

"Why did ya pick Miami?"

"Cause the winters ain't as cold here."

Dolly had to chuckle. "That's real funny, Ella, cause ya know what? That's the very same reason I picked to come down to Miami . . . cause it's warm."

"Yeah, an' easier to find food too cause you kin go fishin' anytime ya want."

"Why don't ya come with me back to my place an' we'll have some soup an' a drink an' we kin talk some more." She looked down at the sea gull on the bench and said, "An' I gotta get this poor bird's wing fixed. He's in bad pain." Dolly picked the bird up and started walking and Ella followed.

The two women walked toward Dolly's small apartment only a few blocks away.

"Where do ya live, Ella?"

"Oh, I don't really have a place of my own yet . . . I stay on the streets most of the time. I found this nice place under the 79th Street Bridge where I kin catch all the fish I want."

Dolly felt sorry for Ella. It was hard to believe that she would end up on the streets. Dolly felt proud to at least have an apartment, even if it was small and shabby. "Well, didn't yer sister leave ya nothin'? I thought she had all that money. Oh yeah, an' I'm real sorry to hear that she died."

"Margaret did have quite a bit saved but it all went to er husband. He even told me to leave the dresses that my sister gave me cause they was part of er estate. So I left with jus' a few things an' he paid fer my ticket to Miami."

"Why that louse! He litterally jus' kicked ya out like you was some kinda ol' dog er somethin'!"

When they reached the door to Dolly's apartment, Ella stopped for a moment before going inside. "I was wonderin', Dolly. What happened to ya? Why are ya livin' like this?"

"Oh hell, this is the Waldorf Astoria compared to livin' on the streets! Come on in!"

Dolly went directly to the sink and put the bird in it. "Will ya hold em down while I git a stick?"

Ella walked over and placed her hand over the bird in the sink while Dolly fished around in the drawer next to her bed.

"This'll work." She held up a pencil then went back over to start setting the bird's broken wing. "This would be right up Jacob's alley, huh Ella."

"Oh what a nice young man he was. I remember him comin' to the house lookin' fer ya all the time. Half the time you'd go hide from em an' ya called em as pest. But when ya got bigger ya started bein' nicer to em. I always liked Jacob . . . but I couldn't stand that Matt Kilgore."

Still working on the bird's wing, Dolly looked up at Ella and said, "I never told ya this before but I had a baby . . . . by Matt Kilgore. He raped me, Ella. I jus' wanted to make em want me an' then leave em like he did me."

"I know about the baby, Dolly. It was all in the newspapers, remember? An' I knew it was Matt's cause Abby wrote to me an' told me when ya went to Boston to have the baby her friend took care of ya."

"What friend?"

"She said a nurse . . . Ronda er Rose er somethin' like that."

"Rosie Stringretter?"

"I think that might be it. Yeah, she was the nurse who took care of ya at that home. Abby knew er from the hospital in Boston."

"I wonder if that's where Jack Wade, the reporter who wrote all that stuff, found out 'bout me havin' the baby."

"Abby said her friend, the nurse, moved to New Orleans shortly after ya had the baby. I wouldn't be surprised if that reporter did talk to er. Ya know how reporters are. They seem to find out anything they want. Er maybe that nurse found the reporter . . . who knows?"

"There ain't nothin' sacred nomore. Everthing I ever did got in the newspapers. Well those days er over now, Ella. Dolly finished taping the pencil to the gull's wing. "Now I'm gonna put this bird back outside."

She went to the door and threw it into the air. It fell back onto the ground with a thud. "Aw shit! I thought it could fly away!" She turned to Ella and laughed, "Did ya ever eat gull before?"

Dolly slammed the door, leaving the bird to fend for itself.

"But Dolly, I thought ya loved animals," said Ella.

"I do. I was jus' jokin' . . . but I reckon I jus' don't wanna be bothered with no damn bird . . . or any other kinda animal fer that matter. I still love em . . . I jus' don't have time fer animals no more. Ya gotta feed em an' I have a hard time jus' feedin' myself. When I get a little bread sometimes I go over to the pier an' feed the gulls jus' so they kin entertain me fer a bit. Now . . . let's have a drink!"

Dolly poured two small glasses of beer from the icebox and handed one to Ella.

Ella's trembling hands quickly grabbed the glass and she gulped it down. "Dolly, tell me why ya left the circus."

"The booze . . . Jacob gettin' killed . . . gettin' pregnant . . . oh jus' everything. Mr. Bailey couldn't deal with me no more an' jus' got rid of me." Dolly plopped down on a chair and looked over at her scrapbook on the table. "I heard the Ringlin' Brothers joined Mr. Bailey an' the traveling circus is bigger then ever. Oh how I miss it too. I loved the attention an' the expensive liquor." Dolly's eyes sparkled.

"I see ya put on a few pounds." Ella's bug eyes moved down to Dolly's thick middle. "But yer still as purdy as the day I met ya. So tell me, Dolly . . . what happened to ya? How do ya live?"

"I reckon I drink too much an' it's depressin' but all my clothes got worn out . . . er maybe I jus' got too fat fer em an' anyways I have a hard time keepin' a place to live." Dolly didn't mind telling Ella about herself. "Men still look at me an' sometimes they give me money. Ya know . . . fer special favors. That's how I live," she said as she picked the dirt out from under her fingernail. "I jus' been bouncin' around from one place to another all these years. I buy beer with every nickel I ever git my hands on. An' ya might say I have it rough but I'd rather give sexual favors fer money rather then resort to beggin'."

Ella didn't seem surprised with what Dolly was telling her because she knew how honest she was. The thought crossed her mind however that Dolly might be a little crazy like she'd heard but she didn't care if Dolly was crazy or not. "Ya really are somethin', Dolly Wafford . . . Oh, I mean . . . Crystal."

"Ya never told me how ya found me. How did ya find me anyways?" asked Dolly.

"Oh, it wasn't hard. Not too long ago I found this old newspaper . . . I put a newspaper over me at night to keep the dew off . . . I really keep up with all the news that way too. Oh . . . an' you remember Sky Walker with the Ringlin' Brothers?"

"Yeah. I didn't even know he went with them. What about em, Ella?"

"Well one of the things I read was that he fell off the wire an' got killed a while back. They said he was too old to still be doin' what he was doin'"

Dolly felt a twinge of heartache. "Ya know, Ella? I loved em like a brother at one time. I fergot all 'bout em an' he was a real good friend to me." She looked down and sighed, "I wonder what ever happened to Grant."

"Grant who?"

"Oh, that was Sky Walker's midget lover."

"Ya mean her name was Grant?"

"No, I mean his name was Grant. Sky was queer ya know.

"Well, I did read somethin' about a midget in that article. Let's see . . . I think he was the one . . . yeah, the midget created a scene at Sky Walker's funeral. It said a midget tried climbin' in the coffin an' made it fall over. I wasn't gonna tell ya this but

Sky's body rolled right out an' landed on the midget's feet. It said his body was stiff like a board when it fell out an' the midget jus' screamed an' screamed till they had to take em out. I think it said they put em in the nuthouse an' he might still be there fer all we know."

"Ella, this is quite upsettin' to me ya know. We gotta talk 'bout somethin' else." She reached into her mouth and pulled out a tooth and continued, "Now tell me how ya found me."

"What was that ya jus' pulled outta yer mouth?"

"Oh, my teeth er all loose an' one jus' comes out once in a while," Dolly laughed. "I'm gettin' used to it so don't fret none fer me. Now tell me, Ella! How did ya know where I was?"

"You know . . . with these newspapers over my head every night I see everything, like I told ya. Anyways, I saw yer picture in that one paper. It didn't say who ya were but it showed ya sittin' with the pelicans on the pier . . . right where I met ya. Wanna see it? I got it right here." Ella pulled the small folded piece of paper out of the top of her dress and handed it to Dolly.

"That's me all right. Let's see . . .", Dolly quietly read the print as she brushed away the tear from each eye for Sky. "It's nothin' but some advertisement fer the restaurant on the pier . . . but they got me in the picture. Ain't that a hoot?"

"Well . . . That's how I found ya, Dolly. I knew it was you."

"Ya look kinda skinny to me, Ella . . . are ya hungry?" Dolly reached for a can of soup from over the sink and began to open it. "Chicken noodle . . . that's all I buy."

"Suits me jus' fine."

"Ya wanna sleep here tonight instead of on the sidewalk?"

Ella slept in Dolly's bed and Dolly slept on the floor . . . Just like her Uncle Thomas would have had it.

Just before Dolly put out the lights, Ella said, "Oh yeah. I fergot to tell ya the news 'bout Abby."

"What about Abby?"

"Well, she worked real hard at the hospital. I know cause she started writin' me when she never heard back from ya. Anyways she got real run down an' picked up somethin' from one of those little orphans that was life-threatenin'. Now I'm not sure I got the story right cause it came second hand from Ed . . . an' ya remember how Ed would exaggerate."

"Ya mean Matt's uncle? Ya talked to em?"

"Well, Ed musta felt real bad cause he let out yer's an' Thomas's secret an' came lookin' fer me up at my sister's in Knoxville. He was real apologetic an' all so yeah, I was nice to em."

"Jus' tell me about Abby."

Well anyways . . . it was a while back . . . she swelled all up an' her eyes started to bulge outta her head. Last I heard she ain't dead yet but they say she ain't never gonna git better. Ed told me that she can't even talk er write an' er husband divorced er. Kin ya imagine that? When she needed em the most he just up an' left er. An' he was a doctor too." Ella reached for Dolly's hand. "I'm real sorry to have to tell ya this since I know you an' Abby was such close friends an' all."

Dolly didn't know what to say. She hadn't thought about Abby in years. She did wonder a time or two what had ever happened to her. All of sudden she felt the sting of tears and sniffed. "Jeez Ella! I loved her a lot an' feel guilty 'bout not tryin' to git a hold of er fer all these years. It ain't too late . . . I'll see if I kin git up enough money to go see er."

"Dolly, ya ain't got no money to git to Europe. Ya can't hardly even afford chicken noodle soup. An' besides she ain't gonna be alive be by the time ya git there."

"Ya know, Ella, Jacob gave me this big ol' diamond ring fer our engagement. I saved it but I don't know where I put it. I been searchin' fer years but it's gone. That ring woulda got me to Europe I betcha. Dolly hung her head and closed her eyes. "Dear Lord, please forgive me fer not bein' there fer my best friend. Help her oh Lord an' help us too . . . amen." She looked up, "Well Ella . . . I guess there ain't nothin' we kin do but jus' pray fer er. Let's git some sleep." Dolly turned out the lights. "Good night, Ella. Sleep tight."

In the dark, Ella knew that beneath Dolly's gruff exterior was a tender heart filled with pain and compassion. She knew Dolly well.

The sharpness of her words, her toughness and her unpredictability were all just a shield to protect her from the pain of reality. She knew that Dolly felt sad for Sky and for Abby . . . and even for the sea gull she'd thrown outside, but over the years of so much tragedy in her life she had to learn to block out all the pain. It made Ella sad that others didn't always see what she saw in Dolly.

They didn't have much but the two women loved each other and stuck together from then on. Dolly continued to make money the way she was forced to do. She managed to keep a roof over their heads and some soup and beer in the house but as soon as the rent came due it was time for Dolly to find them a new place to live.

She found another small efficiency, along the Miami River, that required no deposit and moved her few belongings in along with Ella.

Dolly continued going out at night, wearing her heavy make-up and outrageous costumes. Ella often wondered about how Dolly felt about prostituting but never said a word until one evening when she conjured up the nerve to ask.

"Dolly . . . Do ya mind what ya do fer a livin?" asked Ella as she wrinkled her nose.

"Hell no . . . I ain't gotta choice anyways. But it's okay cause I reckon I'm gettin' purdy used to it now. At first I was scared cause it made me think about Uncle Ernest but it ain't so bad. Of course I don't really enjoy it much. I jus' do what I gotta do to eat an' besides . . . . I like workin' fer myself."

Over the next several years they moved twenty-six more times. They drank as much beer as Dolly could afford with the little money she made. She wanted to do more for Ella and she had to remind herself from time to time that it was the best she could do. They spent their days talking about the past, about Uncle Thomas and the old house in Ridgetop . . . back when they were happy. It worked out to be a perfect union between the two women. Ella depended on Dolly to take care of her and Dolly needed someone love her.

"Look what I got today, Ella!" Dolly came through the door with a phonograph in her arms. "An' I got a record of Billy Murray too!"

Ella smiled and said, "How could ya afford it?"

"Oh, it didn't cost me nothin'. A nice old man took me to his house today an' said he got a new one so I could have this one. An' I didn't have to stay there with em very long cause he couldn't get his private parts workin' right. But it plays real good an' the phonograph record is new cause he bought it fer me. He said this here is a Victrola phonograph an' it cost a lot of money but he was a rich doctor so he could afford it."

"Well wind it up an' let's hear it!"

Dolly put it on the table and turned the crank. "Now let's see now. Ya jus' put the record here . . . an' oh yeah . . . ya jus' lay this here thing like that an' there ya go."

Dolly began shaking her shoulders to the tune of "Oh You Beautiful Doll" while Ella sat on the bed smiling.

She sang and danced around the room, kicking her legs high but soon lost her breath and had to stop. "Guess I ain't in no shape to do this no more!" Dolly panted.

"It sure is good to hear music again. I wish I could dance but I'm afraid my heart jus' can't stand it."

"Guess we're jus' getting' old, huh Ella? Well anyways, I'm happy I met Larry an' got this Victrola."

"Was that his name, Larry?"

"Yep an' he was a doctor too. I think he had a last name like Saloman er somethin' like that."

"Ya mean Dr. Larry Solomon?"

"Yeah, that was his name. Why, did ya ever hear of em before, Ella?"

"That's who Abby was married to Dolly! Don't ya remember? Dr. Larry Solomon!

"Shit no!" shrieked Dolly as she plopped down onto the bed next to Ella. "How in the hell do we even know it was the same Larry Solomon . . . an' even if it was . . . how did he wind up down here in Miami? I never did think of his name an' I only met em once with Abby long time ago. But ya know, Ella? I thought there was somethin' familiar 'bout his face. Aw shit!"

Ella gradually became pale and more weakened by her bad heart. Dolly did everything she could to try to help her but Ella only got worse. One morning Dolly woke up and found her dead. She knew that she couldn't afford to bury her so she moved out and left Ella there.

CHAPTER 26

Years passed and the attention from strangers dwindled. Dolly ached inside from loneliness as she continued to walk the streets, having sex with anyone who wanted to pay for it. She'd let herself go for so long that the few men that took her to a bed or behind a tree were generally fat or old.

On the day of Dolly's fifty-fourth birthday, as she stood in front of the mirror, two sad crystal blue eyes stared back at her from the face of an old woman. She was wearing no make-up and had dark bags under her eyes. Her thin red hair was speckled with gray and she was fat. She'd never noticed what a pitiful old woman she was turning into until that day.

"Oh", she moaned. "Where did ya disappear to, Dolly Crystal?" She tried to fluff her hair out the way she did when she was young but there wasn't enough hair left anymore. "Well . . . hell. It's time to git her back again."

Dolly reached into the kitchen cabinet and found a bottle of red food coloring. "Oh, this'll be perfect," she said as she leaned over the sink and poured it over her head. She rubbed it in until her hair was saturated with the bright cherry red food coloring.

When she looked in the mirror she was pleased with what she saw but something was missing. She reached into the top drawer of the dresser and took out her make-up box. She began patting the white powder over her face until she looked like one of the clowns from the circus. Without giving up she applied rouge then her false eyelashes. She finished with exaggerated penciled-on red lips while her hair dried. She stepped back from the mirror to examine the results. She did not see the sagging eyes and orange teeth in her reflection. What Dolly saw, in her drunken splendor, was a beautiful young woman with bright red hair and silky smooth skin. "Oh, there ya are! I found ya again, Dolly Crystal!"

She continued dying her hair bright cherry red with anything she could use . . . iodine, beet juice or Ritt Dye for fabrics. Anything suited her as long as it turned her hair red. She painted her face religiously every morning, using heavier make-up each time.

Dressed in her tight-fitting faded costumes and dirty ballerina slippers she ventured out into the crowded streets of Miami where she reigned as Queen.

Dolly often stopped strangers on the sidewalk and started telling stories about her past. Sometimes she'd hold a stranger's arm and they would have to shake her loose.

One morning after applying her thick make-up she walked out of her tiny rented shack into the front yard wearing only an apron. As cars went by they honked their horns at her. Dolly was a sight to behold. She danced in circles on the patchy front lawn and every time she'd turn around she'd expose her white pasty behind to the onlookers.

She loved being in the center arena again and never thought for a moment that people were laughing at her.

It became more difficult for Dolly to get money. No one wanted her anymore and she became desperate. Struggling without food most days, Dolly, for the first time in her life thought about stealing.

At the grocery market she picked up four cans of chicken noodle soup and stuffed them into the front of her dress. She managed to get a small roast into her underpants and held a bag of potatoes between her thighs. As she began to walk out, a man grabbed her by the arm at the front door.

"Okay Lady. Whatcha got under your dress!"

"Jus' a little food I needed. I was gonna pay ya but I ain't got no money. I suppose ya want it back . . . but kin I jus' keep one can of soup? I'm real hungry."

"Okay. You can keep two cans of soup but I want ya to put the roast back."

Dolly spread her legs apart and the bag of potatoes plopped to the floor. "I got these too but you kin have em back." She lifted her skirt and retrieved the roast from her underpants and passed it to him. She reached into the top of her dress and pulled out four cans of chicken noodle soup and handed them out to him. "Ya said I kin keep two of em, right?"

The storekeeper pushed all four cans back at her. "I never want to see you in my store again. If you show your face here one more time I'll have you arrested."

Dolly's soup was gone and she was hungry but she hated stealing. Her rent was four months past due and her thirst for alcohol consumed her. She tried to think of a way to make more money.

Dressed in her best tattered costume she paraded down the street with a cup in her hand. She held it out in front of every person she passed and said, "Do ya remember me? I'm Dolly Crystal, Queen of the Circus!" She looked pitiful and silly but still funny enough that some people threw some pennies into her cup.

"I thought I'd never resort to beggin' . . . but what the hell," she muttered to herself at the end of the day while counting her pennies. She counted seventy-three cents and headed straight for the liquor store.

That evening while Dolly was dying her hair with iodine she heard a knock at the door. "Aw shit, who's that botherin' me this time at night." She wrapped a towel around her head and answered the door.

"I'm here to collect five months rent. You owe me fifty dollars, Miss Wafford," the man said.

"Well I got fifteen cents left. Ya kin have that . . . but I ain't got no more."

"Then you're going to have to vacate by day after tomorrow."

"Kin ya wait here fer a minute?" She went over to the sink and started looking in the drawers. "I know I got that diamond ring. Jus' gotta remember where I put it."

"Quit stalling. You don't own any diamond ring."

"I do so! An it's real big an' expensive an it would pay my rent fer over a year! The only thin' is I can't find it."

"Just be out by Saturday." The man stepped out and left.

Dolly went into the bathroom and removed the towel from her head. She looked in the mirror and her hair was dark orange. "Aw shit! Now I gotta start all over again!"

Saturday morning came. Dolly painted her face, pulled out another tooth and laid it on the sink. She put on one of her tattered costumes, not remembering that she was being evicted that day, and slipped out the door with her cup.

When she returned home with forty cents in her cup, she found her things strewn all over the sidewalk in front of her shack. Her clothes were stuffed into paper bags and her Victrola was lying upside down on the sidewalk. She couldn't understand why someone would do this to her.

She gathered what she could in her arms to bring back inside but the door was locked. "How in the world did I do that? I don't even have a key . . . an' fer that matter, I don't even have a lock on my door."

As she stood there trying to figure out why the door was locked it flew open and there stood the man who had asked her for rent. It wasn't until then that she remembered.

"Get your things and find another place to live," he said with a cold look.

"I got noplace to go to. Ya think maybe I could stay jus' a bit longer?"

He slammed the door in her face and she backed away.

Dolly took a grocery cart from a nearby parking lot and went back to fetch her things.

She loaded up the grocery cart then pushed it for several miles looking for a place to sleep. She was just about ready to give up hope when she spotted a doorway with a sign that read, "Home of the Homeless."

"I jus' knew you would lead the way fer me, dear Lord!" Dolly opened the door and pushed her cart inside.

A short old black woman approached her and said, "Hello. My name is Mrs. Sherman. Are you in need of a place to stay?"

"I reckon I am in need . . . so show me where I sleep."

"I need you to come over here to answer some questions first."

Dolly nodded and followed her to a table.

"Please tell me your name and why you are in need."

"I'm Dolly Crystal, Queen of the circus . . . do ya remember me? I'm very famous ya know." Dolly lifted her chin high, striking a pose in hopes that the woman would recognize her. "As ya probably know I ain't with the Barnum an' Bailey circus no more an' I run outta money so I ain't got noplace to live no more."

"Well, here we can provide you with a clean cot, breakfast and one hot meal at six in the evenings for as long as you need us to help . . . but there are some rules."

"An' jus' what rules are ya talkin' 'bout?"

"The first rule is that for as long as you are staying with us you must diligently be seeking employment. The second rule is that you be in by ten O'clock PM every night except Saturdays. On Saturdays you can stay out as late as midnight. If you have anything of value we ask that you let us hold it for you for your own protection."

"The only thing I have of any value is a ring but I can't find it. It must be in my stuff somewhere. When I find it I'll give it to ya. Okay? Now where kin I git some food around here?"

Dolly thought about trying to find employment but bareback riding and prostitution were the only jobs she knew and she was too old to do either. Begging in the streets gave her very little money and some days she came back with an empty cup.

She spent the few coins she had on beer but when she had no money she had to steal it. She hated herself for having to steal but some days she just had to do it.

It was January 16, 1920 when Dolly went to the grocery market to fetch her daily beers as usual. She was prepared to slip a few bottles under her coat as she approached the cooler but when she looked down it was empty. There was a sign that read, "Sorry. No sale of alcohol due to the Eighteenth Amendment." Oblivious to the prohibition movement that had been going on she could not figure out what had happened.

"Hey! Ain't ya got no beer?" She asked the merchant.

"You didn't know? They made that law go into effect today. I'm sorry, Lady."

Dolly felt her throat tighten up and gulped, "Well, hell. Nobody ever said nothin' to me!" She needed that beer. Dolly felt angry and afraid all at once. "Do ya know where I kin git any?" she blurted out loudly as she wiped the drool from the corner of her mouth.

"Nobody's going to sell you any today. I know that," answered the man behind the counter as he rolled his eyes back. "Tomorrow I can sell you some wart. All you have to do is add it to yeast and you can make your own beer . . . . but it's not very strong. I'll be getting some other low alcoholic drinks in tomorrow too, if you can wait till then." He noticed that the funny looking old woman was shaking. Feeling sorry for her, he stepped out from behind the counter. "You really need it . . . don't you. I'll tell you what. Go see this man." He handed her a slip of paper with an address on it.

"Where's this?" asked Dolly as she clutched the paper in her trembling fist.

"Just go up to the corner and turn right. It's on the right side. Just look for the number."

Dolly hurried out, not thinking about how much money she would need. She followed his directions until she found herself in front of a wooden door with number 2224 on it. She anxiously hammered on the door for over a minute until a man opened it.

"What do you want?" demanded the bald, fat man.

"They said I could git some beer here."

"Who's they?"

"The man at the store. Please. I jus' gotta git me somethin' to drink."

The fat man looked both ways before letting her in. "Okay, walk into the other room."

There were five men sitting around wooden crates filled with bottles. The room had no windows and it was lit by a single light bulb dangling from a cord in the middle of the ceiling.

"How much do ya charge?" asked Dolly, reaching into her coat pocket for her change.

"Probably more than you have," commented a well-dressed man wearing spats.

"Who is she?" said another man.

"She's harmless. Just an old lady lookin' for something to drink," said another.

The fat man turned to Dolly and said, "Well, Old Woman, all we got is rum. Is that what you want?"

"Oh yeah. Anythin'! Here. I got eleven cents." Dolly slapped the pennies on the table.

The men laughed. "Oh give her a bottle, Tony. Look at her. Her tongue's hangin' out."

Tony reached over and handed Dolly a dark, plain bottle and slid her change from the table and put it in his pocket. "Okay, Old Woman, there ya go. Now get outta here an' don't come back."

The men burst into laughter as Dolly scrambled for the front door and hurried away toward the shelter.

She opened the bottle and swallowed a big gulp before she got to the door. When she walked in she was the only one there. She took another swig. "Ahh," she sighed as she flopped onto her cot. She reached over and cranked up her Victrola to the tune of "Oh You Beautiful Doll," her favorite.

Savoring every sip and not thinking about where she'd get her next bottle, she drifted off into a deep dream.

There was Jacob and Uncle Thomas with Ella. They were laughing at her. Dolly was wearing a circus costume and had her long thick ringlets tied up with a pink bow . . . but her face was old.

Jacob put his arm around her shoulder and said, "Dolly, you're still the most beautiful girl in the world to me but you are a pathetic drunk." Then he laughed at her and pulled away.

"Jacob! Don't ya love me no more?"

He turned his back to her and said, "Get out of here, Dolly Wafford. You disgust me."

"Uncle Thomas! Ella! You love me don't ya?"

They only glared back at her with red glassy eyes and said nothing. Dolly screamed and woke up with a lump in her throat and began to cry.

The rum was almost gone by that next evening. Dolly had to think. Where could she get some more? She dressed in her finest tattered clothes and applied heavy makeup over what she had worn the day previously before slipping back out onto the street with her cup.

The following morning she took the few coins she had collected and headed straight for the grocery market to buy some yeast and wart.

September of 1926 Dolly moved to a shelter on Miami Avenue. She'd heard that it was much larger but the food was more plentiful. It was an old brick warehouse that slept seventy-five people in one large room with cots lined along the walls and two rows in the middle. There was a small open kitchen at one end and a bathroom next to it.

Upon her arrival, Dolly was thrilled that many of the homeless people at the shelter remembered her as the queen of the circus. They welcomed Dolly's stories in the beginning but over time they began to avoid her because she never knew when to stop talking. That was except for one blind man named Hugo who couldn't get enough of her stories.

Dolly played her Billy Murray record over and over again until one of the volunteers finally told her to put it away because it annoyed them. He told her to pack it away in her pink wooden storage box under her cot and to never to bring it out again or they would have to ask her to leave the shelter. Dolly felt lost without being able to hear her Billy Murray song every night but the others were relieved that they didn't have to listen to it over and over again.

It was midnight when Dolly was awakened by the loud winds roaring outside. "Do ya hear that?" she asked the lady who slept on the cot next to hers.

"Yeah, it's starting."

"I didn't hear nothin' 'bout how big it's suppose to be. Did you?"

"They say it's a rough one but we're safe in this building so don't worry and go back to sleep." She yawned and rolled back over.

Dolly tossed about on the cot and tried to sleep but couldn't close her eyes. The wind grew louder and the rain pounded hard against the boarded windows. She lay there sliding her locket along the chain remembering when Uncle Thomas put it around her neck. She'd not taken it off once since that day. Her thoughts shifted to Jacob and finally she drifted off to sleep.

Dolly was awakened by an abrupt sound of the strengthening winds. The walls were creaking and her cot trembled beneath her as the violent winds started to peel the boards loose from the windows.

The lamps went on and people were moving about the room nervously watching the two vulnerable windows. A moment later the lights flickered and went out. Dolly heard people chattering and praying but the room was so black she couldn't see one face.

"Anybody got a candle?" she heard.

A minute passed before she saw the flicker of a flame six feet from her. More candles were being lighted and she could finally see again. The blind man, Hugo, who was two cots over from Dolly had a look of terror on his face. She got up and went over to him. "We're gonna be jus' fine, Hugo."

"Will you tell me a story, Dolly?" he said as he took her hand.

"Well, did I ever tell ya 'bout when Jumbo got killed by the train? When I ran outta my boxcar to go see em that poor ol' elephant was jus' rockin' his head back an' forth layin' on his side an' . . . . Oh Lord help us!"

There was a thundering crash from a tree limb flying through a window. Pieces of plaster and paper started to dart toward the broken window and were being sucked to the outside.

"Oh my God!" shouted a voice.

"This place is gonna go!" someone else yelled just as another window blew out.

Glass and debris were being tossed about the room. Dolly watched as two volunteers ran over with a pressed cardboard dressing screen and held it up to one of the windows. "Find some nails and hurry!"

In a matter of minutes they were hammering around the broken windows until the winds were finally blocked.

The man next to Hugo said, "That was sure a close one, huh? Scared the livin' daylights outta me."

"Well, it ain't over jus' yet," said Dolly. She knew they were in for a long night. She let go of Hugo's hand and said, "I'm gonna git back to my cot now. Ya try not to worry cause I'll be close by."

The wind was still whistling through the blocked windows and Dolly wondered how long it would hold. She grabbed her scrapbook and held it under the blanket with her.

Just as Dolly had predicted the cots blew off of one window and at the same time the screen blew off of the other. Lamps and shoes were flying around the room like swarming bees. Dolly sprang up when she felt something hit her cot. She looked up and saw the ceiling buckling in and out as if it were breathing. The candles were quickly being snuffed out one by one and the room was almost black again. She tucked her scrapbook into her bosom and felt her way back over to Hugo. "Come on," she said, "Git down on the floor!" Hugo rolled off of his cot and onto the floor with Dolly.

A man staggered and fell on the floor next to them in the blackness. Dolly reached for his hand and said, "Jus' stay down here on the floor with us, Honey, an' you'll be safe."

They stayed in the same spot on the floor, helplessly listening to the moans and screams of everyone around them all night long.

The winds finally subsided and daylight began to seep in enough for them to see.

Dolly's eyes moved toward the man lying next to them. She said, as she started to roll him over, "Are ya alright, Honey?" Then she screamed, "My Lord, Hugo! This man ain't got no head!"

She stood up and said, "This poor man's head's layin' over there! Oh my Lord! Yer lucky ya ain't able to see all this."

"Tell me what you see, Dolly."

As her eyes scanned the room she cried, "Oh I kin see hurt people layin' all over the place with blood on em an' some er probably dead. Everthin's busted up an' there's a big hole in the roof an' a wall is half missin' too!" She felt faint and had to sit back down on the floor next to Hugo and the headless body.

"Are you okay, Dolly?" asked Hugo as he got to his feet and held his hand out to her.

"Yeah, jus' give me a minute. I feel like I'm gonna puke." She turned to the side and vomited. She wiped her mouth with the back of her hand and said, "I'm fine now. Come on, help me up."

One of the men went to the door and opened it. "It's safe to go out now," he yelled. "We gotta go get help!"

Dolly yelled back, "Don't go too far cause this storm ain't over yet!" She remembered the hurricane in St. Augustine when the winds stopped but then came back again forty-five minutes later.

"You crazy? Look outside. It's over with!" said another man.

"Well, I got a feelin' it ain't safe jus' yet. Sometimes it comes back again when ya don't expect it. I think we're in the middle of the storm where it's calm an' peaceful . . . an' I believe there's an even bigger storm brewin' on the other side."

"Oh horse shit!" whistled an old toothless man.

"Yeah, horse shit! Look at it out there. It's over and ain't coming back," said another man as he stood halfway out the door.

People went outside, paying no attention to what Dolly was trying to tell them. She heard them walking away from the shelter and said, "I sure hope they don't git too far an' look out fer more shelter when the storm comes back."

Dolly went from one injured person to the next, trying to help as much as she could, while others went for help. A man died in her arms making her feel helpless but then she decided that she was doing the best she could do.

A half-hour had passed and many of her homeless friends that left hadn't returned. The street outside was filled with people walking around and looking at the damage. Ten people had been transported to the hospital and eleven had died. Only fourteen people had returned back to the shelter. Dolly worried, as the winds began to kick up outside, that she might never see some of her friends again if they didn't come back.

The fourteen who stayed behind took Dolly's warning seriously. They boarded up the windows again and filled as many containers of water as they could. The dead bodies were moved to one corner.

Without warning the wind suddenly picked up full hurricane force.

"Jus' hold on tight cause this is gonna be ferocious!" Dolly yelled just as both boards flew off the windows like an explosion. She looked up and saw that part of the roof was lifting off and she scrambled to scoot down under her cot next to her pink storage box, making sure her scrapbook was still tightly secured in her bosom. Everyone started screaming and running for a place to hide. Dolly knew her cot wouldn't give her enough protection from the flying glass so she rolled out from under it while holding her hand over her scrapbook and ran to Hugo.

"We're gonna die!" Hugo yelled.

"No we ain't!" said Dolly as she reached for his arm and pulled him down next to her. "Let's git over to that corner! It's sturdier over there!" In a squatting run she quickly led Hugo to the corner wall and they crouched down.

The heavy rain pounded in through the broken windows and Dolly could feel the sting against her skin. She held her face down on Hugo's chest while clutching him tightly.

The rest of the roof flew away and boards started flying through the air. A piece of the ceiling hit Dolly on the back hard enough to knock the breath out of her. She gasped for air until she regained her breath before she felt the pain. Cots were being tossed around like feathers and Dolly could hear the sounds of people outside screaming for help. "My God people are getting' blown 'round like they was made of paper!"

An old woman ran into the middle of the room screaming, "God help us!" Dolly looked up and saw a broom shoot across the room and pierce the old woman in the chest.

"Ya stay here, Hugo!" Dolly ordered as she started to crawl across the floor toward the old woman. "Hold on Honey, I'll help ya!" A piece of glass jabbed Dolly in the leg as she tried to reach the old woman. The flying debris was so thick Dolly could hardly see. She grabbed the old woman by the arm and pulled her back to the corner with Hugo. The old woman was still alive but the broom handle had gone right through her.

"Am I gonna die?" said the old woman.

"Ya might. I don't know yet," said Dolly as she held on to her.

The wall started tearing away in the middle of the room and soon there were only two walls left. As they huddled in the corner Dolly watched as the walls that once protected them were crushing people like tomatoes.

Several long hours the winds finally quieted down but the pounding rain continued. Most everyone in the rubble was either dead or dying around her and Dolly cried out, "Somebody! Somebody help us!"

The horrifying moans of the half-dead filled air as she looked down at the old woman. "It's over now, Honey." But the old woman was dead.

Hugo had a small blade of glass stuck in his back so Dolly pulled it out and examined the wound. "It looks sorta nasty, Hugo, but it ain't too deep so I think ya might be alright." She pushed away from the dead woman and stood up to pull the piece of glass from her own leg.

People started to slowly move about. Most of the ones who were able to stand up couldn't wait to get outside. A few stayed with Dolly to help the injured.

"Is she still alive?" asked a man as they pulled a woman from beneath a large beam.

"This one's gone too," said another.

Dolly looked over at where her cot used to be and spotted the heavy wooden pink box that she'd kept her things in still in tact and leaning against the one standing wall. "What a miracle," she said. She patted her chest to make sure her scrapbook was still secured and ran over to her pink box to pull out the bottle.

After taking several hardy gulps Dolly felt better but didn't know where to begin. There were more injured than there were helping. Looking at all the crushed and bleeding people around her made her feel shame for hanging on to her scrapbook. "Please fergive me Dear Lord fer thinkin' 'bout this old scrapbook at a time like this."

Dolly started to feel dizzy then looked down at her leg and saw that she was losing too much blood. She had to sit back down in the corner with Hugo. She tore a piece from the bottom of her dress and tied it around her right leg then stood back up again.

The wailing cries and the bloody bodies were almost too much to bear. She picked up her bottle and took another big swig.

"Ya wanna a drink of some good bootleg whiskey, Hugo?"

"You're damn tootin' I do!" Hugo grabbed the bottle with trembling hands and took a long drink.

"Come on, let's go see if we kin help out there." She helped Hugo to his feet and led him outside into the street.

Dolly brushed her thin hair back away from her face and she looked around as the stinging tears came to her small bue eyes.

"What do you see, Dolly?"

She took another swig of whiskey and cried, "Oh there's buildins' gone an' trees layin' on their sides an' oh, Hugo, people er layin' everwhere . . . on the road an' even hangin' outta trees. There's two feet I see stickin' out from under a truck that's upside down . . . Oh, the poor souls," she cried, "I tried to warn em."

CHAPTER 27

Ten years had passed and Dolly lived in a homeless shelter on 79th Street along with Hugo. She was relieved when they finally lifted the ban on alcohol because she would never have to buy wart or deal with bootleggers again. Though she hated herself for it, she went back to stealing her beer. It was easy, and besides, she could use the little money she had to buy her cigarettes.

Dolly was out begging for money on 79th Street when she spotted a young woman walking by with a little boy. His hair was blond like Matt Kilgore's and it made Dolly think about her son. She wondered what he looked like and what ever happened to him. Did he know about her? Where was he? Who adopted him? Was he still alive? So many questions flooded her mind but knew she'd never find the answers. Would God forgive her for wanting to kill her unborn baby and for giving him away? She remembered what she had told Sarah Martin on that New Year's Eve, mouthing the exact words, "At least I never got pregnant an' killed my baby!" What she did was even worse than killing an unborn baby. Old Dolly felt ashamed for the first time.

The day after her best and only friend died she was out making her rounds with the cup she decided to walk a little further than usual. She had a lot of remembering to do along the way. She sadly thought about Hugo and how she'd miss him. She had to think about Jacob again too. Lost in her own world she walked for miles.

She finally stopped when she realized that she was in a part of Miami she'd never been to before. It was then that she discovered the welfare office and went inside.

Now that Dolly had a steady income from the government she would no longer have to live at the shelter or accept money from strangers.

It was 1941 when Dolly moved into the small efficiency in back of Joe's bar. She had become too old and riddled with arthritis to walk very far. She never went further than the Lighthouse grocery store or the post office to pick up her check.

Her thoughts were always lost in the past. She remembered Jacob's face and how she lived with his ghost because she couldn't bear to let him go. When she played her Victrola she was with Ella again. She heard Uncle Thomas's voice telling her he loved her when she opened her scrapbook to his picture. Her memories of the past were sharp in every detail but she could not remember what month or year it was.

She was too fat for her old costumes so she wore dresses she'd hand sewn from flour sacks that Mike had given her. She drew her brows in a high arch over her thick false eyelashes and painted her lips much larger than they were.

Mike did not like Dolly. She was too loud and crude for him. He was a quiet Jewish man who worked hard. He'd bought the grocery store only a year before Dolly moved to Twenty-Seventh Avenue. He cringed when Dolly came into the store, knowing that she would ask to charge something or she would talk his ears off.

"Hey Mike, ya got somethin' I kin sit on out front?"

"Why do you need something to sit on?"

"Cause I got noplace else to go except my place an' it's too hot in there. I figure I kin sit out here by the door where the shade is an' look at my scrapbook while I drink my beer."

Mike handed her an apple crate from the back. She took it outside and placed it by the door then sat down.

She'd opened her scrapbook on her lap and wait for someone to show it to.

She'd ask strangers, "Do you remember me? I'm Dolly Crystal, the Queen of the Circus!"

People laughed at her, thinking she was nuts, or they would ignore her but she believed they were only too shy to approach her. Dolly appeared to others as a lonely old woman living a miserable existence but she did not see it that way. To Dolly, she had it all. She reigned as Queen and everyone adored her.

It was sunner of 1952 when the old woman first met the two little barefoot girls pulling a wagon full of bottles. "Do ya remember me? I'm Dolly Crystal, the Queen of the Circus!" The little girls stopped and looked at her. "Do ya wanna see my picture of when I was in the circus?" Dolly patted her scrapbook.

"Yeah, I'd like to see," said the little blond girl, My mama told me you were a famous circus queen a long time ago."

As Dolly opened her scrapbook she asked, "What's yer name Honey?"

"I'm Ida and this is my best friend, Dixie."

"Well, sit right down here an' let me tell ya how I came to join up with the Barnum an' Bailey Circus."

From that time on Dolly would stop Dixie and Ida everytime she'd see them. The girls could not figure out why Dolly would always ask, "Do ya remember me?" when she'd told them stories only days earlier. Dolly never remembered their names and only referred to them as the barefoot girls.

It was June of 1953 when Dolly walked to the post office to pick up her welfare check and found the letter from Boston. She trembled as she slowly opened it.

> "Dear Miss Dolly Crystal,
>
> I'm sure you remember me even though you've never met me. I was born sixty-three years ago in Boston. I don't even know if you ever think about me but I want you to know that I am doing fine. I have a successful law practice here in Boston and am married with two grown children and one grandson. I've been trying to locate you for many

years. I do not want to meet you. I don't think it would be a good idea. I hear that you are not doing very well and I just wanted to send you the enclosed.

Best Regards,
Your Son, David."

Dolly opened the enclosed oblong card and found a check in the amount of five thousand dollars. She took another swig of beer and swallowed the lump in her throat. She choked back a tear and folded the letter and tucked it into her scrapbook along with the check.

"Your Son, David." It sounded odd to her . . . "Your son." She had no feelings for him but she did feel guilt and was filled with curiosity about him.

A month passed. Dolly walked into the Lighthouse Grocery Store and asked, "Kin I git a beer an' pay ya tomorrow, Mike?"

"You know I don't like that. Aw . . . go ahead . . . but don't forget to pay me!"

"Oh yeah! An' kin ya throw in a pack of Old Golds too?" She asked as she walked to the icebox to retrieve a bottle of Schlitz.

"Yeah, sure, "said Mike as he smacked his lips. "Here's your Old Golds."

She opened her beer with Mike's bottle opener then snatched up her pack of cigarettes and said, "I got a son. He's a lawyer an' lives in Boston. Did ya know I had a son, Mike?"

He looked at her without smiling; "You never mentioned that before, Dolly."

"Well, I do . . . an' his name's David." She reached into the back of her mouth and pulled out a bloody tooth then tossed it into the wastebasket behind Mike.

"What was that thing you just pulled out of your mouth?"

"Oh, jus' a piece of old candy . . . I got a letter from my son a while back." Dolly's tiny blue eyes sparkled beneath the false eyelashes that were coming loose and sticking straight out, waiting for some kind of a response from him.

Mike didn't say a word. He was disgusted with Dolly and wished she'd never moved to Twenty-Seventh Avenue. He turned to his cash register and started counting change.

"Well, I guess I'll tell ya more 'bout em later, Mike. See ya in a while."

She found her old apple crate leaning against the back wall of the building and dragged it over by the front door and sat down. She pressed her lashes back down before opening her scrapbook.

"Dolly!" Joe yelled over to her from across the street.

She had no idea why Joe would be calling her. Maybe he was calling someone else, she thought. Dolly sat without budging from her apple crate throne.

Joe didn't like being disturbed but he ran across the street to the Lighthouse Grocery to fetch Dolly anyway. "Dolly! Didn't ya hear me calling you? You got a telephone call . . . someone who's lookin' for you. Hurry up! It's long distance!" He charged ahead of her to get back to his unattended bar.

Dolly knew who it was before she answered the phone.

Her son asked, "Why didn't you cash the check I sent you last month?"

Dolly answered, "Cause I don't deserve it. I never gave you nothin' . . . Son."

"But I wanted you to have it. That's why I sent it to you. Don't you need it?"

"Oh . . . no . . . no, I don't need no money. I got plenty of it, way more then I kin spend."

"I read in the paper that you were living on welfare."

"What do ya mean . . . ya read it in the paper?"

"Exactly that. Every week they've been running a column on the history of the circus and you're mentioned all the time."

"Well, how in the hell did they know I was on welfare? How do they know all about me?"

"Oh hell . . . they've got their ways Mother." David slipped and called her Mother, without thinking.

He sounded just like his father, she thought for a moment. She didn't know what to say. "Well, Son, I gotta hang up now so goodbye."

Dolly's heart was pounding so hard she had to sit down. This had been a good day for her, she thought. If Dolly Crystal was still being mentioned in the newspapers, that meant she was still famous. Then she said under her breath, "An' I been called Mother at least once in my life now," and smiled.

CHAPTER 28

The old woman's memories were clear and crisp on that stormy August night in 1953 as she stretched herself out across the bed, feeling very tired. She'd had a full life, she thought. She pictured the faces of the two young girls who listened to her stories and knew they would always remember her.

The howling wind grew louder outside as the rain picked up strength and pounded hard against the window above her head. Every detail of her eighty-seven years all at once flashed through her mind with a single bright surge of lightning.

Dolly remembered back when she'd first met Jacob at the church in Ridgetop. "Dear Lord, where did all those years go? It feels like they was jus' minutes I had with em. Time is a funny thin'. It goes so slow fer a while then it picks up speed an' before ya know it . . . time's all gone."

Dolly's eyes rolled back with pain for an instant then eased again. "An' Lord, ya gave me a lot in my life. I had everythin' any girl could ever want. I had glory an' fame an' love an' riches an' I thank ya fer it all. But most of all, dear Lord, ya gave me courage to tackle all the thin's I did an' the strength to git through em all. I'm grateful to ya an' don't want nothin' else except to be able to take all these good memories with me when I come to join ya."

She reached over and turned on the scarf-covered lamp, propped the pillow behind her back and pulled her scruffy old scrapbook to her lap. Her head felt heavy as she strained her neck to see the pages and opened her scrapbook one last time. Another sharp pain hit her hard then subsided. She looked at the picture of Ella standing in front of the house in Ridgetop holding Pronto's rien. "I'm really sorry, Ella, about leavin' ya like I did when you was dead. It wasn't right what I did but ya knew I didn't have no money an' I know ya forgive me. Ella's big round eyes sparkled back at Dolly from the yellowed photograph.

She tried to sit up but a jabbing pain in her chest pushed her back down. The light in the room flickered and she could hear the crashing of street signs blowing down Twenty Seventh Avenue as the whining winds gained force.

She strained again to lift her head far enough to see the picture of Uncle Thomas standing in front of the old house in Ridgetop. She gently laid her hand over his image, feeling his warmth as she cupped her locket in her other hand. As her tired head fell back onto the pillow the light went out and the room was pitch black.

"Dolly?" She heard the voice loud and clear but couldn't see anyone. Again she heard, "Dolly Wafford." A brilliant light suddenly appeared on the ceiling. She could smell the sweet fragrance of cucumbers and felt a warm breeze cross her body as he spoke. "It's peaceful here, Darling. Please hurry. I've been waiting for so long now."

She stared up at the white light until she could make out Jacob's face smiling down on her. Her heart stopped for a moment as she watched his green eyes fade back into the blackness of the ceiling. "Jacob, come back an' take me with ya," she said in a weak voice.

The whistling winds grew louder but to Dolly they sounded far away and dim. The crushing pain in her chest lasted only for a moment. Her tiny pale blue eyes became flooded with tears of joy and relief then she laid her head down to rest.

No one missed the old woman, except for the two young girls. Her body wasn't discovered until two weeks after the hurricane when someone passed by her broken window and noticed the stench.

The day after they found Dolly's body the two young barefooted girls passed by the old apple crate by the front door of the Lighthouse Grocery where Dolly once sat.

"I think Mike musta put that apple crate out there for Dolly in case she ever came back," said Ida.

"Aw I don't even think he missed her. You know how Mike is. He works so much he never pays attention to what goes on. That crate's sitting there only cause he forgot to bring it in.

"Yeah, maybe you're right but ain't it funny that it never blew away in the hurricane?"

"Yeah, that's really strange. Oh, and you know what else?" said Dixie as she looked at the apple crate, "We forgot to ever give Dolly her mangoes. I feel so sad cause they're still sitting in that bag by your front steps."

"Yeah . . . they're all rotten now." Ida replied shamefully.

"Hey Ida, I heard that cop say they found a check for five thousand dollars in her old scrapbook that she never even cashed. And when they found her she was wearing a huge diamond ring on her finger that was probably worth over two thousand dollars. Strange, huh?"

"Then why was she so poor, I wonder?"

"Do you think she stole the ring?"

"Somebody musta given it to her because I know Dolly wouldn't have ever stole anything," said Ida.

"An' I wonder what ever happened to her old scrapbook?"

"Mama said she had a son so I guess he musta gotten it,"

Dixie thought for a moment. "Yeah but my mama told me she never even met him," she said as she scratched a scab off of a mosquito bite on her skinny arm and put it into her mouth. "I betcha he won't even know who all those people who are in it."

"Yeah, I bet we're the only ones who really know who they were. An' I bet he'll probably just throw it out too." Ida's eyes sadly gazed across the street at Joe's bar." I wonder what she looked like when they found her," as she squinted her nose at the morbid thought then took another bite of her candy bar.

The girls held hands and walked over to cross Twenty-Seventh Avenue. They glanced back at the empty apple crate throne and knew that they'd never forget the funny sweet old woman who would say, "Do ya remember me? I'm Dolly Crystal, Queen of the Circus."

BVG